Totally Bound Publishing books by Jayce Carter

The Omega's Alphas
Owned by the Alphas
Shared by the Alphas
Saved by the Alphas
Protected by Her Alphas
Caught by Her Alphas
Tamed by the Alphas
Claimed by the Alphas
Exposed by Her Alphas
Trained by the Alphas
Reclaimed by Her Alphas

Ready or Not
Fake It 'til You Make It
Opposites Attract
Third Time Lucky
Enemies Closer

Grave Concerns
Grave Robbing and Other Hobbies
Hell Raising and Other Pastimes
Saving the World and Other Bad Ideas

Dark Sanctuary
Bound by Fear
Trapped by Doubt
Buried by Despair

Nemesis
The Corpse Princess
The Resurrected Queen

Larkwood Academy
Silenced
Whispers
Screaming

Flocking It Up

OUT OF MY FLOCKING MIND

JAYCE CARTER

Out of My Flocking Mind
ISBN # 978-1-80250-746-1
©Copyright Jayce Carter 2024
Cover Art by Kelly Martin ©Copyright August 2024
Interior text design by Claire Siemaszkiewicz
Totally Bound Publishing

Published in 2024 by Totally Bound Publishing, United Kingdom.

Totally Bound Publishing is an imprint of Totally Entwined Group Limited.

OUT OF MY FLOCKING MIND

Dedication

To all the people who get quiet after asking what
I do for a living—apparently 'I write porn' wasn't
an expected answer.

Chapter One

Home might be where the heart is, but more importantly, it's where my vibrator is.

My time on the run had taught me to appreciate how nice it felt to go to my quiet house and enjoy a lovely orgasm or two all on my own. No annoying men, no other complications. Just me and bliss!

I'd spent most of the past two weeks since my entire life had gotten turned upside down, since I'd cleared my name after getting framed for murder, since I'd gotten a seat on the council doing just that.

Despite the messiness of, well, everything, I'd taken my ass back to my own little house and shut the rest of the world out.

Not that it had mattered. I'd gotten a visit from Galen — the pack alpha who still seemed determined to talk me into becoming his mate — but I'd refused to answer. And fuck, I had never worked so hard for a climax as when I'd pretended *not* to hear him knocking at the front door. I couldn't let him win, though, and had refused to let him steal even one moment of joy from me.

My phone vibrated, which was not the specific tool I needed to do that at the moment. Still, I rolled over and picked it up from my nightstand, frowning as I read the screen.

I wanted to ignore the call, but my finger moved without me thinking it through to answer.

"You've ignored me for over a week." Ruben's voice came out annoyed as ever, with him speaking as though already mid-lecture.

"And? I didn't know I had to answer to you. You aren't my boss anymore, right?"

The long moment before he answered had me smirking, wondering if I'd finally gotten the better of him. "You don't have to leave your position as a courier. Besides, even if you choose to do so, as a sitting council head, you still must answer to me. You are not immune from my authority."

I moved my lips along, mocking him without making a sound. I didn't need him to realize just how childish I could be.

"Stop acting like a child."

I sat up, then peered around. "How did you know? Are you spying on me or something?"

"I have better things to do than sneak into your pigsty of a home and peep on you. Your naked body lacks the appeal for me to sink that low. I simply know you well enough to predict you couldn't just behave yourself."

"Wow, rude much? You, for sure, won't see me naked now." I pursed my lips, then tried to shake off the annoyance. I needed to focus so I could get off the phone and back to my own little orgasm-filled world. "So, why are you calling me?"

He paused then, which made me want to laugh. I knew that pause, the one that said he wasn't sure what to say next.

Of course, where I expected such things from people like myself, people who often ended up in situations over their head that they hadn't planned for, hearing it from Ruben was beyond weird.

I had to fight the urge to ask if he had a fever or had somehow lost his mind. I had a feeling that even if either were true, he wouldn't tell me.

Finally, he let out a breath that could have almost been a sigh. "After everything that happened, you really wonder why I might call you?"

I pressed my lips together, then leaned back in my bed, tossing the trusty vibrator aside. Ruben had a deep voice sexy enough to help in my fantasies, but unless he stopped lecturing me or I grew a kink for that, I had a feeling I was getting nowhere until we finished up our little conversation.

"So this is a 'hey, how're you' call? Well, I'm just peachy keen, thank you very much."

"You have been ignoring all calls, from what I understand."

"Haven't seen a reason to speak to anyone."

His censure came down the line without him having to utter a word. That was the strength of his disapproval aura, though. I'd bet it could bend space and time to make someone feel bad. "You show up and turn the system on its head, then think you can disappear as though it had never happened? You added a seat to the council, Grey, a seat *you* now occupy."

"Technically, *I* didn't create it. That guy did."

"Speaking of, would you happen to know who he is?"

"I figured you'd know better than I would. I know I'm a weird guy magnet, but I don't have all the answers. He made me, and I never saw him again in person until he showed up at the trial. He said I could call him Knot, but beyond that? He never even told me he was coming." I let out a soft laugh at that, at how he'd saved me and annoyed me at the same time. "How can you not know? You know everything."

Ruben let out a rough, disgruntled sound full of frustration. "I know what is in the old books, the forbidden ones, but there are still countless tomes locked away even from me. I've found that the old stories say there were gods other than the four represented by the council seats. Some died, some were killed, some simply had no wish to participate. They each have a color of their own, but those colors are not listed anywhere I could find to identify."

"So no who's-who of the Spirit world?"

"It seems not."

"I guess it doesn't matter. It doesn't tell us anything important because those books are written about nonsense. I mean, most people still think that the old gods are just stories, but there one stood, very lively for a story."

He said nothing back, and I could almost see him grinding his molars through the line.

I chuckled. "What? Did I stun you by being right for once? Don't worry, you probably won't need to get used to it."

"How are you feeling?" he responded, as if unwilling to admit my point. No doubt he'd rather change the subject than suffer such humiliation. "You went through a lot. Are you okay?"

"Yeah, I'm good. I mean, it's not like I'm going to sprout an extra arm or a penis just because we found out I wasn't some weird anomaly."

"Technically, you still are an anomaly. Anomaly means something new and unique. Even if we know

now that you were created by a different god, it doesn't make you not an anomaly."

"Remind me never to come to you for a pep-talk. You suck at them."

A shrill cry from outside made me sit upright. It was the sort of noise I'd heard before, but not from my overly prim neighbor. I went to the window and peered out, but no light escaped from the closed curtains across the narrow strip of desert landscaping.

"What's wrong?" Ruben asked.

"I think my neighbor is having very noisy sex," I answered.

"Please tell me you aren't trying to watch her through the window?"

"If she didn't want an audience, she shouldn't have made so much noise. It's like chewing loudly when other people are starving—expect staring." I narrowed my eyes, trying to catch a glimpse of something just as another yell came through. "Well, someone must be doing something very right or very wrong. Are you a yeller, Ruben?"

"Excuse me?"

"I bet you aren't. You seem like the strong and silent type, huh?" I pressed my forehead against the cool glass of the window, not finding a car in her driveway or any sign of her partner.

She could have been alone, but she seemed rather lively to be playing all by herself.

"I'm going to have to let you go," I said.

"Why?"

"Well, I *was* busy when you called, and now I have some mood music, so have yourself a lovely evening because I plan to do the same." As I ended the call, I could hear his voice echoing out, scolding me, as though that would have changed a single thing.

Silly man.

I opened my window, staring out at the neighbor who hated me endlessly. She was in her forties, working as a realtor after her husband had run off with his secretary.

I had no idea if that bitterness was the reason she hated me — or maybe it was because since I moved in, her lawn gnomes were always getting moved like some twisted elf on a shelf year-long game. Either way, she had that fake smile when she spoke to me, the one that said she loathed me and talked plenty of shit the second I was out of earshot.

Which was fine with me. Little Miss Karen next door was hardly my idea of a good time, anyway.

However, it made me wonder what had happened to cause *this* change. With the window open and the narrow space between our houses, it was easy to hear more. I caught moans and whimpers, all hers, which further implied that she was alone over there.

I glanced at my vibrator, wishing I was that good at it. Hell, that woman was having the time of her life all on her own. My own solo sex life felt rather empty all of a sudden.

Teach me, sempai!

Another shout echoed through the space between our places, but this one made my hair stand on end, the skin at the back of my neck tingling. That was *not* the sound of pleasure. Not even the kinky pleasure-pain that people liked. It held a wealth of pain, and a broken, soft whimper came afterward.

I grabbed my pajama shorts off the end of the bed and pulled them on, hopping on a single foot as I did so, trying to rush as fast as I could. Something in the noise drew me, forcing me to rush. It sounded like a wounded animal stuck in a trap, and I couldn't stop myself from going over.

She could hate me all she wanted — I couldn't ignore that sound.

I rushed down the stairs, toppling down the last few before catching myself on the front door. The chill of the night, with Christmas coming soon, drew goosebumps all over my bare legs and arms. Rushing out in a thin tank top and night shorts was a terrible idea, but it was nowhere close to the worst of my bad ideas.

I went through the rocks that separated the thin strip of land between our places, the houses so close I could have reached out and touched both at the same time. From this spot, I was sure that there were no cars. It meant if she wasn't alone, the person had either walked or arrived with her.

Maybe this was an online hookup gone wrong? Or gone *very* right if it was just a bit of roleplaying. If that was the case, the bitch deserved an award.

I knocked on her front door, but no answer came. No lights turning on, no rustle of clothing as two caught people tried to dress before answering. Instead, about fifteen seconds later, another scream, this one worse than the last.

I moved to the side of the door, to a cracked open window on the ground floor. I pushed on the screen, then lifted it, sliding it out of the groove that held it.

I'd snuck out enough times as a teenager to know exactly how to get a screen free. I pushed the window open further, the lack of a squeak telling me she was on point with her maintenance. The metal of the window frame dug into my hands as I gripped it, then hefted myself through the narrow space.

I'd never seen the inside of her home, and I had to admit, the woman knew how to perfectly recreate the stifling feeling of a housekeeping magazine. Not a single pillow appeared out of place, all of them with that silly center crease and none of it implying anyone ever actually used the room.

The layout mirrored my own, just like all the places in the community. Funny how something almost identical in structure could look and feel so different.

Another scream, this one weaker, cut off my little internal tirade and got me moving. I went up the stairs at a run, trying to breathe softly despite the exertion. At the top of the stairs rested the hallway, and the door to the master bedroom sat open with only darkness beyond.

I tiptoed down the hallway, fear beating against me as hard as my heart. Once I reached the doorway, I tried to stare through the darkness, and it took a moment for my eyes to adjust and take in the room.

Only to find the bed empty, and instead, my neighbor's body on the floor. No one else was beside her, and she rolled like caught in some nightmare. She had her hands clasped to the sides of her head, as though she could hold it together by way of grasp alone.

"Stop," she whispered, curling into the fetal position, the soft word full of pain.

Was she having some sort of mental breakdown? And here I figured I'd be the one between us to go through that. I thought about calling my friend and sometimes counselor, Ignis, and asking her what to do. However, this was probably outside of her wheelhouse.

I went to take a step inside the room, to go to her side, when an unfamiliar voice stopped me.

"Why fight? It'll only hurt you more." Along with the masculine voice, a shadow moved inside the room. It shifted away from the wall and toward my neighbor, then crouched beside her. "I'll take every last thought you have, savor them all, get drunk on them. The more you try to hide any of it, the harder I'll yank, and the more damage'll get done."

My neighbor stared up at him, her eyes wide in horror, and there went the last of my patience.

I spotted a very fancy and expensive-looking lamp on the table in the hallway, which seemed large and heavy enough to be useful. I wrapped my fingers around it and pulled the cord from the wall, the sound hidden by the whimpers of my neighbor.

I didn't bother masking my steps anymore, not when I was this close. I lifted the lamp, holding it over my shoulder for more power. If I was going to hit someone, I planned to do it right. It was like shooting someone— if I had to do it, I'd make sure they stayed down.

Nothing was more dangerous than a wounded opponent.

I swung the lamp, aiming for the man's head. One good crack and he'd go down hard.

Except, before it hit, he twisted, so fast it startled me. The lamp didn't strike him, and it took me a moment to figure out why. He'd wrapped his hand around my wrist, his grip so tight it hurt, and the lamp slipped from my fingers, shattering against the floor.

He stood, forcing me to look up at him despite not making out any of his face in the darkness. It seemed almost familiar, but I didn't know why, the room so dim that I couldn't identify any specific details.

He tilted his head, as though confused by me. "You're different," he said, his voice low and rough and somewhere between interest and accusation.

"People usually call me special, but they don't mean it as a compliment," I answered, the lame joke all my brain could come up with.

He caught my chin with his free hand, holding me still, and I only had a moment to fear before an intense pain echoed through my head as though someone had driven a spike through my temples and the world faded out around me.

* * * *

I woke with the world an absolute mess around me. It seemed disjointed and my body both hurt and hung, almost weightless.

Was this a dream?

No, not enough hot naked men to be a dream of mine...

"Your brain's different." I recognized the voice as belonging to the man from my neighbor's house. However, when I twisted, I couldn't find him in the surrounding darkness. "Why? What are you?"

"I'm just me," I answered, buying time. "What are you looking for, and maybe I can help?"

"What do I want? I want to taste you."

"If you mean like a meal, no thank you. If you want to taste somewhere else, well, who am I to say no?" My chest ached as I struggled to slow my racing heart.

"I don't give a fuck about your flesh" —his words still gave me no idea about what he meant— "but your mind is a different story. That's where the real flavor of a person is, in their memories, their thoughts, their desires and their fears."

I recalled the way my neighbor had rolled on the floor, a sinking feeling pulling me down. Was this a Mind Spirit? Some of the more powerful empaths and telepaths could access old memories, and a few of the really crazy ones weaponized it. I'd never experienced such a thing, but I had a feeling it wasn't all that pleasant.

"You're a Mind?" I asked.

"So you aren't just some human. Figured as much when I felt the fucked-up way your mind works, but I've done this to humans, to Graves, to Natures, to Weres, to other Minds, and none of them feel like you. So what are you?"

"A problem, mostly."

"Make all the jokes you want—they won't help. I'll dig down as deep as I can, until your mind shatters into a million little pieces that I can taste, that I can swallow and steal and savor." His words sprang from his lips like snakes and slithered across the edges of my mind.

Which was where we had to be, right? The lack of any actual space around me, the way I couldn't find the floor or walls or reality, it meant we had to exist inside my mind.

It's a lot less cluttered than I would have expected…

I mean, it wasn't a nice neighborhood or anything, but it wasn't the teardown I'd pegged it for, either.

"You're trying to distract yourself."

"Usually I'm distracting to others."

A shadow came closer, but even still, I couldn't make out his face at all. It was as though my brain blocked it out. Or perhaps that was something he managed? Either way, it unnerved me to hear his voice, to see his form, but not be able to tell who he was. I didn't think I knew him, despite a strange sense of familiarity.

"You like to use jokes to mask your actual feelings, don't you? You laugh and play off any situation so no one figures out how terrified you really are."

"Being afraid takes being smart. My mom always said I wasn't smart enough to be afraid."

"You're still hiding. You might be the most frightened person I've ever met, afraid of everything, especially what's inside your own head."

I gulped, hating the way it felt as though he stared right through me.

"I wonder what your first memory of fear was. What was the first time you hid behind a laugh? The woman you interrupted my time with was already growing boring, but you? I have a feeling I could feast on you for months or more."

I shook my head and tried to back away, but I couldn't seem to move, or perhaps I did, but he moved faster? Whatever it was, I couldn't put any space between us.

"Show me," he whispered, causing the world around us to shift and twist, the darkness folding in on itself and reforming so fast that my stomach rolled like I was on a carnival ride. The world was bright again, and it took a long moment for me to recognize where I stood.

"This is my old home," I said, then spotted a young girl on her knees, in front of a faded coffee table, a broken, worn-down crayon clutched in her tiny fist. She scribbled on the coloring book before her, not coming close to staying inside the lines. She focused on the page, staring so hard as though to block out the world around her.

And what a world to block out...

The place was clean but run down. Dark spots — signs of repeated roof leaks — stained the upper walls and ceiling. Dingy linoleum squares covered the floor of the trailer and sweat trailed down the girl's forehead since they had no air conditioning.

"That's you, isn't it?" the man asked.

I nodded before I could help it, watching the girl I'd been. I wanted to crouch down and tell her it would be okay, that things would get better. I wouldn't have believed it back then, of course. Back then, my entire world had been just this, just a dirty trailer and hours alone, as my mom did everything she could to support us on her own. Hell, a four-year-old shouldn't have been home alone, but what choice did she have?

A noise at the door made the younger me twist, her familiar blue eyes wide in fear. I didn't remember this, but as I watched it, it felt true. This had happened even if my conscious mind couldn't recall the details.

The girl got up and rushed behind the couch, crawling into the narrow space between the wall and the old piece of furniture, then into the small space inside the frame of the couch. Watching her go, I remembered how dark it was inside the couch, how cramped. I rubbed my hand against my arm, a scar still there from when I'd gotten caught on the sharp edge of a spring there.

"You spent a lot of time there?"

"My mom knew about the hiding place, told me to go there if anyone showed up." I whispered the answer, feeling the same fear that rested inside young me.

Not a moment after the girl concealed herself, the door to the trailer opened with a crash as it slammed against the counter inside. The faces of the people were hidden from me, probably because I'd never seen them. I'd only spotted their feet from my hiding place, after all.

Three people — men, from what I saw of their shoes — entered the trailer.

"Check the bedroom," one said.

Steps signaled that one obeyed, heading back toward the one bedroom that my mother and I had shared.

The shadow stepped up beside me, and the way he stared at me made my skin feel too tight on my frame, as though I could sense his gaze like an unwelcome caress.

"Bitch isn't here," one man said.

"What about the kid?"

I felt my younger self shiver at the threat in those words. They'd come knowing about me, looking for me if they couldn't find my mother. This version of me, of my mother, felt so far removed from who were now that I'd tried to block a lot out.

"Place seems empty. Kid is pretty young—probably with a babysitter."

One man picked up the picture I'd been coloring and the broken crayon rolled off it, then over the edge of the table and to the floor. "You know why I'm so successful at collecting debts? Because I know the trick is finding a person's weak spot. If you can find that, you can apply pressure and get exactly what you want." The man bent forward and drew on the paper with other crayons on the table, the scratching of the colors loud in the silent room. "Let's go. I think she'll get the message." One loud bang echoed before the men left.

Younger me remained in her hiding place, shaking, for another few minutes before crawling out. It was then I spotted what the men had left.

"A little on the nose, isn't it?" the shadow asked.

I swallowed hard as I stared at the picture. The yellow girl I'd been drawing remained, but other things had been added. Black X's now covered the eyes and aggressive red lines slashed through the body. A knife pinned the picture to the wall.

Younger me stared at the knife, at the picture that even at my age I'd understood for the threat they'd meant. It had been the first time I'd really understood the dangerous world I lived in, when that sense of security children have had shattered.

I'd understood that no matter how much my mother loved me, she couldn't protect me. I'd realized that locked doors and adults and hiding in couches didn't actually keep people safe.

"Oh, that's a pretty fear," the shadow purred. "Your pain is almost sweet, so much better than most. Why is that? Why are you different? Your brain's like a maze I want to spend forever lost in, tearing apart each memory, each pain, each pleasure, all of it. Why?"

The feeling of helplessness swamped me, so strong that I struggled to pull in a single breath. It was like it was still as large and overwhelming as it had been when I was a child, as though it had grown along with me until it crushed me. My hands shook, my gaze locked on that knife.

What if they'd found me that day? What would have happened? I watched as the younger me—braver than current me, apparently—ran up and yanked down the picture, shredding it into a million pieces, then pulled the knife from the wall. She ran out of the living room, and the memory of hiding that knife, not wanting my mother to see it and worry, made my knees weak.

I collapsed to the ground, the weight of so much on my shoulders. Despite my fear of those men, of what they might do, my priority had been protecting my mom, not wanting to see the pain on her face when she found out.

It was the feeling of isolation, of recognizing how truly alone I was.

"Is that what rests at the center? Are you that afraid of being alone? Oh, how much fun we'll have together exploring it." Something brushed the side of my face, a touch so cold it made me tremble.

As soon as it happened, however, it stopped. Something on the edges of my awareness came through, a feeling, a ripple through the world that caused the trailer to waver.

The shadow shrank back, then let out a hollow laugh. "Seems our time's over today. Don't worry, though, I'll come back for you."

His withdrawal hurt as much as the initial attack had, as though he tore a wound wider by pulling away so fast. The surrounding trailer collapsed, the memory falling around me until it faded away, and with it, my consciousness.

My last thought before it all went dark was just how ominous his last words really felt.

I should have stayed home and just masturbated…

Chapter Two

Usually, I woke up a bit like an old man getting up off the couch. There was a lot of groaning and took far longer than it should have. Maybe it was because I didn't care for getting up, most of the time, but it was *never* easy.

Which was the first thing that clued me into a problem when I bolted out of bed as though I were one of those horribly annoying morning people.

I stared around me, trying to make sense of my surroundings. I found myself in my own room, standing beside my bed, with light pouring in through the open window.

I twisted, coming to a stop when I spotted someone in the room. At first, they seemed like just a shadow, a form I couldn't identify. Fear hit me, as though such a shadow were beyond terrifying. As my brain woke up fully, I recognized the person.

And immediately found myself even more confused.

"Harrison?"

The blond man sat in the chair before my desk, staring back at me as though it were perfectly normal for him to sit there and watch me sleep, or like he had any good reason to be here, in my bedroom.

I opened my mouth to say something rude when the memories from the night before crystalized in my head, reminding me of what had happened.

The fear and pain that had swarmed me back then threatened to overwhelm me again.

"Breathe slowly," Harrison said.

I wanted to snap at him, but the panic beating at me wouldn't allow it, so instead I tried to do as he said. I leaned forward, bracing my hands on my knees as I tried to draw air in slowly.

And fuck him, because it helped.

"What happened?" I asked when my throat loosened enough to let me speak.

"You were attacked."

"Yeah, I figured that much."

"How do you feel?"

I rolled my eyes at the way he asked me something without answering my question. "I feel great. Can't you tell?" I twisted my head, still bent forward, to glare at Harrison, who hadn't moved in the least. "Besides, you already know how I feel, don't you?"

"No. I told you before—I can't feel your thoughts or emotions."

"Then how did you know to tell me to breathe slowly?"

"Because you panting like a racehorse was a fairly obvious indicator."

"Rude. Besides, you try to get cardio in however you can when you're as busy as I am."

He twisted his head, glancing over at my bed. Despite the fact he must have put me in there, he had evidently left the vibrator in its place, where it still sat there like a joke.

"It's called self-care," I snapped, then picked up the vibrator and tossed it into the drawer in the nightstand. "So who the hell was that last night?"

"I don't know who it was."

"Then it was pure luck that you showed up?" I frowned, feeling as if I were making far too many leaps in my thought process. "Wait, did you scare him off?"

Harrison nodded. "Yes, I did. And as for why I came, it was because I've been searching for specific blasts of mind power. I tracked it there."

"And me being there was just dumb luck?" I thought back to what had happened, then shuddered as I allowed myself to sit on the end of the bed. "Maybe luck was the wrong word."

He didn't smile, as though that were not funny at all. It felt a little harsh, but I supposed everyone was a critic when they wanted to be.

I sighed, trying to ignore the pain in my head and the way my stomach rolled and my knees still shook. It was hard to tell myself I wasn't there anymore. The memories of living there, in the trailer…the fear and panic still existed inside me, bouncing around and threatening to pull me under.

"You seem to often end up in the wrong place at the wrong time," he said. "However, I doubt you'll have another issue."

"Really? Because the asshole said he'd see me again."

That got Harrison's attention. His focus snapped onto me so strongly, I flinched. Even with that, he didn't lighten his expression in the least. "He said that?"

I nodded. "He said he'd never found anyone like me before, that he wanted to see what I *tasted* like." I shuddered at the phrasing, at the way he'd said it, the sickening lust inside it. I still didn't really understand what he'd meant, but I knew really fucking well it spelled nothing good for me.

Harrison dropped his gaze to the floor as though thinking. "He won't target you again."

"You say that like you know him."

He shook his head. "I only meant that people who do this typically do whatever they wish and move on. The victim rarely survives, but I have never heard of someone actually returning to the same victim more than once."

"Which tells me you know exactly what happened."

"It isn't your business."

I poked myself in the temple and winced as soon as I did it. *Still sensitive.* "Seeing as someone just took a lovely little stroll through my brain, I feel like that makes it my business, don't you?"

Harrison stood, his actions slow and bored, as though he'd already grown tired of this conversation and me. "No, I don't, any more than someone who gets splashed by a puddle during a chase still has no business in the chase. If you are awake now, you will recover, so no lasting harm was done. Drink water with salt to help you recover more quickly." He nodded once, then turned to walk out.

"Wait one minute." I caught his arm, annoyed by the fact he felt it was okay to walk in here and just drop shit like that. Clearly, he was involved in this nonsense, and now he thought I'd just ignore it all? That I'd pretend it hadn't happened? "You can't just leave like that."

He didn't turn around fully, instead twisting his neck enough to peer over his shoulder at me. "I believe

I can. This is also a poor way of showing thanks. I believe this is the second time I have saved you."

I opened my mouth to argue, then snapped it shut. He was right, no matter how much it annoyed me. He'd saved me once before, when he'd realized I had hidden in that box as a crow during a council meeting, when he'd snuck me out safely. Now he'd apparently scared off the fucker who had attacked me.

Knowing that didn't help, though, since I still had no idea who that someone was, or even why it had happened.

"I called someone over to clean up the mess. Your neighbor's body will be discovered later today and they will rule her death a suicide."

"Body?" The word hit me hard, the acknowledgment that my neighbor hadn't survived it.

Why had I, then? Because Harrison had interrupted him, or because of what I was?

Harrison nodded but showed no signs of sympathy, as though he didn't give a fuck about her death or my feelings on the subject. "Most don't survive such an attack. Humans never do, and most spirits who survive the initial don't do so…whole. That you are not a raving madwoman says you did, however."

"Or maybe it's harder to see, given how I normally act?" I let out a weak laugh as I released him, shaken to the core by the realization of how close to death I'd been.

He paused, as though considering just how to handle this. Was he thinking about saying something else? Comforting me? I couldn't imagine that, which was why when he nodded one last time, then walked out, it didn't shock me.

The opening and closing of the front door echoed up the stairs, telling me Harrison had left. My home, the place I normally loved, where I felt like I could let my guard down, suddenly didn't feel nearly as comforting as it had before.

My little piece of personal heaven, my den, my nest—it felt trampled upon. Even though that shadow hadn't come in here, it seemed tainted, like he'd touched it and ruined it all at once. The idea made me sick, made me want to scrub the place top to bottom, but I knew that wouldn't help.

It didn't matter how much I did, how I cleaned, how I bleached it all, it wasn't my home that had gotten dirtied.

That shadow hadn't put his filthy hands on my home, but on my mind, my past, my memories and my emotions. He'd riffled through them, watching them as though they were his own personal form of entertainment.

I slid to the floor, my body weak and my mind in chaos. I'd always felt like no matter what happened, my mind was my own. It was the only place I could have complete control, the only thing I knew was mine and mine alone, but that shadow?

He'd taken that security and torn it away, he'd slipped into my memories and that fact terrified me.

He'd tainted the one thing that truly mattered to me. What an asshole.

* * * *

I scraped the butter knife across the toasted bread, smearing the jelly over it all. It was one of those fancy jellies they called fruit spreads with little bits of actual fruit in it, but I could forgive Galen for that.

"You know, sneaking into a werewolf's house is—"

"Dangerous—I know. The real question is why do you only buy this weird healthy stuff?"

He glanced at the jar then shook his head. "It's made with no added sugars."

"Watching your weight?" Even as I asked, I glanced back at him, rewarded with a look at a body that didn't need to lose a single damned pound—*lucky bastard.*

"Sugar's bad for you."

"You're immortal. Why do you care?"

"Immortal or not, unhealthy food leaves you feeling unhealthy. Also, don't you think it's rude to complain about the food you're stealing?"

"Stealing is rather extra, don't you think? *Mi casa es su casa*, right?"

He pressed his lips together, then shook his head as if deciding that arguing with me was far from worth it. It had taken him a long time to come to that decision, but I felt a little pride at the fact he'd finally gotten there.

Instead of arguing, he moved past me and to the fridge. He pulled out a large gallon container and poured the dark liquid into a mason jar, adding ice at the end. "We'll eat outside." He didn't ask my opinion, just carried the drink past me and set it on the table out back.

I finished making the toast, put the jar back into the fridge, then followed Galen out.

He'd left the drink at an open spot, suggesting it was for me. I took him up on the offer, then tried the drink.

It made me smile, the familiar flavor of the sweet tea calming. Despite the chill of December and the light sweater I had on, there was something so comforting about the cold tea that lingered in my mouth even after I swallowed.

"Thanks," I offered, my voice soft, meaning more than just the tea.

He had no idea what else I meant, of course. I hadn't let him in on the little run-in with that shadow and Harrison last night. He'd only worry and bitch and moan—and I sure didn't love those sounds.

However, just coming here made me feel better, like the filth that still seemed stuck in my mind couldn't touch me here.

"You promised me before that you'd see me the next day."

I took a bite of the toast, taking far longer to chew it than I needed to, just to buy time. When I swallowed, I considered taking another bite just to procrastinate more.

"Grey…" Galen said, the name one hell of a warning.

I set down the toast on the plate, giving in. "I wasn't ready."

"You should have answered my calls, at least."

"If I did that, you'd know something was wrong with me." I flashed him a smile, trying to lighten the mood.

Except, Galen didn't seem all too willing to play along. His gaze moved down from my face to my neck, lingering on where I knew scars still rested. Despite Kelvin's little trick not quite working out, the marks hadn't gone away.

"Maybe you've been busy with Kelvin." Galen's tone was flat, as though he tried *very* hard not to show any feelings that might frighten me. It made me wonder just what rested beneath that carefully curated exterior.

And no matter how much I wanted to prod at him, how I wanted to play up the clear upset he had, I didn't.

30

Was this what it felt like to grow up? Or maybe I'd just had such a rough night I lacked the energy.

"No. I haven't seen or spoken to Kelvin since the trial." I laughed softly. "He hasn't tried to contact me, either."

Galen narrowed his eyes. "Aren't you his thrall?"

"Not really. You were there—you saw that I didn't become a Grave."

"You might not be a Grave, but that doesn't mean you aren't bound to him." Galen leaned forward, moving so slowly it felt like a joke, as though he wanted to ensure I could pull back if I wanted to. "The fact that these marks remain tell me that he created some sort of a bond."

I shivered at the stroke of his fingers against the marks. Why did that feel so damn good? As though some line connected those marks right to my clit? My voice came out breathy as I responded. "I can't form bonds like that because of what I am."

"Maybe not a normal bond, but that doesn't mean there isn't any. Be careful, Grey. You have no idea what a bond like that could do to you—or what Kelvin might do because of it."

I snorted. What exactly did he think Kelvin was? Some romantic idiot? "Yeah, well, seeing as he hasn't reached out at all, I don't think there's much to worry about there."

He blew out a long breath, his shoulders drooping in something that almost seemed like relief.

It made me frown. "Why are you so happy about that?"

"I didn't like you going to him," Galen admitted softly. "After I'd offered, and you rejected me, the idea of you choosing him and binding yourself to him didn't sit well." He refused to meet my gaze, instead staring at the floor, until he let out a quiet chuckle. "I probably sound pretty pathetic, don't I?"

"Maybe a little," I admitted, charmed despite my best efforts. Something about Galen sounding like a jealous teenage boy was rather sweet, to be honest. "Look—I didn't go to Kelvin, either." I paused, then shrugged. "Well, I went to the vampires to find the real killer, and he caught me when I was there. In the end, when it seemed like there weren't any other ways out, Kelvin made me his thrall all on his own."

Galen lifted his gaze to mine then, a darkness in his eyes that seemed so at odds with his youthful face. "You're telling me he *forced* that on you? That he made you a thrall by force?"

I froze in the face of that anger, the threat his words made obvious.

As quickly as he'd startled me, though, he jerked his gaze from mine and stared off, as though giving me a bit of space. It let me swallow once and shake off the nerves from seeing him like that.

Somehow it still startled me each time I glimpsed that other side of him, the Spirit that rested inside him. It wasn't him, was nothing like his normal personality, and I damn well knew it. It meant those times when it slipped free, I had to come to terms with the truth—that he wasn't just one man, but two different souls. Worse, as arguably the most powerful of the Weres, at least in this country, his wolf was far from something innocent and sweet.

"Sorry," he muttered, his voice barely above a whisper.

Acknowledging his apology would have forced me to admit he'd bothered me, so I ignored the words and moved on. "Kelvin was trying to do what he thought was best."

"So you'll just forgive him for trying to take your free will away?"

"Forgive? Fuck, no. I just don't think you need to get so pissed. I can get mad all on my own, thank you very much."

Galen snorted, the sound breaking some of the tension between us. "You never change, you know that? Even when you're in trouble, when you need help, you always refuse to take any. You are, without a doubt, the most frustrating person I know."

"I'll take that as a compliment."

"You really shouldn't."

"But if I didn't take insults as compliments, then I'd never *get* any compliments," I pointed out before picking up the toast and taking another bite, savoring the contrast between the crispy bread and sweet, cold jelly. Maybe I needed to take back my complaints about the healthy fruit spreads he used, because this was actually pretty tasty.

We didn't speak for a while as I ate my make-shift breakfast and drank the sweet tea he'd given me. It felt oddly comfortable, as though none of the last few weeks had happened. I'd never gotten put on trial, hadn't almost gotten myself killed—a few times—hadn't ended up on the council.

Nope, it was just me and Galen here. Me being a nuisance and him somehow not killing me over it, just like old times.

"So what are you going to do now?" he asked.

I could have acted as though I had no idea what he meant, but why drag it out anymore? "Ruben said I could still be a courier."

"Even with your position on the council?"

"I'm the leader of a group of one. I guess no one's really worried about me causing problems—at least, no more than usual. Besides, I need the money. Mama needs liquor and porn, and those don't come cheap."

Galen rolled his eyes but didn't respond to my joke, which was only partly a joke. "So when will you start?"

"Ruben put me on contingency. I can work when I want to. I'll probably go back in a week or so."

"You could just come here."

"Are you offering to buy me liquor and porn? Because if so, I want to see you go in and buy it." I smirked at the thought of the youthful looking and strait-laced Galen walking in anywhere to buy such things. It would be a sight worth partaking in, for sure.

He looked my way again, his expression serious. "I'm serious, Grey. You wouldn't have to work, to deal with the Justice Department. You could stay here and it would take away most of your problems."

I tapped my neck. "Didn't this teach us that that sort of thing doesn't work?"

"So you don't officially join my clan? I don't care. I'll still protect you."

And just like that, I sighed, leaning back.

It always came down to this, didn't it? Every person in my life seemed to want the same thing — to own me in some way. They wanted me to give up what I had and accept a place by their side, like that was winning the lottery. They thought me trading my life for theirs was a step up I should take gratefully.

And why did it still disappoint me so much? Why was it still so upsetting to hear that? Maybe because I'd taken so much time trying to stand on my own, because I cherished that freedom so much, so when the people who should have understood me didn't?

It hurt.

But I couldn't explain that because it felt like bearing a fresh wound, like admitting to my own weaknesses, and I hated that.

So I did what I always did. I plastered a smile on my lips and pretended like nothing hurt me.

Chapter Three

There was something uncomfortable about spending time with Ignis. I mean, there was the disconcerting feeling that came with hanging out with a person whose job comprised analyzing the thoughts of people for a living.

Maybe that would have bothered me more if I'd worried about my sanity, but the truth was I knew exactly how shitty my choices were. It didn't take someone with a PhD to recognize that.

Despite that, however, I still adored my time with her. She managed to make me feel as though someone could tolerate me even with all my nonsense.

"Another!" I called out loudly after gulping down the shot, barely giving myself time for a grimace before demanding more.

"Don't you think you should slow down?" Ignis asked.

I pursed my lips and blew a raspberry, sputtering both saliva and liquor as I did so. "Slowing down is the *last* thing I want! We came out to have fun."

"Actually, we 'came out' because you claimed you were in crisis," Ignis said, though her tone held no actual upset.

"I am in crisis."

"Being bored isn't crisis."

Before I could respond, the bartender brought over another four shots and placed them on the table. He sure attended to us quickly, but the flashy credit card I'd given to him earlier opened a hell of a lot of doors, I'd found. It was thicker than most others and made of metal. It was black, and had Kelvin's name along the bottom.

Was it petty to run up his card?

Maybe.

Did I plan to stop?

Well, ask that to my new, fancy outfit and the embarrassingly large bar tab we'd run up so far tonight.

The moment I flashed that card, however, people started acting a hell of a lot nicer. Money really did open doors, and I planned to walk my ass through them at Kelvin's expense.

"So what's with the drinking?" Ignis asked. Her words weren't as crisp as they were when sober, but she also hadn't held up her end of the drinking games. I'd probably gone two or three for every one of her drinks.

Not that that was all that uncommon. For as much as I adored Ignis, she wasn't much of a drinker.

I wasn't either, a lot of the time, but today? Today the idea of getting black-out drunk sounded fan-fucking-tastic. Hell, maybe liquor then a quickie with a handsome and stupid man who took directions well to top off the evening.

"Grey?" Ignis' voice reminded me of her question.

"Rough couple days," I admitted.

She nodded. "I heard from Harrison about what happened."

I flinched at first, thinking about the attack, about that horrible feeling of someone slithering into my mind to unlock everything inside.

"Grey?" Warmth on my arm made me jerk my head up to realize Ignis had been talking to me.

I blinked quickly, trying to clear the intrusive thoughts and memories that I'd hoped I'd drowned in alcohol already. I smiled. "When was that?"

"The other day," she said, the words causing a rush of relief to pour through me. The other day meant he must have just told her about the council nonsense.

And what sort of life did I lead where all of that mess was nonsense?

"Something else happened," she said, her gaze sharp. For a moment, she looked like her brother.

"I told you before—it's rude to pry into other people's minds."

"And I told you, I can't sense your emotions. I'm just good at reading your face. What else happened?"

I waved her off, then picked up another glass and downed the contents in one big, burning gulp. After slamming the glass on the bar, I offered her a wide grin. "Nothing that needs repeating. Now, come on, I didn't come here to mope."

Ignis gave me one hell of a look, one I knew all too well. It was her, 'I disapprove of your poor coping methods' look. However, she was here as my friend, not my therapist, so I shrugged and grabbed another shot glass.

Drinking this much might fix nothing, but it would let me forget about it all for a while.

That was the only thing I had to look forward to anymore.

* * * *

A few hours later and I was delightfully drunk. The music in the bar thundered through my ears and I swayed my body to the music.

Ignis had gone home an hour earlier, after trying to load me into a cab that I had promptly escaped from. I didn't blame her—she'd tried her best to keep me under control. Then again, if men like Kelvin, Galen and Ruben hadn't brought me to heel, Ignis had little chance of it.

The bar wasn't the type made for dancing, but when had such trivialities ever stopped me from having myself a good time? So I stood alone, by the neon-lit jukebox, dancing my black little heart out to the same song I'd put on at least twenty times.

"Knock that off!" a man from the bar yelled, annoyance all over his features.

He was the sort of man who'd been in good shape when he was younger, but time had eventually caught up with him. He was tall and had put weight on so instead of being lean and fit, he was just large.

Not that it mattered—just outweighing me by a hundred pounds put him in a good position no matter how fit he was.

Also, size differences didn't really matter to me.

So I smiled at him, and the idiot misunderstood that as some sort of flirting. I fixed that misconception by lifting my hands, middle fingers extended, all the while never missing the beat as I danced.

He narrowed his eyes, then got up and headed my way. He swayed, but his was because of alcohol rather than the music.

"You've been playing that song for an hour already," the man said, his voice low. "How long are you gonna play it, for fuck's sake?"

I shrugged. "You know when the world is supposed to end? I'm gonna play this for about an hour after that point."

"This ain't your personal bar, little girl."

"Little girl?" I laughed at his insult. "You're the one arguing about music with a little girl, aren't you?"

He pressed his lips together and took another step closer. The crow inside me fluttered, already on cloud nine. Making bad choices, drinking too much, insulting men twice my size, those were all things that it adored.

Anything to put me in a place to get into trouble pleased it.

"That's enough," called out the bartender. "Sit down, Tony."

"But she—"

The bartender offered one hell of a glare, cutting the man off with that look. "She's been paying well and tipping even better all night. If she wants to dance, let her dance."

The man curled his lip into a snarl before turning around, the words "*rich cunt*" leaving his lips under his breath.

I waved at his back while he retreated just as my stomach growled.

Huh. When I thought about it, I had no idea when I'd eaten anything beyond liquor. It had to have been the toast that morning with Galen.

After the time I'd spent here, seeing what I had, there was no chance I'd eat here. Food poisoning was the sort of trouble even I didn't want to screw with.

So I slid the black card once more through the jukebox and selected the same song to play on repeat.

If that guy hated me now, I had a feeling when the song played for the next—I tried to read the screen despite the way everything spun—four days or so, he'd like me even less.

And that sure put a hop in my step as I exited the bar.

I tried to glance at the time on my phone, but everything seemed far too blurry to make sense. I blamed that on my phone rather than the alcohol, figuring from the empty streets that it must have been around one in the morning.

I reached for the wall as I stumbled down the sidewalk, using my fingertips to maintain my balance as I went. The sound of cars and the cool air against my drunken, flushed skin felt amazing, and they all felt a bit like a music of their own.

The wonderful numbness in my head, the cloudy thoughts, they all helped erase…well…everything.

It made my uncertain future fade away, made the memories of the attack cloudy and helped me ignore the footsteps that followed me.

Wait, that last one might be important…

I tripped, stumbling against the trunk of a tree planted in the sidewalk, the sort of thing supposed to make it look less like a concrete jungle. I had to force my brain to focus on that last thing.

Footsteps.

Right, there *were* ones, that had been following me since I'd left the bar. Was it the man I'd flipped off? The idea made me laugh. It shouldn't have, but something about it just seemed so fucking funny.

Though that was probably due to the liquor more than anything else.

The streets weren't empty, but neither were they exactly bustling. On the weekends, it would have been busy, but at this time of night during the week, few people remained outside.

Not that I was the type to go to others for help. It reminded me of what Ignis had said earlier, the same thing Galen said, the same thing *everyone* said. I wasn't trying to be difficult, though. I just knew better than to reach out.

Drowning alone was far preferable to knowing someone I trusted and reached out for didn't try to save me.

So, nope. The idea of running to anyone else didn't even occur to me.

My phone vibrated in my hand, so I hit the green icon on the screen after three failed attempts. "Hello?"

"You ran away from Ignis."

I smiled at Harrison's voice that somehow managed to sound both annoyed and yet flat at the same time. "She isn't a big drinker. Did you know that?"

"Alcohol makes it harder to filter our powers," he said. "Few Minds drink because of that."

"Boooooring." I drew out the word to drive home my point. "Why don't you take her place? I bet you'd make a fun drinking buddy."

"As I just said, Minds don't drink. That includes me."

"*Fine*, you could be the designated driver. Take me place to place! With a face as pretty as yours, I bet we'd get into every club." I tripped over an uneven paver on the sidewalk, but this time there was no tree to stop my downward path. I groaned at a pain in my knee, not entirely sure what happened, but fairly sure I'd scraped it.

"What happened?" Harrison asked.

"Stupid sidewalk moved."

"I doubt that happened. It seems more likely that you simply have no idea about your own limits. Where are you?"

I rolled over so I sat, the idea of getting back to my feet about as daunting as climbing Everest. A glance around me at the few still lit signs told me I'd only made it down about a block from the bar. "I'm on the strip, just past that old piercing place. Oh, come down here! We'll get matching piercings!"

"I don't want a piercing."

"But we could *match*. Or we'll go opposites. I'll get the left nipple done, you get the right. No! Wait, I'll get the right done. My left is more sensitive."

A low rumble came through the line, the sound something between annoyance and incredulous, like he couldn't quite believe the sound had come from him. "Just stay there."

"You're going to come save me?"

"If I don't, and something happens to you, my sister will never give me a moment of peace again."

"Ignis can be mean." I folded my legs, ignoring the few people who did pass as they made sure to not lock eyes with me. Then again, I was a drunken blue-haired girl sitting in the middle of the sidewalk at one in the morning. I guess I wasn't what others considered good friend material.

"Why do you do this?" he asked after I thought he might have hung up.

"Do what?"

"Drink yourself to this point. Ignis said she tried to get you to go home a few times, but you slipped her grasp. You clearly did it on purpose. Why?" He paused, then asked, his voice softer, "Was it because of what happened?"

"I'm not smart enough for trauma," I said, not feeling the laugh I hung on the words like a costume. "I just felt like a girl's night was in order."

He made a soft sound, one that implied he didn't believe me. That was fine—who did?

Pain in my head made me wince, and for a moment, I wondered if it was the alcohol. Was this some aneurysm caused by my horrible habits? Maybe my body was giving up the good fight, like the victim in an abusive relationship who had had enough.

Except, as quickly as I'd thought that, I recognized that shooting pain through my temples.

It was like that night.

I gasped, dropping the phone to grab my head for all the good it had done me before.

"Grey?" Harrison's voice came from the speaker, but it seemed miles away.

Instead, the rushing of that pain was all I heard, at least until that *other* voice echoed in my skull. "*I told you I'd see you again.*"

I whined softly, trying not to respond even as that voice whispered to me, "*To think you'd go out alone so quickly. How stupid can you be? Or do you have some sort of reckless death wish? Maybe you wanted to meet me again and came out here for that reason?*"

I shook my head, unable to utter any words. I wasn't sure if the alcohol numbed the pain or the pain pushed back the alcohol, but I felt less drunk than I had earlier.

"*What should we explore this time? I saw fear from you before, but you have so many layers, so much hidden. Let's see what else I can find.*" After he said that, like a soda can opening, panic bled through me.

This time I saw myself at fifteen, in the back of a car with a handsy boy I'd thought liked me, who I'd gone with thinking it was the start of some beautiful romance. Instead of that, however, I'd found myself parked in the middle of nowhere with Handsy-McGee yanking my skirt off.

Now I could laugh about it, about my own stupidity, about the whole fucking thing, but in the moment? I recalled the fear — no, not just recalled, I *felt* it beating at me. That helplessness, the way he'd held me down, the disgust he'd looked at me with like I were trash, just a toy for him.

"Even crows can bite." The voice of the man who had made me slithered to me, beneath the panic, through the shadow's voice, all of it.

It gave me the moment I needed, and my crow stretched her wings inside me. It wasn't much, but it was just enough to slam shut that memory, to lock it away.

A cry echoed in my head, one that said the shadow hadn't guessed me capable of that. To be fair, I wasn't sure how I did it, either.

I blinked, waking from that horror, to someone crouched before me.

And I couldn't stop myself from letting out a scream when I found myself face to face with Harrison.

Chapter Four

I couldn't seem to scrub that memory from my mind. It was worse than the one I'd gone through before, because this one I clearly recalled on my own. I remembered after that, how fucked up I'd felt, the way I'd showered and scrubbed and thrown away the clothing I'd had on. Maybe for someone else it would have been some defining moment, but it almost felt worse that it wasn't.

Someone touched my shoulder, causing me to jerk away, my eyes peeled wide. I could still *feel* that memory, the way that asshole had grabbed at me, the sensation of his warm, sour breath on my face.

Harrison pulled his hand away and took a step backward. His expression showed no signs of hurt, as though my overreaction didn't matter to him, though he still gave me space.

"Sorry," I muttered, then forced myself to put on that mask I always wore, the one of the jokester who nothing ever affected. "Who would have figured I'd become a germaphobe, huh?"

He shook his head as though disappointed by the weak attempt, then set a drink before me. I didn't ask what it was before picking it up and taking a sip.

And immediately spitting it back into the cup. "What the hell is that?"

"Tea."

"I've *had* tea. It isn't this gross, bitter leaf juice."

"You've had sweet tea, Grey. That is not the same thing. Now, drink it."

"No, thank you."

He lifted one of his light-colored eyebrows as though unused to people telling him no. "You were attacked by a Mind for the second time in less than a week. That will throw your body out of sorts and can cause low magnesium. Thus, the tea is made with a magnesium supplement to counter that before you suffer from the effects, which can include anxiety, trouble sleeping and muscle cramps." He gestured at the cup. "Now, *drink.*"

I thought about arguing again—the taste really was horrible—but the idea of having added anxiety on top of the mess in my head seemed worse. I gave in and lifted the cup, staring it down like an enemy. Thankfully, it wasn't that hot, so I did it the same way I did cheap liquor, gulping it down like a shot before slamming the cup on the table.

Harrison sighed—*loudly*—before taking the cup away. "Was that my own little glimpse into what you look like drinking?"

"A lady never tells. Besides, you could come bar hopping with me if you want. I bet you're fun after a few shots."

"As I said—"

"Yeah, yeah, yeah, I know." I paused, then furrowed my brows. "Why does Ignis drink, then?"

"She's far less powerful, so it doesn't affect her as much. It just causes us to have trouble controlling our powers, but it doesn't increase them. For her, it causes headaches, and she feels the emotions of those around her more, but it isn't nearly as troublesome or dangerous as it would be for me."

"You have those subtle brags down, don't you?"

"It is hardly a brag—subtle or not."

"Yep. *Poor me, I'm just a super powerful and handsome Mind. You should feel so bad for me.*"

"That is the lamentations of those who misunderstand the stresses of power. Ignis may live where she wishes. She can interact with who she pleases, shape her life as she wants. For me, that is not possible."

I glanced around his massive living room, the décor sparse and modern. "Yeah… I feel really bad for you in your mansion."

"Do you know *why* I live here?"

"Because you're filthy rich?"

"Because this property sits on five acres, giving me enough space to not worry about neighbors."

When I didn't seem to understand what he meant, he sat in a chair across from me.

"I have lived here for ten years, but it was not my first home on my own. I lived closer to the city at first, in a smaller place with neighbors to each side. I had thought I'd learned enough control to make it safe. However, as the days passed to weeks then months, the community around me changed. That softness that existed before, the closeness between the residents, it cracked and left jagged edges. Couples split up, families fought, children suffered, but still I assumed those things the normal goings-on beneath the surface of all places. It was four months after moving in when I awoke to the flashing lights of police on the street." He crossed one of his legs over the other, resting his ankle on the opposite knee. Despite his flat, careful words, a tremor vibrated beneath them, a sign that it affected him more than he let on. "The father in the house to my left had been a sweet and quiet man. He'd lived his life doing everything he was expected to. It took only four months of living beside me for him to take a gun and end the lives of his wife, his three children, then himself."

I sucked in a quick breath, the story worse than I would have even guessed. The horror of such an action was bad enough, but the realization that he was responsible for it? A weight that heavy could easily end a person.

He nodded, then jerked his gaze from mine to stare out of the large window that showed the open land between him and any neighbors. "So you understand now why I live where I do. People can spend short periods of time around me, but eventually they all become affected. No matter how strong a person, spending time around me *will* turn them to their darker feelings. They will give in to the darkness inside them because that is what my power does – it infects those who come in close contact with me."

I frowned as his words – full of so much self-hatred – hung in the surrounding air. And, even if his reasoning was different, even if the effect he had on others was different from my own, I understood that isolation.

My crow did the same thing, didn't it? Hell, I'd been annoying even before that, but since changing? I thought about my place, full of stolen trinkets I'd been unable to *not* pocket, the times I'd annoyed others just because I couldn't help it.

How much worse would I feel if my actions had caused actual harm to others?

But I knew better than to come out and say that. Harrison was proud, just like me, and he wouldn't appreciate that from me.

So instead, I brought my legs up and crossed them in front of me on the couch. "So why'd you bring me here?"

"You being attacked was my fault."

"Pretty sure you didn't do it." I paused, a nagging concern I couldn't quite identify refusing to go away. "You didn't do it, right?"

He tilted his head as though he couldn't make sense of my words.

"I mean, you did show up *both* times I was attacked, and you are a Mind, right? So, you didn't do it, did you?"

He blew out a slow breath as though I were a lot to deal with. "No, Grey, I did not attack you. I am apologizing because I never thought you would be targeted. You told me what the attacker said, and I disregarded that. For that reason, you being attacked a second time is my fault."

I waved my hand at him to dismiss his worries. "Please. I get attacked often enough that it's hardly anyone's fault. You can't take that on your shoulders."

"Regardless—you are being targeted by someone who is under my command. That makes me responsible. If he has attacked you twice, I see no reason he wouldn't make a third attempt. For that reason, you should remain here. Under my protection, you will be safe."

"What happened to the whole — *I am an island, I must live alone* – thing?"

"You do not appear to be affected by my powers. I can't read your mind or feel your emotions and you don't react to my feelings. You seem to be perhaps the only person who can remain this close to me."

I pursed my lips as I thought about it. That was *almost* some weird romantic notion, like fate had bound us. Maybe it had? Fate was one random ass bitch, after all.

"What if I don't want to stay?" I asked.

"I won't force you. You can leave if you wish. However, there is a very good chance that you will be attacked again if you do. Given your reaction this time, I suspect you'd rather that not happen?"

I snorted at his high and mighty tone. "You know I have other friends, too, right? You're not my only option."

"Actually, I am. Minds attack in a way that other Spirits cannot defend against. A vampire or a werewolf or a justice or even a druid could do nothing to keep you safe. However, no Mind is stronger than I am, and I would immediately sense them before they even got close. Also, this one has fled from me twice, so I doubt they'll approach while I am here."

I exhaled in a quick rush, feeling entirely outmaneuvered. "Fine," I said when I could come up with no other option. He was right that I didn't want to experience that hell again, so I lacked any actual choice.

Harrison nodded, then rose, reminding me he was taller than I realized. "I expect that I will handle this issue within the month, at which point you can return to your old place and your normal life. Until then, I will try to make this as easy a process as possible. You must be tired—and still drunk—so follow me to your room."

I did as he said, because it was far from the first time I'd had to be put to bed to sober up. Of course, it wasn't usually in a strange house with a man who probably wasn't going to sleep with me.

This was shaping up to be a really fucking boring sleepover.

* * * *

He was touching me *everywhere*. It made me want to scream, but nothing came out of my mouth, fear tightening my throat. I shoved, but he grabbed my wrists and held them in a single hand, making me curse the fact that men were so much stronger.

The sharp edge of his belt buckle dug into my thigh since he hadn't removed his pants. This wasn't important enough for him to do that. So instead of bare skin against mine, it was just rough cloth and droplets of sweat.

"Relax, Grey," he whispered. "Just let it happen."

Just accept it. Just do what I was supposed to. Stop being so difficult. I'd heard it all my life, the vicious words that had carved out so much of my soul.

"Grey," the voice repeated, the tone slightly different. I shook my head and tried to push away both the man and the voice. The calling of my name went on, shifting from that breathless, vile, lust-filled voice to a more familiar one, though the edge of panic was new.

"Grey!" That last shout got through, and I bolted upright.

I stared around, having no idea where I was for a long moment. Light streamed in through a window, the warmth of it a nice way to wake — my racing heart aside.

On the other side, standing next to the bed, was Harrison with a strange expression on his face. Fuck, I didn't know his face could *do* that. Normally he had little to no emotion, so bad that he reminded me of older women who paralyzed their faces to the point they couldn't move them anymore. Maybe that was why the way he looked at me was even more startling than my nightmare.

"What a way to wake up," I muttered, leaning forward on the bed to catch my breath.

"You were crying and whimpering," Harrison said. "Why?"

"What, you've never heard of a nightmare?"

A line appeared between his eyebrows as though he had to do some serious mental gymnastics to make sense of his own thoughts. "I have never seen you make such faces or noises. I found them…distressing."

I laughed softly. "Well, I'm so sorry for distressing you."

He sat on the edge of the bed beside me. "Such noises don't bother me generally. I feel people's emotions already, even if I attempt to ignore it, to block it out. It's normal for me, so why is it that when *you* do it, I feel…uneasy?"

I had no idea what to say, so instead I took a moment to study his face. It somehow looked different than it had before. I recalled when I'd first argued with him at Ignis' office, the way he'd stared at me as though I'd been nothing.

No, that wasn't quite right. I'd thought it was pride or arrogance before, but I knew better now.

It had been fear.

Fear of getting close, fear of feeling too much, those had kept him distant. However, sitting beside me, he didn't seem nearly so far away.

He seemed really fucking annoyed about it, too.

"Was the nightmare because of another attack?" I asked.

"No. I would have felt that. Was the nightmare the same thing from the attack?"

I nodded, shuddering as soon as it brought back the sickening feelings from the nightmare. My stomach rolled, and I worried for a moment I wouldn't be able to keep it down.

All the alcohol I'd drank the night before probably worsened the situation.

I wasn't some freshman co-ed who'd never drank before, though, so I swallowed to settle my stomach and drew my hands into tight fists.

"You flinched last night."

"What?"

"When I touched your shoulder, you jerked away. Minds can not only go through the memories of a person, but can create horrors of their own. Which was it that they made you see?"

"My own memory."

He nodded, still not looking my way. "I thought so. There's a type of pain between fantasy and reality. False horrors are terrible, but memories? Knowing it happened? Those hold a different level of panic. What was the memory?"

"Yeah, thanks, but I'm not really interested in tearing open that wound for you to dig around in."

He sighed, the sound making my chest ache. Why the fuck should I have felt bad over not wanting to tell

Harrison every last little painful event in my life? Hell, I barely knew him, all things considered.

Before I needed to explain myself, however, he spoke again. "I understand. However, you should sleep more."

"After that dream? Not happening."

"I was thinking—I can't feel your emotions or thoughts normally, but perhaps if I attempted it, I could help?"

"No thanks." I tapped my temple. "This is a clear VIP members only, and I'm the only VIP on the list. I like to keep this mess private."

"I wouldn't try to read you, just to ease you back to sleep. I think I could keep any additional nightmare away."

I took my bottom lip between my teeth, unsure. The last thing I wanted was another nightmare, but the idea of relying on him, of trusting him, that felt even scarier than the dream itself.

I shook my head to refuse. "Thanks, but I'll be okay."

"I just want to help, and that isn't something I normally want to do."

"I know, and I mean it, thanks for the offer. I just…" I sighed, then forced myself to answer truthfully. "I feel like someone has already walked all around in my brain, and the last thing I could handle right now is for someone else in there. I need to feel like my mind is my own."

He sighed but nodded. "I understand. I don't like it, but I understand your reasoning. Well, if you won't go back to sleep, then go ahead and use the bathroom, then dress. There are some items hanging in the closet for you to use, and we will stop by your place today to pick up the things you need. You have an hour before we leave." With that, he rose, the softness between us disappearing as though it had never been there at all.

It made me wonder just how much that man was hiding, because he sure as fuck wasn't telling me everything.

Chapter Five

Walking around outside helped clear my mind.

Doing it beside Harrison reminded me of all the shit I'd rather not think about, though.

He had spoken little after my shower. In fact, by the time we left the house, he reminded me far more of the man I'd gotten used to before. He seemed closed off, his words careful and flat.

Was that because he had to focus more when out and around others? Was the glimpse I'd gotten of him at the house the real him? The one beneath the layers of control and shields and power?

Ever since leaving, he'd hardly looked my way. It felt as though he had little idea I even existed beside him. Despite walking along together, he didn't seem to pay any attention to me.

My toes caught on the sidewalk—not all that uncommon, really—and I braced myself to hit the ground as usual. Instead, strong arms caught me.

I twisted to find Harrison with his arm around me.

So much for thinking he wasn't paying attention to me…

He released me as quickly as he'd saved me, though. "You need to pick your feet up more when you walk."

"That's not the problem."

"Then what is it? Will you blame the sidewalk?"

"Not the sidewalk — my crow."

"You blame a bird?"

And *wow*, was that a mocking question.

"Not just any bird. You saw — I am evidently the Clan of Chaos. Things around me just go wrong. That means things break around me and my feet will almost always find any little imperfection in a sidewalk."

"Is that why you fell last night?"

"No — that one was all tequila."

He shook his head before continuing on, not waiting as though he knew I'd catch up either way.

Which I did, despite my short little legs.

"So where are we going?" I asked when the boredom got to me. We'd driven to an area off the strip, and Harrison had parked the car in a large, public lot. It was strange to see him around so many humans.

Usually, I saw him either in terms of the council or alone. Seeing him in the midst of the busy sidewalks made him stand out.

He really was handsome…

Fuck, the man could have been a model. His pale skin and perfectly formed jaw would be totally fitting on the cover of a magazine. I imagined him talking about his workout regimen and how he drinks gross tea and meditates when at home. The bright sun made his hair appear an even lighter shade of blond, and the curls made it seem wild.

"We are going to meet with a group of Minds."

"Why?"

"I have to check in. It is part of my duties, and given our search for your attacker, it makes sense to touch base with a few of my people."

"Great. Spending time with a bunch of people who can crawl around in my head is exactly what I was hoping to do today. I thought the whole point of being with you was to prevent that."

"You worry too much. You will be under my protection, so nothing will happen."

As much as I wanted to argue—the memories of the times that fucker had riffled through my brain like a pervert in a panties' drawer still far too fresh—I couldn't.

Doing nothing wasn't going to help, after all, and showing fear was so not my style.

So I tucked my hands into the pockets of the dress I had on, the one I'd borrowed from the selection Harrison had in the guest closet. It was loose and long, easy to move in, and I'd thrown on a jean jacket from my place when we'd stopped to pack some of my stuff.

The meeting place, as it turned out, was the upper floor of a standalone building. The bottom floor was a liquor store—I filed that away for later—and upstairs was a DUI lawyer on one side and a clock repair place on the other.

We went into the clock repair place, which I figured I probably had far less of a need for compared to a lawyer.

"Harrison," the employee behind the counter said, rising from his seat in a rush. "I didn't know you'd come today."

Harrison folded his hands behind him, not reacting, as though the panic on the other man's face wasn't there. "I saw no reason to announce my visit. Is the meeting happening as scheduled?"

"Yes, of course."

"How many?"

"Six. Just the regulars." He turned his gaze to me, a question there. I had a feeling if it had been anyone else, he'd have asked about me. His fear of Harrison must have kept him quiet.

I waved. "Hi. I'm Grey."

His eyes opened wider, answering whether or not he'd heard of me. I'd started getting this reaction more and more as news of the new council seat became more widespread. "O-oh. Okay, well, welcome."

It would probably be damn rude to laugh when he was so clearly terrified, but I couldn't help it. Who the fuck was *ever* afraid of me? If only I could leverage this reaction for my own gain. I'd probably have a lot fewer problems if people were that afraid of me.

Harrison made a soft noise though his expression didn't change at all. In fact, if I hadn't heard it myself — the soft, mocking snort — I wouldn't have believed he'd done it all.

Wasn't that just like him, though?

The man gestured toward a door behind him. "Well, go on in."

Harrison didn't acknowledge the offer, as though he had every right to go wherever the fuck he pleased. That arrogance was annoying, but somehow at odds with the Harrison who had spoken to me last night and this morning.

Still, I followed him as he went into the back. At first, I found what I expected — a room full of clock parts and shit I didn't quite understand. However, to the left sat another unassuming door. Harrison didn't hesitate before turning the handle and walking in.

The room was brightly lit and open — nothing like the cluttered and dusty storage room or the front of the shop. Instead, this reminded me of the sort of place someone might hold a self-help meeting. Fuck, there was even a table at the back with coffee and pastries.

I immediately headed that direction. I'd skipped breakfast and just the sight of something sugary made my stomach rumble. It was the perfect thing to soak up the rest of the nonsense in my stomach after drinking so much last night.

I had a muffin in my mouth before I realized we weren't alone, turning mid-bite to find six people in the room staring at me like I was some weird aberration.

That seemed rude, since I felt like Harrison would stick out *far* more than I did.

So I waved before swallowing the poorly chewed bite. "Tasty."

Harrison sighed, then turned toward the group, who had seemed to just notice him as well.

"Harrison," a woman said, her voice only slightly less terrified than the man up front had been.

All the people sat on folding chairs placed in a circle, all different ages and with no single feature the same among them.

Men, women, young and old, some dressed in nice clothing and others looking as though they hadn't slept under a roof in weeks. In short? I wouldn't have guessed these six would have anything in common.

However, given Harrison's presence and his previous statements, I had to guess they were all Minds.

Which were so not my favorite people currently.

Harrison didn't sit, but standing there made me feel entirely on display. Instead, I inched forward and took an empty seat, nibbling on the muffin, trying to blend into the background. At least with them noticing him, I'd become less interesting.

"Why did you come?" the woman asked.

"Do I need a reason?" Harrison responded.

She jerked her head back and forth, as if trying to immediately backpedal. "Of course not. You just rarely come to these. I was worried you might have come today because there was a problem."

Harrison shifted his gaze, taking in each of the people seated in the room, a heaviness in his look that implied there were other facts I wasn't privy to. It felt more like an interrogation than a simple meet and greet.

And when I had no idea what else to do, I lifted the muffin to my mouth and took another noisy bite.

The sound made Harrison look my way and narrow his eyes.

"Sorry," I said around the mouthful of sweet, tasty goodness.

Still, the action broke the tension and it almost seemed as if everyone took a deep breath.

"I am sure you have heard about the recent attacks by Minds," Harrison said.

The woman nodded, fidgeting in her seat—not the best sign of innocence. Then again, I was pretty sure almost every person would shift like that under Harrison's harsh gaze. "I've heard about them, but I can assure you, no one here is involved."

"Are you certain?" Harrison took a few steps closer, stopping just beside the chair I sat in. "Everyone in this room is a Cloud addict, after all."

Cloud?

The word meant nothing to me beyond the vague place where people sent files from their phones.

However, I had a feeling me speaking up would only hinder the whole conversation. Better to stay quiet and piece it all together on my own—at least until I got a bit more information.

Just the mention of this cloud stuff had everyone avoiding Harrison's gaze, just like when a personal trainer talked about desserts. Still, the woman spoke up, her voice shaky. "That's why we're here, why we meet every week no matter what. If we were using, would we be here?"

Harrison nodded. "A fair point. However, backslides happen. People believe they can have just one more taste, then stop yet again. How many have joined such groups as these only to disappear one day? Now, I am not here to accuse those here today—I wish to know if there are any who have recently stopped coming."

The woman sighed, her shoulders dropping. "There are always those who come once and never again."

"The person I'm looking for would have stopped coming two months ago."

I twisted to look up at Harrison. Two months ago implied he'd been aware of the person that long, which he hadn't said a word to me about. It said he'd tracked this person since before my whole mess with the vampires.

Which said he'd left a lot more victims than I realized.

The woman shook her head. "No one stands out, but I'll give you the records I have." She hesitated, then asked, her voice softer. "I heard about a few deaths. Do you think it's the same person?"

I expected Harrison not to answer. In my experience, he was fantastic at not giving the information requested when he didn't want to. However, he did the unexpected and nodded. "I believe the same addict has been targeting people for the past two months. Given the attacks occurred before an influx of Cloud, I believe the person manufacturing it is the same who is using it. Thus far, twelve have died and one victim survived, unharmed. All evidence suggests they had the same perpetrator."

"A survivor?" The woman leaned forward, her attention rapt. "I've never heard of someone surviving intact. Were they a Spirit?"

"Yes, they were."

"What clan?"

"Chaos."

The woman frowned, then darted her gaze toward me.

"Is this where I introduce myself?" I asked.

Harrison set his hand on my shoulder, the weight surprisingly comforting. "This is Grey, the head of the Chaos Clan. The perpetrator attacked her *twice*."

The woman got to her feet, her gaze sharp and surprisingly terrifying for such a small woman. "She survived *two* attacks? How is that possible? Cloud victims don't recover."

"She is unique. I believe that is why the attacker has targeted her multiple times. The structure of her brain must be different enough to entice the suspect, because he appears to have fixated on her."

The woman stepped closer, her bright blue eyes locked on me in a way that made me want to back away. Something about that look rooted me in place, though. A strange sensation ran through me, like someone stroking across my mind with feather-light touches.

"I wonder what that feels like," the woman whispered, her tone sounding as though she spoke only to herself. "I wonder what she tastes like."

And *fuck* did I dislike that familiar phrasing. I got to my feet that time, knocking the chair backward, especially as the light touches turned to pressure. It wasn't the same pain I'd experienced before, not the stabbing through my temples. That had felt like a sledgehammer, whereas this was a flick.

Though, given the woman's gaze, I doubted she held back on purpose. It must have shown a difference in power—or maybe this Cloud thing?

I found myself jerked backward, the action finally breaking the contact. Harrison pulled me closer to his side, and being so near felt oddly like he'd taken me within his protection. Suddenly, the woman could no longer reach me.

"Enough," he snapped, his voice rougher and lower than usual.

The woman blinked quickly, as though waking up, and the moment she came to her senses, she gasped and covered her mouth. "I didn't mean to," she rushed out. "I just wondered what someone would see in her to do that and before I knew it..." Her voice trailed off, her body trembling. She didn't look a bit like the terrifying thing that had closed in on me, once again appearing frail and small.

"You just attempted to attack someone with your powers, someone I had afforded my protection to. You thus forfeit your life."

"Her life?" I pulled away from Harrison, placing myself between the two, my back to the woman. Right now, she seemed the lesser danger. "Whoa, whoa now. Let's not get quite so murdery right off the bat, huh?"

"She attacked you. Had I not been here, there is no telling what might have occurred. I cannot let that go unpunished."

"Pretty sure it's my life and what little is left of my brain we're talking about, right? That means it's at least a little my business. You can't kill someone over giving me a very slight headache."

"She knew the risks. If I allow this to go without retribution, such behavior will continue."

One glance up at Harrison's face made me want to back away. Sure, Harrison was a stick in the mud, but I hadn't viewed him as all that dangerous before.

I should have. He headed his clan for a reason, and that reason was his power.

This was the first time I really thought he might actually use said power, though. And for this reason? *Insane.*

"She didn't hurt me. You really think someone should die because they had a split second of thinking about something that *never happened?*"

He pressed his lips together. A tic in his cheek said that was exactly what he thought but voicing that would make him look like a monster. *Ah, good old social conditioning.* People didn't like to look heartless. "Very well," he muttered, his words sullen. "I'll let you decide, since you were the victim. However, if anything occurs afterward, it will be your fault."

"Enough stuff is my fault that I probably wouldn't even notice." I let out a breath when Harrison folded his arms, a sign that he wasn't going to go all brimstone and vengeance.

It let me turn around to face the woman, who hadn't moved an inch. She reminded me of a kid whose parents fought. The last thing she wanted was to draw that sort of attention to her. "Thank you," she whispered. "I didn't mean to..."

Harrison shook his head. "You made this choice— you deal with it." He left those words for me before walking out, though I had a feeling he wouldn't go farther than the storage room.

It left me alone with the others, but the threat of Harrison remaining so close would keep me safe. *Probably.*

The best I could hope for was probably.

"I really am sorry," she said again. "And thank you for stopping him."

I shrugged before grabbing another muffin—a blueberry this time—and sat down again. "No harm, no foul in my book. I've gotten an actual taste of what one of you can do. I can let anything short of that slide."

The woman sat as well. "My name is Reba."

"What is this Cloud shit he was talking about?"

She furrowed her brows as though surprised I wouldn't know, but didn't call me out on that ignorance. "It's a drug that enhances the abilities of Mind Spirits. However, it also creates a euphoric high and removes their abilities to control themselves. Minds on that drug, especially at high doses, often kill others."

"Why would anyone make something like that?" I went with that question because it felt more polite than asking why any idiot would take it, sitting in the room of addicts.

"Being a Mind is difficult in a way the other clans don't deal with. We are not human, but we have to live

67

human lives. We don't age slower, we aren't immortal, we are as likely to fall sick or injured as any human. Additionally, our powers can't be turned off or ignored."

"How does increasing a person's power help that?"

"Because for that bit of time, we get to revel in what we are. It's like…bloodlust for a vampire. It strips away all the questions, all the fears, everything. Instead of feeling all those negative things myself, I get to taste them from someone else." As she spoke, her eyes glazed over.

I'd seen that look before, from alcoholics who knew how terrible liquor was for them, but still missed their fond memories of it. At least this time, she didn't seem likely to attack me over it.

"So if no one has been here that you think could have done it, you can't offer anything. Thanks anyway, sorry for interrupting your meeting." I rose, feeling as though we'd made little progress.

"Wait," a boy who couldn't have been over sixteen said. His voice was soft, as though he had to fight with himself to force the words from his throat. He trembled, and my chest ached as I looked at him.

A kid that young shouldn't be here, shouldn't have that terrified look on his face. He should be chasing girls and going to school and worried about little beyond a party that weekend. How the fuck was he here, in a meeting for addicts?

I said nothing, pausing to give him the time and space to gather his courage and speak.

Finally, he lifted his gaze to mine. "There's more Cloud coming through lately, and it's stronger than before."

"How do you know that?" Reba asked.

The boy flinched, rubbing his hands together as though to dispel his nerves. "People talk. I know more and more Minds who have tried it out lately." He shook his head, then rushed out, "But not me. I'm done with it, I swear. I just hear about it."

Reba offered a smile more reassuring than I thought she could make. It seemed she wasn't quite as cold as she'd seemed before. Then again, I had a feeling Harrison could bring that negative side out of people pretty easily. "I know that. Just tell us what you know."

The boy nodded, shifting uncomfortably in his chair. "A year ago, no one really knew about Cloud. It was just whispered about in bad areas. Now, though? I don't think I know almost any Minds who haven't had at least a tiny taste. Cloud is really hard to make. Not many people can do it—it's almost an art. Lately, the stuff that has been coming out all has a sparrow on it."

"You're telling me people sign the drugs they make now?" The idea seemed like something out of a shitty crime show. "Isn't that stupid?"

"People want to make money," the kid said. "They want credit for what they do. The issue with Cloud has moved around a lot, it's usually only a problem at one place at a time. I think..." He paused, as though he wasn't sure how to say it, before taking a deep breath and just putting it out there. "I think there's only one main maker of cloud. The other stuff, it's like replicated—and not well—but the good stuff only shows up one place."

"So you're telling me the main distributor of Cloud is here now?"

"That's my guess."

"So if I can find that main distributor and stop them, then the person after me won't be able to get anymore

Cloud and will just have whatever he's already bought?"

"Cloud doesn't last more than a few days. It decays fast. So if you can stop the person making it, after a few days, you'll be safe," the kid acknowledged.

Finally, some good news, a plan, a possible way forward.

Who said kids were useless these days? As it turned out, they knew where the drugs were!

* * * *

My head ached, no matter how hard I tried to ignore it. It wasn't a hangover, not anymore.

Maybe I had a cold coming on? I tended to be hardier than humans, but I still could catch the nasty bugs when they went around.

"You are frowning," Harrison said. "Are you bored here? I know people can be uncomfortable being alone so much."

"No. I don't really mind that part, especially with how crazy my life was for a while. It's kind of nice, honestly."

"So why are you frowning?"

"I'm not feeling great," I admitted. "I was thinking I should go over to Galen's."

"Why?"

"He's a good mother hen type. I bet he'd make me soup and fuss over me."

Harrison dropped his gaze, as though deep in thought. "You don't think I could take care of you?"

"You don't strike me as the nursing type." I shrugged as I said it, not expecting him to take it too hard. We all had to accept the things we were good at and the things we weren't. Harrison excelled at that silent glare, and was evidently extremely powerful, but a caring, mothering type?

Nope—not even a little.

Maybe that was why it surprised me to see him frowning. I'd said *far* worse to him before and he hadn't so much as blinked, but somehow *this* bullshit marked the end of his world?

I might have cared at another time, but I really didn't feel well. His fragile ego was not my problem, especially right now.

"I'm going to go lie down," I said as I got up and off the couch.

"You should eat dinner first."

I shook my head. "Food sounds like a no-go right now. A little sleep and I think I'll feel better." I didn't wait for an answer before heading for my room.

I slept in fitful spurts. An hour here, thirty minutes there, but each time I woke, I felt the same. My head ached, my skin felt warm to the touch and, in general, the last thing I wanted was to wake up and do anything.

However, when the sun had set, a knock on the door told me my time of hiding away had ended.

I didn't answer, but Harrison still walked in as though he owned the place.

Which, considering this was his house, I guess he sort of did.

Still, annoying.

I didn't bother even rolling over, instead staying cocooned in the blankets of my bed. At least, I did until a heavenly scent hit my nose.

The world could be a frozen tundra of unhappiness, and I'd still venture out in search of the source of a scent like that.

When I rolled and sat up, I found Harrison there, a bowl in his hands.

"You need to eat," he said.

"Did you order that?"

He furrowed his brows, his expression peeved. "Does it matter? When a person is sick, they should eat well. As a Mind, I am more susceptible than most Spirits to things like illness, so I know how to take care of it."

I narrowed my eyes, not trusting him at all. It felt like a tiger bringing food to their prey — probably just a ploy to fatten me up.

However, one glance at the soup made it clear I was easily bought. The surface was translucent, with floating white ribbons of egg in it. "Is that egg flower soup?"

He handed the bowl to me, using one finger to hold the spoon in place. "It is. This soup is warm and gentle on the stomach. You need energy to beat such illnesses, and you need to eat to get that."

The first taste told me I should apologize for what I'd said the night before. Even if he had ordered it, what did that matter? And while my smart-ass mouth wanted to make fun of him for this, I wouldn't risk not getting more of this heavenly goodness.

I ate more quickly than I probably should have, but I couldn't stop or slow myself. The tiny bites of corn inside, the subtle chicken flavor, it all blended perfectly and warmed me up from the inside out.

"You look better," he said as he took a seat on the bed beside me. "The food and sleep must have helped."

I nodded, speaking despite my mouth full and my cheeks puffed out like a hamster. "I'm still not a hundred, but I don't feel like death anymore. Why? Do we have plans?"

"Not today, no, but tomorrow we do."

"And what plans are those?"

"Do you fancy going back to school?"

I thought back to my olden days, when I'd gone to school, and shuddered. "No fucking thanks."

"Not a fan of those days?"

"You've seen the trouble I get into now — do you really think I did well in a highly regimented environment like a school?"

"I thought you didn't become a Spirit until later?"

I took another bite of the soup, hating that my spoon scraped the bottom of the bowl since that meant it was almost gone. "I've always been difficult. I think that's why that asshole picked me. He did it because I already had that sort of personality. It means I got worse, sure, but I'm not all that different." I considered the odd things I stole, the desire to wreck everything I saw, and sighed.

Maybe I am a bit different…

I lifted the bowl to my lips to drink the last of it, savoring the warmth and complex flavors. When I finished, Harrison took it from me. He probably knew if he didn't, I'd lick the bowl clean.

Which I absolutely had planned.

"How were you changed?" He set the bowl down on the dresser before turning back toward me. "I know the man who showed up changed you, and that Galen later saved you from a werewolf, but I don't know exactly what happened."

I thought back to the ugliness of those days, the confusion, the uncertainty. Changing, becoming something entirely different, it was a hard thing to accept or know how to handle.

There weren't any, 'So Now You're a Crow!' books to help me along the way.

I didn't love having to go back, to remember that period in my life. Sure, most of my life didn't seem all that wonderful, but at least I'd gotten my feet under me now.

I considered that I worked as a delivery girl and had just been framed for murder and thought...maybe not as in control of my life as I liked to pretend.

Still, he had brought me food and I did feel slightly better because of the sleep, so what was a story in exchange?

"I was lost one night and wandering through the desert."

"Lost?" He cocked up one of his blond eyebrows in a knowing expression.

"*Fine.* I was slightly drunk as well. I'd planned on walking to the store and, well, the desert is surprisingly easy to get lost in. I ended up in an area I didn't recognize, and spotted three guys following someone else. It was pretty obvious they weren't planning on just selling him some baked goods or anything. Looking back, I should have minded my own business. I should have turned right around and gone the other way."

"Why didn't you?"

"That's the question, isn't it? Why didn't I leave him to his own problems. Fuck knows, I had enough of my own." I sighed, sitting back. "I've never been good at that, though. I've never been able to just leave things well enough alone. I think it's because I know how it feels to be alone, to have no one there supporting you.

It's hard, and it sucks, and I don't want other people to have to deal with that."

I knew that was an understatement. A huge number of my problems in my life had occurred because I couldn't keep my nose to myself. I walked right into shit I had no business in because I didn't like what was going on.

I went on, trying to keep my tone light despite my feelings about that night. "The man didn't seem to care about the three punks. In fact, it seemed like they amused him, like they were the same type. However, when one got behind him, they lifted this stick to hit him in the back of the head. That sort of cowardly shit is something I hate, so I rushed in and shoved the guy out of the way. I got hit in the temple." I touched the mark that still remained, the scar on my left side that went to my eyebrow. It didn't hurt anymore, but something about it forced me to remember everything.

Harrison caught my chin, twisting my head while taking my wrist in his other hand. He pulled my fingers away, staring at the tiny scar there.

It was funny, because it wasn't like I didn't have other scars. I'd lived a pretty hectic life, and every scar was from a damn good story. Not that the stories were all fond memories, but in my experience, some of the worst times in my life made for the best stories.

At least, after the wounds healed.

The same did not hold true for that tiny mark, though.

Harrison narrowed his eyes as he stared at the faded scar. "Did it require stitches?"

"It probably would have, but not that night."

"Because of what that man did?" Harrison released my chin and wrist, allowing me to nod.

"I fell down after I got smacked, and those three started mocking me. I expected the man to run off."

"Even after you helped him?"

"In my experience, people don't stay by your side, at least not once shit gets real. Most times they take off then, because people care about themselves the most." I shrugged, hating how fucking cynical I sounded. "Not that I blame them. I mean, that's how we all are, right?"

"Not you. You helped him when you had no good reason to."

"And look where it got me?" I laughed, the sound bitter even to my own ears. "Anyway, so when the asshole who hit me the first time went to swing again, I flinched. Except, nothing landed. I opened my eyes to find the man there, the end of the stick in his hand like he'd caught it. Even as the punk tried to pull, he couldn't get it free. That should have probably been my hint that something was different, but fuck, I'd just gotten smacked hard. I wasn't thinking straight."

The night came back to me so clearly that I could almost feel the dribble of blood down my face, the throbbing in my temples, all of it. I recalled how the man had locked eyes with the one who had swung on me, and asked, "Should I kill him?"

It hadn't made sense at the time, but when he'd turned his head toward me, I'd realized he'd asked it of me. "Do you want me to kill him?"

I had shaken my head, unwilling to have someone's death on my hands. He'd snorted, then shoved his hand out, sending the other man flying.

I left that part out of the story, since it felt like a strange moment between the man and me. "He ran the three off, then crouched in front of me. He'd said I was different, that I'd caused chaos in his life, that not enough people do the unexpected."

"And then he asked if you wanted to change?"

"Yeah, he isn't the sort of man to ask anyone anything. He set a hand on my forehead and the world went dark around me. I woke up later in that same spot, the wound at my temple having healed, the man gone."

"He didn't stay and tell you anything?"

"Not a single thing. I didn't have a clue what he'd done until about a week later." I paused, then sighed when I realized that probably made little sense to him. "See, because of what I am, I crave mischief. I end up tense, like this noise that keeps getting louder and louder in my head until I can't ignore it if I don't do something. Sometimes it's just adding googly eyes to random stuff, or pocketing some things that don't technically belong to me, and if I ignore all that, then the stakes keep getting higher. I didn't realize that at the time, though, so I ended up seeing someone — a man who didn't look all that safe — and I taunted him. I didn't know why I did it, but something inside me said I should. Well, long story short, that man wasn't a man but a werewolf — a stray, at that. Turned out he was more than halfway to crazy all on his own, and I guess my other side knew that provoking him would cause a little chaos. It did, of course."

"And that was when Galen saved you?"

"Yep. The wolf chased me and I ran into an old building. Galen had been trailing him already — one of my few lucky breaks. When I was trying to escape him, I turned into a bird. It was like this sense of fire licking over my skin, and between one second and the next, I was a crow. It let me crawl into a vent, and that was where Galen found me. He assumed I was a Werecrow, but, well, you know what happened when he tried to have me sorted at the council meeting." I lifted my shoulders in a quick shrug, as if to signal the end of the conversation. There wasn't really anything else to say about it, was there? He'd heard the whole stupid, ridiculous story.

When he said nothing in return, when the silence got too heavy, I sighed and tried to speak again with as light a tone as possible. "But that unpleasant walk down memory lane helped. I don't feel nearly as bad." I lifted my gaze from my hands to Harrison, finding his eyes locked on mine.

Did he sense how uncomfortable that made me? He must have, because he tore his gaze away and looked off to the side. "I'm glad you feel better. Our work would be far more difficult if you were ill."

"Well, it wouldn't be the first time I made a job more difficult."

He shook his head, the action telling me he didn't appreciate my attempts to keep us from talking about anything too real. He rose, then gathered the empty bowl. "You should rest a little longer, then you can shower. We will leave at first light."

"See, this is the nice thing about hanging out with non-vampires. With vampires, it's always at dusk. I swear, I lost any tan I ever had spending time there."

Harrison didn't acknowledge me that time, instead leaving me alone in the room. At first I didn't appreciate it, the quiet feeling too loud, as though the space closed in on me.

Except... The smile fell from my lips. Without anyone else there forcing me to keep it plastered on, without someone I needed to hide from, the memory of that night, of how many things were stolen from me then, it all washed over me and I had no reason to keep it at bay.

So for the first time in so long, I couldn't even remember, I didn't smile. I didn't laugh, didn't joke, didn't minimize the rough emotions that poured through me. I felt them, every last confusing, horrifying one.

The things I'd lost, the life I couldn't have anymore, the troubles and dangers I faced now, it *all* rushed through me until I trembled.

Because fuck, there was a good reason I'd run from them all. Mainly? Because they sucked, and right now I remembered exactly why.

Chapter Six

I always thought I was young until I got around actual young people...then I realized I was old and could really go for a nap. And now, surrounded by teenagers, I felt *really* old.

It had been far too long since I'd been in a school, and I sure hadn't gone to one this nice.

Harrison slowed in front of me, allowing me to catch up.

"Did you go here?" I asked as we approached the main door. It was still early, so the day hadn't started, meaning kids still milled about.

"Of course."

"Because you're rich?"

"Among other reasons." The subtle lift of his eyebrow told me the other reason.

Often, Spirits went to private schools like this one, at reduced rates for those who needed it. The Spirits who inherited their skills needed extra help, and the human children of Spirits often required additional understanding. Things like full moons could cause havoc in a pack household, after all.

"Nice place." Stone covered the outside of the enormous building, reminding me of the old-school Ivy League universities. It made sense because, for those who wanted it, this place was basically a pipeline there. Still, compared to my school, which had used portable buildings that remained there for thirty years, it was a whole different world.

Then again, when I spotted the kids, it wasn't as different as I'd have excepted. Sure, the kids drove fancy cars or had drivers who dropped them off. They wore designer clothing, had expensive phones, and all around had things I had only ever dreamed of. Still, despite all that, the underlying behavior was just like every other teenager.

They complained about their parents, about their teachers, about their schoolwork. They gave Harrison and me side eyes, and no doubt they snickered about the new people on campus.

So it seemed no matter how much money people had, they were, at their core, the same assholes as the rest of us.

Harrison held the door open for me, the chivalrous act strange. Still, I didn't need to draw more attention to myself, so I walked through. The interior of the main office mirrored the other décor. Marble floors, fancy decorations, expensive artwork on the walls. It was like a five-star hotel except for the spoiled brats who went there.

Not that I bet they realized just how lucky they were.

"Would you please refrain from looking as though you are casing the joint?" The way Harrison said that last part forced me to resist the desire to laugh. He sounded like a terrible parody, trying to emulate a criminal but having never lived such a life.

"I'm not trying to 'case the joint'," I pointed out. "Though, if I were, there's some nice shit here." As soon as I said that, a student turned their head my way, as though the curse word drew her in. I smiled and shrugged, to brush off her surprise.

Harrison merely shook his head and continued walking, taking the lead since he hadn't given me details. Sure, I knew we were going to work at the school to try to find some sign of the person selling Cloud — and use that to find the person making it — but beyond that?

Not a fucking clue.

I didn't love being out of the circle when it came to plans, but I also didn't love that condescending look Harrison liked to give me when he didn't appreciate me asking too many questions.

What was it about the men in my life that they felt the need to constantly underestimate me?

At least it meant I could get in close if I ever needed to bury a knife in them.

"I don't think I care for that smirk," Harrison said despite not turning around. He couldn't have possibly *seen* my smile, could he? Or, hell, for all I knew, maybe he was just that good at guessing what I would do or how I would react.

Either way, I didn't remove my smirk. If he didn't care for it, maybe he shouldn't have acted in a way that made me feel as though casting him out in the middle of the ocean was a completely viable communication plan.

We stopped in at the main desk, but the receptionist seemed to know exactly who he was. She handed over two name badges with our photos and names already on them — *when the fuck did he get this picture of me?*

I stared at it for a moment, then cursed.

The asshole had taken this when I'd fallen asleep on the couch the other day, hadn't he? Damn it, I hadn't been feeling well and that should have been a sacred time! Worse, because pictures didn't work well for me, it was smeared and barely recognizable.

Once the bell rang, the hallways emptied. The sea of kids disappeared, leaving the previously packed spaces now abandoned. Only the rare slackers still appeared, and fuck, those were *my* people.

Harrison and I followed a guidance counselor who took us on a tour of the school grounds. They were even more massive than I'd expected, honestly. Despite having a fraction of the kids compared to a public school, it was easily four times as large. The school filled that space with a few tennis courts, massive learning facilities and a cafeteria that could have had its own spot on the best places to eat. This was more resort than school.

"So, Mr. Harrison, you will be in room forty-three."

I snorted. "What are you teaching?"

Harrison didn't respond — fuck, he didn't even turn my way. Instead, the counselor answered for him. "He is working as a special lesson instructor for social-emotional learning."

I cocked my eyebrow at Harrison, trying to ask without speaking.

He turned, as though he heard my expression aloud. "I will be fine."

"Wasn't you I was worried about," I muttered, keeping my voice low enough that the counselor wouldn't catch it.

Harrison narrowed his eyes, then turned his back on me to end the conversation.

Still, while I wasn't besties with Harrison or anything, I knew him well enough to guess he wouldn't endanger a bunch of kids. If he said he could handle it, I trusted he could.

Not like I had other choices.

"And what am I teaching?" I asked, immediately picturing everyone calling me Ms. Keystone and looking at me like some sort of authority. Oh, the things I could teach kids!

The councilor stuttered — never a good sign — then spoke slowly, without meeting my gaze. "I wasn't told you were coming on as a teacher."

"I'm not? Then what am I doing here?" I peered over at Harrison, wondering just what nonsense he'd come up with. "Please tell me I'm not a lunch lady or something."

"Not exactly…" the counselor said. "You'll be a proctor."

"What the fuck is a proctor?"

She actually *flinched* at the curse word, like it had leapt from my lips and slapped her in her face. "That means you will oversee the children when they are not in the classroom. During passing periods and lunch, for example."

I frowned as I made sense of her words, then cursed again under my breath when I figured it out. "Wait a minute. You're telling me I'm a yard narc? *Me?*" I looked over at Harrison, trying to get some back up for how ridiculous an idea that was.

And for one of the rare times, he smiled. Well, it was a curl of his lips so subtle others might not notice the change at all. I sure did, though. "Well, I thought if anyone could connect with delinquents, it would be you."

My response was just one finger, and I had a feeling he could understand that without any of his powers.

* * * *

Kids suck.

The longer I spent in the midst of them, the surer I was about it. I used to hate the way old people bitched and moaned about the younger generations, but right about now?

As I watched two kids throwing bottles over and over again, trying to get one to land upright, I shook my head. Either kids were getting dumber or I was just old.

Today marked the second day of so-called work. Harrison got play the part of respected teacher while I was supposed to keep order outside of the classroom, which felt more like wrangling wild animals than anything else.

Also, I said so-called work because I sure as fuck wasn't doing that. Who cared if the kids were chewing gum or making out? I wasn't getting paid nearly enough to play cock-block for teenagers.

Wait, am I getting paid?

I had better get paid for this nonsense.

Of course, if I found out I wasn't…

I thought about all the rather nice items I'd spotted lying around. A few of those would sell for enough to make wasting my time worth it.

Across the way, someone caught my attention.

Maybe it was my passenger — my crow — or maybe it was just my own personality, but I could always tell when someone was up to no good — especially if they were nervous about it. It was something in the way they walked, the way they held themselves, and my senses zeroed in on them like that first sniff of coffee in the morning.

Sure enough, across the quad, one such kid darted their gaze around as though watching for a tail. Of course, they were shitty at it, because they didn't notice when I got up from my place and headed their way.

The kid — a girl who looked far too uncomfortable to be some career criminal — moved past the line of buildings toward the undeveloped area near the fence line. For how nice most of the school was — complete with greenery and lawns that had to cost a fortune to keep up in the desert — the outer areas were as trashy as any poorer area.

I peeked around the corner of the building to spot Little Miss Innocent standing there with a boy.

If this was yet another hook-up attempt, I was going to be pissed.

"Do you have it?" the girl asked, her voice soft and nervous.

The boy smirked — and boy did I recognize *that* look. He was the one used to being in trouble, the sort who thrived on it. He was my type of person and far more promising.

The boy lifted one of his dark eyebrows. "Depends. Do you have the money?"

The girl nodded and reached into the back pocket of her jeans, then pulled out a roll of bills. The twenty on the outside suggested it was a couple hundred dollars.

Clearly, I'm in the wrong damned profession.

He grinned wider, like the money was some aphrodisiac. He didn't have a trace of uncertainty, as though the idea of selling her something dangerous didn't even scrape against his conscience. He reached into his own pocket, then pulled out a small baggy with a clear crystal substance and a sticker of a lion on the front.

Bingo.

I didn't wait any longer before leaving my hiding spot. I mean, I was dealing with teenagers here — not hardened drug dealers. I didn't need to be quite as careful as I might otherwise.

Not that I ever was.

In fact, a part of me heard Galen's voice in my head, lecturing me about my bad choices.

Neither of the kids noticed my approach — they really weren't equipped for doing shady-ass shit like this, were they?

I plucked the money from the girl's hand and the baggy from the boy's.

"What the fuck?" the boy asked, reaching out for the bag I'd stolen as though he might snatch it back.

I twisted, keeping it out of his hands and ignoring the fact that even as a teenager, he was a lot taller than I was.

The girl, at least, had the good sense to look afraid. Not that I'd hurt her, but the thought of someone ruining her perfect little life was more terrifying. I could almost see the way she thought about everyone finding out what she'd done, her parents getting pissed, all of it.

However, given the way she reacted, I doubted she'd done this before much. That made her pretty much useless for my purposes.

In fact, I had a feeling the longer she remained here, the better the chance of her fucking it up rather than helping. For that reason, I motioned to shoo her away.

"You're just letting me go?" she asked.

"Unless you want to stay here and have me ask more questions?" I lifted the baggy, waving it to draw attention to the evidence that would not help her in the least.

She shook her head and hurried off just as fast as her little designer-jeans clad legs could carry her, leaving me and the boy alone.

"I knew that girl was a mistake," the boy said and crossed his arms, looking put out by the entire ordeal. Even now, with the drugs in my hand, he didn't seem worried.

"You want to know a secret? Don't sell to girls who could play the lead in a teen drama. Never ends well." I lifted the baggy toward the sun, watching the way the light poured through the crystals. They were clear, which twisted the sunlight until it came out in rainbows.

If I didn't know exactly what this shit could do, the pretty sight might have dazzled me.

"So what now? Did you let her go because she has such a bright future?" The boy snorted. "Not the first time I get the blame for everything."

I tore my gaze from the crystals to peer over at the boy. "Please. That girl will get knocked up by some rich boy and be unhappily married within a year of graduating—trust me. Besides, I'm not planning on turning you in, either."

"Why not?" He narrowed his eyes, and his suspicion confirmed that the boy wasn't stupid. Only an idiot would blindly trust someone in my position.

Especially because I still planned to use him to my own ends.

"Because I need some information from you."

"What kind of information?"

I waved the bag at him. "Who supplies this to you?"

His mouth shut, as though he were afraid the name might escape through his lips and he couldn't let that happen.

In addition to that, however, a spark of fear rested in those eyes. Clearly, he didn't want to tangle with the person.

Given they evidently created a dangerous drug and used kids to sell it, it was probably pretty fair to be wary of someone with so few scruples.

He swallowed hard, then shook his head. "Sorry, but that information comes with *way* too high a price. I'd rather face another suspension than risk that."

I flicked the baggy. "You sure about that? Because last I heard, this shit is pretty risky. The Minds don't look too kindly on people who sell this."

He swallowed hard, his gaze darting around as though he'd just realized I wasn't merely some yard narc. "You know what it is?"

I tried to stop myself—I really did—but a shudder ran through me as I recalled the way it had felt when someone had sifted through my thoughts with the gentleness of someone forcing tomatoes through a sieve. "Yeah, I sure do. The leader of the Minds seems *pretty* pissed about this shit."

The boy shifted dirt with the toe of his boot, the first real break in his composure. "It's not like I sell to Minds on purpose. In fact, I try to avoid it."

"Why would other people use it?"

"It works on all Spirits, just not as strong. Gives other Spirits a high and a very mild affect—just enough to sense other's emotions. Not nearly as addictive to them, not as dangerous. That girl just now, she's a nymph."

"And you?"

"Were," he muttered.

"You're a wolf?"

"There's more Weres in the world than just wolves, you know," he muttered, the annoyance in his voice enough to make me laugh. I sure as fuck understood that, after being looked down on for not being one of the big four. It helped me to understand him a bit more.

"Boy, do I know that," I said, thinking about all the others I'd dealt with—including how I fit into the world. "How long have you been selling?"

He shrugged, tucking his hands into the pockets of his jacket. "I've always sold whatever people can't find. It was candy and soda when I was a kid, cigarettes later, but now people want more."

"So now it's Cloud?"

"There's a market for it, so why not? Not like I force anyone to take anything or trick them. If they don't get it from me, they'll get it from someone else. What are you, some do-gooder who's here to tell me what damage it's doing by selling? You should stay off my ass."

"What's your name?"

"Trey. You want to give me some heart-to-heart about how my choices are going to ruin my life?"

"No. You want to ruin your life? Go right ahead—better you do it than someone else. This shit, though? It's dangerous," I said.

"People make their own choices—"

90

"It's dangerous to *other* people. The first time you feel the way a Mind on this shit picks through *your* brain, you can sit there and tell me it's not a big deal." I tried to go for unaffected, but just talking about it made that old headache come back, the pain through my temples a sure sign that I was far from over that little ordeal.

The boy had the decency to look bothered by my words. However, pity wasn't something I wanted — and sure as fuck not from some kid — so I shook my head to clear the memory and the mood.

"I'm not here looking to pin anything on you. You're a dealer — no offense, but you're small fish to me. I'm after the person creating this."

He sighed. "Even if I wanted to tell you, I couldn't. The person who makes it, they don't exactly go around announcing themselves, you know? That's a fast way to short career when it comes to drugs."

"So you don't know who they are? How do they get you the product, then? How'd they even find you?"

"I meet up with them when I need more. I pay upfront for the product, then price it as I want and the profits are all mine."

"So you have a number to contact them?"

"Nah. I just leave a note at a dead drop, and they call me the next day with a meeting location."

"So you've met them in person?"

He nodded, then frowned. "Sure, but I couldn't tell you anything about them."

"Why not?"

He scratched his temple, gaze troubled. "I don't really remember. It's like he uses a filter of some sort, and I can't remember most of the meeting."

That sounded strangely like my own powers, but I'd never met anyone else like myself. According to the asshole who made me, there weren't any more like me around.

That suggested it had to be a Mind Spirit, didn't it?

It also meant the boy wasn't all that useful, at least in terms of information.

The disappointment had me tapping my foot as I considered my options. I could try to get the boy to contact the supplier, then follow him to the meeting. However, if it was a Mind, they'd probably spot me before I could do anything useful. In fact, it was possible that their powers would impact me as well.

But would it affect Harrison? As an exceedingly powerful Mind, he could probably resist anything someone else did.

However, given that they usually could spot one another, he'd probably get spotted well before we could make our move.

Which meant what I really needed was to have a reason for the supplier to come to *me.*

I pressed my lips together, an idea hitting me. It had to be one of my worst ideas, all things considered, but that was a pretty low bar already.

The boy took a step backward, as though he could just read on my face how much he didn't want to be a part of whatever I had planned.

Which was fair.

I'd done a lot of fucked-up shit before, things I wasn't all that proud of, but who knew that my next step would be becoming a drug dealer myself?

Talk about moving up in the world…

Chapter Seven

"You have got to be kidding me," Harrison muttered for what had to be the hundredth time that night.

"If you're going to keep complaining, can you at least make it entertaining?"

"How can this be entertaining?"

"*Anything* can be entertaining," I pointed out. "I mean, you're talking to the girl who makes pap smears a party!"

Harrison gave me a deadpan look that called me an idiot with no words needed to get the gist.

I rolled my eyes and leaned back, my head still killing me.

"Headache?" he asked, his gaze back on the work before him. It was almost impressive how he could do something so technical while somehow paying attention to me and my state.

"How can you tell?" I closed my eyes and rubbed at my temples. "Can you sense that?"

"Usually, yes. I can feel not only the emotions of those around me but also the physical issues."

I opened one eye to peer across the room at him. "Does that mean you get off if others are having sex?"

He narrowed his eyes but didn't look my way, answering the question for me.

"Well, well, well, who would have figured you for a voyeur? It's always the quiet ones, I'm telling you. I'll make sure to have some solo fun while in the same house. You could use the excitement."

"You know, normal people don't bring that sort of thing up in mixed company."

"Yeah, well, when have I ever been normal? What's the point in that anyway? Normal is boring."

He shook his head, closed his eyes, and moved his hands across the items in front of him. He had a metal tray out on the large dining room table, his body hunched over it.

It had started as sugar, but after a very boring and complicated process that had involved me ignoring it and napping a few times, now resembled the clear crystals I knew Cloud to be.

"This is a mistake," he said again, his voice soft, as though he couldn't help saying it even if he knew it would do no good.

"This is our only choice. If you have a better idea, go ahead and tell me," I pointed out—again.

He let out a short huff but didn't respond—proof that he couldn't argue with me over it. The fact was that we were stuck.

We needed to find this supplier to track down the person using the Cloud. Given what I'd learned from Trey, it was clear that the supplier was a powerful Mind, so sneaking up on them was unlikely.

It meant creating our own product to add pressure to the supplier. Giving him a rival would draw him out, and mad people made mistakes.

Given Harrison was the only Mind I knew who could actually make this shit, he'd basically volunteered himself.

"You know," I said, my eyes closed again. "I'm surprised you know how to make this."

"It's not easy to do, but it isn't all that complicated. It is more a matter of available power. Few Minds have blood powerful enough to actually create it."

"It won't hurt you, right?"

"What, are you worried about me now?"

"Nope, not at all. You're just my current shield. If something happens to you, I'm a sitting target again."

He snorted, the sound calling me a liar. Still, he didn't come right out and say it, moving on instead. "No, using this amount of power won't harm me in the least. By morning, I will have replenished anything I use, especially because I've made this batch differently."

"Differently? Did you flavor it or something? Personally, I'd go fireball. Kids today love fireball."

"I reduced the mental effects while increasing the euphoric sensation."

"You can do that?"

"Of course. Cloud is created using the powers of the Mind who makes it, along with their blood as a binder. With enough power and control, they can steer the effects. I made this batch with the purpose of drawing in users without offering them the increase in power that can put others in danger. The last thing I want is your little plan to backfire and harm others."

"You might just have a future as a chemist," I said with a laugh. "Why don't we both quit the council and become drug dealers?"

"This has less risk, but far from none. Someone could still overdose on it, and another powerful Mind could tamper with it. Make no mistake — I don't care for creating this. I've seen what Cloud can do to Minds, and I dislike putting more of it out there, even if I don't have any better idea or plan." His tone was low, as though sulking.

Still, I understood. I'd never really liked drugs, and I sure as fuck didn't care for the idea of selling them at school.

However, it would put us exactly where we needed to be, like it or not. Sometimes we had to do some shitty things to deal with a bigger problem. It took me back to Trey's words, to the idea that no one was *forcing* anyone to take it. If doing this got the really bad stuff off the street?

I'd lived with worse.

The conversation dwindled, and before I knew it, exhaustion pulled me under. I slept fitfully, waking every hour or so to find Harrison still hunched over the table, hard at work.

Yet, something about him there helped to ease me, as though he took some of that stress from me. I knew I shouldn't have felt safe there, but he made me feel it whether or not I wanted to.

The headache refused to ease, and I'd taken enough ibuprofen that any doctor would have lectured me for it. That didn't seem to even help, anymore. My skin felt feverish, like a cold I just couldn't kick no matter what I did.

"Grey?" Harrison's voice came from so close, whispered and oddly sweet. He normally spoke to me so coldly, but I had to admit, I rather liked this tone.

It was strange to hear, sure, but I found myself turning toward it in pleasure. Warmth touched my cheek, and I nuzzled against it.

"Grey, wake up."

That time, the words drew me back to consciousness. The throbbing headache that ran through my brain made me instantly regret it, however.

How was it possible for me to *still* feel this horrible? Just sleeping should have helped.

"You're still hurting." The words weren't a question, and I doubted he needed me to confirm it. Instead, I forced myself to sit up, aided by Harrison's hand on my back.

I peered to the side, toward the light through the window. It told me that the sun had risen, which meant I'd slept through the night. A look at Harrison's face — and the dark circles under his eyes — said he hadn't. Guilt hit me for a moment before I pushed it away.

When had guilt helped anything? Never. It hadn't done anything for me, so why waste my time with such nonsense?

So instead, I looked toward the table where he'd worked.

"I finished," he said, clearly knowing my next question.

I forced myself to my feet, hating just how bad I felt. Not that it mattered — I could whine and bitch later. For now, I needed to work. I headed for the table, finding not the mess of the night before. Instead of the sugar, the now clear Cloud was already in a number of small bags, the same size and shape as the ones sold by Trey.

The main difference? I picked one up, impressed that it appeared even more pure than the shit Trey had sold. On the front was a different sticker, white with a line art image that made me give Harrison a dirty look.

"Really?"

"I thought it fitting."

Hard to argue that as I peered at the simple design of a crow, the lines flowing and ethereal. "I guess you have a point," I admitted. "It's not like this will work if they can't track the product back to a single supplier."

"This is your bad idea—I thought you'd want your symbol on it."

I shook my head, too tired and my headache too bad to argue with him over it. Instead, I sighed and looked at the baggies. "How much is there?"

"I created thirty-two bags. Cloud is only good for a few days after created, so making more than we can sell will do us no good. This much should get the other supplier's attention, however. Assuming you can find buyers, that is."

"Are you doubting me now? Trust me, I can find people to buy it all. No problem. I'm good at that."

He pressed his lips together, seeming far less sure than I felt. Then again, Harrison struck me as the type who had no idea how many people would buy shit like this. The truth was, finding buyers wasn't that difficult, not when it came down to it. So long as the product was good, buyers would always be lining up.

And no matter how much I enjoyed ribbing on Harrison, I had zero doubts that he could make a good product. If it really was all about the power of the Mind who created it, then he'd have no problem making some good shit.

"So tomorrow I'll bring this." I gestured at the bags on the table. "If it only lasts a few days, by the end of the week, the other supplier should catch wind of the new players."

"Which means you need to remain vigilant," Harrison pointed out. "You need to ensure you are not more than a few hundred feet away from me at any time. A Mind using this could do serious damage in a matter of seconds."

I waved off his concerns. "I get it, but you worry too much. I'll be on campus, so it'll be fine."

He pressed his lips together, then shook his head. "Well, you should sleep more."

"I slept all night."

"Not well, and judging by your pale skin, it wasn't enough."

"You're worse than Galen," I muttered.

"Perhaps, but I can't say I don't better understand him, now. I used to wonder why he worried for you so, why he always appeared worn out when dealing with you. I believe you may have removed years from my life already, and as you know, Minds still have normal life spans. It makes it a more troublesome thing for me than it does for Galen."

I waved off his concerns—or complaints—but I couldn't quite ignore his suggestion.

He was right—I felt like shit. While the thought of sleeping again sounded about as good as cold, canned meat, I knew it was still what I should do.

So I took myself toward my room, ready to fall into my bed and try to finally rid myself of this lingering exhaustion.

Just what the fuck is wrong with me?

Chapter Eight

Sleep had made me feel slightly more alive, but it hadn't fully removed my headache. It wasn't like I could just take the day off, though, so here I was, back at the school.

Except this time, I wasn't just a yard narc. Instead, the baggies in my pocket showed just how useful I could make myself. Three days into our little business endeavor and I only had a few packets left. Maybe I should have felt bad about selling them drugs, but as it was, I did what needed to get done.

I told myself to think of it as the greater good, that this was to solve a larger and more dangerous problem. At least this shit wouldn't put innocents in danger, meaning it was only the user who had to worry. That shouldn't have made me feel better—and it didn't make me feel *much* better—but it was better than nothing. If we could stop the selling of Cloud, it was worth a few stupid kids getting high, right?

That's what I told myself to make me feel better.

I'd spotted Harrison a few times during the day, but we'd only exchanged quick glances, as though he needed visual confirmation that I still breathed. His lack of trust chafed, but that was fine—I was used to that.

I'd managed to not only sell a bit of my own product, but also had handed off plenty to Trey to sell as well. The more widely I got this shit, the better the odds that the supplier would take notice and find it a problem. Did I feel bad for getting him involved?

Sure, but he'd been only too happy to do so. While he wasn't willing to give over any information about the supplier—even if he could remember—it seemed his loyalty didn't go all that far. The thought of having more supply sounded great to him. His supplier didn't give him that much at once—probably due to the difficulty in making Cloud.

My newest buyer scurried off, the small baggy tucked into his pocket. *Idiot.* Anyone taking one look at that walk would know they'd done something wrong. I shook my head, then glanced at my watch.

Three-twenty. School had ended an hour ago, but Harrison had some stupid meeting to attend. It left me wasting time on campus, pretending to watch the kids still there for after school activities. The school had two types of kids still here—the over achievers who wanted enough extracurriculars to look good on a college application and the kids who had nowhere else to go.

It was the second group I'd spotted more of, since the first were actually in the classrooms.

Another kid milled around, one I didn't recognize at first. At least, until she turned, and that familiar blonde hair made me laugh. Yep, it was the same girl who had tried to buy Cloud from Trey the other day. I'd ruined her attempt there, so was she looking again?

She turned her gaze my way, and the way it lingered told me I'd guessed right. *When first you fail, try, try again to get the drugs.*

I nodded toward the bathroom, then headed that way. Her steps followed me, first on the walkway then echoing against the tile of the bathroom. Once inside, I peeked down, beneath the doors, to make sure we were alone.

Once done, I smiled and turned back toward her. "So, you're looking to buy?"

She nodded, shifting her weight from one foot to the other. "I didn't get to last time..."

Her uncertainty rang alarm bells, but I dismissed it. She was probably just worried about how this would go, about whether she'd get caught. However, it made me pause. "Why are you buying this?" I found myself asking even if I told myself I didn't care.

"School is hard," she whispered. "I'm expected to do so much, so I just need a way to relax sometimes."

"And Cloud does that?"

"It helps, yeah. It lets me take it easy and stop worrying about school and college and everything else."

That made me peer down toward the bag of Cloud in my pocket. I'd had plenty of stress growing up, the years before my mom married my stepdad, when things had been difficult. I was alone, in charge of taking care of myself, worrying about where my next meal would come, but it was a different stress, a different pressure.

Would this have been worse? Better? It was so easy to hate the kids who went here, to wish I'd had such first-world problems, but was it really that much better? The way her gaze moved from side to side suggested it wasn't better at all.

I could have lectured her, drawing on one of the *many* lectures I'd gotten from others over my life. I could have told her how she was being silly, that she didn't need to worry so much, that things weren't so bad for her. What was the point, though?

So instead, I took out the bag and held it out to her.

She pulled out another roll of cash—the fact she didn't worry about losing the last amount showed that money wasn't an issue for her—and handed it over.

When she went to take the bag, however, something else moved inside the bathroom. At first, I wasn't sure what it was. It was large and angry—I knew that much—but details?

Not a fucking clue. Instead, I found myself shoved face first against the tile wall with a large, hot body behind me, pinning me into place.

My first instinct was to call out to the girl and tell her to run.

Before I got the chance, however, a low, angry voice rumbled so deep through the bathroom that I felt it through the tile pressed to my cheek, "Get out of here."

That let me exhale slowly, telling me the identity of the attacker.

"Isn't this a fun little reunion?" I asked.

The weight moved away so fast, I nearly fell. I twisted, wincing at an ache in my chest from how hard he'd shoved me.

"What the fuck, Grey?" And I couldn't stop myself from smirking at the annoyed sound of Galen's voice.

Because having a conversation in the women's restroom was probably not great—especially for

Galen—we moved the conversation to an empty classroom.

Galen had his arms crossed and boy did he glare. "Why is that whenever there's a problem, *you* somehow end up at the center of it?"

"Just dumb luck, I guess."

"At least you got the dumb part right."

"Rude." I sat on top of one desk, thankful to sit at least. I still felt like shit. "What are you even doing here?"

"You really want to ask me that when I catch you *selling drugs to children*." The way he said that last part, the emphasis, made me want to laugh. Sure, anything sounded bad when someone said it in that tone.

Not that there was a good way to say that specific set of words.

"It's for a good reason," I pointed out.

Galen shook his head and rubbed his face. "I got word that there was a person at the school selling to Weres. Imagine my surprise to find *you* behind it."

I smiled and held my hands out like jazz fingers. "Surprise!"

Not even a smile… "Come on, Grey, out with it. What are you doing here?"

"She's helping me."

I twisted at the new voice to find Harrison in the doorway. He used a different tone from the one I'd grown used to, the one he used when speaking just to me. It reminded me just how much frostier he was when dealing with others.

And in the same way, Galen's voice dropped lower. What was this, some dick measuring contest?

I could get behind that sort of contest, just so long as I got to be the judge.

Of course, size wasn't *everything*. That was like judging a cake contest without getting to try it!

No, focus!

I shook away the thought, but Harrison's narrowed gaze said he'd probably guessed my line of thought.

"What is she helping you with?" Galen asked.

"It is a Mind issue. I have no reason to answer to you."

"She isn't a Mind," Galen pointed out.

"And neither is she a Were."

"*She*," I said, breaking into their little fight, "is also right here and able to speak for herself."

Both men looked my way, giving me the briefest of glances before returning to glare at each other.

Galen spoke first. "You have her here, endangering herself and the lives of others. I have to guess *you* were the one to make this?" He held up an empty bag with my sticker on the front. "I took it off a pack kid yesterday, and they let me know they'd gotten it here. Just what have you gotten her involved in?"

"I'm pretty sure I'm the one who gets others involved. I'm not some damsel in distress who others have to worry about. I'm not part of the problem—I am the whole damned problem, thank you very much." I crossed my arms, pouting as the two promptly ignored me.

Harrison pulled his shoulders back, a low energy rushing through the room, a warning—which was a really bad sign.

The last thing we needed was these two assholes getting into some sort of fight here. Not only was it bad for our cover, but bad shit happened when council heads got into it. That tended to cause issues like wars, and it was never those in charge who paid the ultimate price for that.

"Let's all calm down," I said quickly, lifting my hands to settle them. "No reason to get testy here."

The look they each gave me suggested they didn't come close to agreeing, and boy, did that *not* help my headache.

"Galen, I'm here because there's an issue with Cloud getting sold to kids here. You've seen that yourself."

"I've seen *your* Cloud sold here," he pointed out the difference.

"That's because I need to catch the attention of the supplier."

"So you're using yourself as bait? Is that the only plan you know of? I swear, anytime anything happens, you dangle yourself out like a worm on a hook for whatever shark is in the water."

"Sharks eat chum—not worms." As soon as I said that, I knew I'd fucked up. Still, I shrugged I went on. "I don't want to see people hurt, so the supplier needs to be dealt with."

"And why is that *your* problem?"

I opened my mouth to tell him the truth, but instantly regretted it. There was no reason he needed to know that. It was a bad idea for him to realize I'd gotten myself targeted.

Sadly, I'd figured that out a split second too late, and the severe look in his blue eyes told me he'd guessed. "What trouble have you gotten yourself into now?" he asked.

"She was targeted by a Mind who uses Cloud," Harrison said, the words surprising me. He'd been rather tight-lipped about everything, so why was he spilling the details now?

"And you didn't feel the need to tell me about that?" Galen asked me, seeming to want to take it up directly with me rather than Harrison.

"It's not your problem. Besides, we've got it handled. We'll find the supplier, figure out his customers, then deal with my stalker."

"*Stalker?*"

Yep, the way he asked that said I should have said less. It was a lesson I should have learned a long time ago, yet never seemed to quite get through my thick skull.

"You're telling me it wasn't just a one-time thing?"

"It was close to one time," I hedged. "I mean, it was two times, which is almost once."

Harrison shook his head. He probably had no idea just how foolish I could be, yet here he was with a front-row seat. He turned toward Galen. "She was attacked at her neighbor's house. The Mind behind the attack seems to have formed an obsession with her. She was attacked again after going out drinking. That is why I have kept her with me — to prevent such an attack from occurring again."

"If it happened twice, why is it you think you can do anything to stop it?" Galen asked.

"Because I am the strongest known Mind. If she remains within my sphere of influence, she will remain safe."

"Convenient," Galen muttered under his breath.

"Not that convenient for me," I said, then looked toward Galen. "I've been selling this for a few days, so I bet we'll have this all worked out by the end of the week. And if you're here, you know exactly how dangerous Cloud is. Are you really going to complain about me doing something about it?"

He huffed, the sound rough, as though he hated I was right. Still, Galen had never been the type to let me have the last word. "What can I do to help?"

"Nothing," Harrison snapped.

And just like that, the tension between them grew yet again. They were like dogs circling each other, and every little sniff in the other's direction set them off. It reminded me how exhausting men really were.

"I don't think there's much you can do," I said, softening Harrison's statement even if I agreed with the basic idea of it. "We've already got a plan. I just need to keep going with what we're doing right now."

Galen's expression softened, his gaze moving between me and Harrison, the meaning clear.

"Can I have a minute?" I asked Harrison.

He nodded, even if he didn't appear that happy with it. He left, though I'd doubt he went far.

"You always manage to slip just out of my grasp," he said, his voice sounded as exhausted as I felt. He lifted his gaze to mine, the look so different from what he'd shown with Harrison in the room. "I keep trying to take care of you, but you just won't let me. Every time I turn around, you just keep moving further and further away from me."

"It's not like I'm going anywhere," I said.

His gaze moved from my face to the side of my neck, to the marks that hadn't faded. He didn't have to say anything for me to know exactly what he was thinking, what he was seeing. It reminded me that as much as I wanted to claim nothing had changed, it wasn't true. Even if that bond hadn't taken, even if I hadn't wanted it, something existed between Kelvin and myself, and now I was living with Harrison.

It would be hard for anyone not to feel bad about that, not to see it as me moving further away from him, that I'd rejected him but run to others.

And as though that realization drew him to close that gap, he came forward, each step slow. Was he doing that after shoving me against the bathroom wall? Like he thought I might be afraid of him?

What a stupid idea—I'd always know exactly how much faster and stronger than me he was. It wasn't like seeing it in person—again—would change that.

He stopped when he was just in front of me, and his warm fingers brushed the marks at my throat. He touched them as though they were open wounds— maybe they were, for him at least. "Do you have any idea how much you terrify me?"

"Me? I'm not usually that scary a person," I said, a soft laugh in my voice.

"Not much scares me because of my position as alpha. You, though? It seems each time you're out of my sight, you disappear, and when you show back up? It's with new enemies, new wounds, new troubles. You have no idea how much I wish I could lock you in a room and throw away the key."

"You're not the first to say that," I said. "But you worry too much. No matter what happens, I always come out on top."

"Until you don't. No one can *always* come out on top. If anyone understands that, I do." He shifted his hand to my cheek, rubbing his thumb against the flushed skin there. Of course, this time I knew that warm feeling had nothing to do with feeling under the weather. "I've been alpha for a long time, Grey, and I know how the world works. People only remain on top for so long, and all it takes is one lucky shot for them to fall. You've survived so far, but that doesn't mean you always will. One of these times, something will get lucky. It'll only take one good swipe, and that's something that can't be taken back."

His words were so soft as he spoke to me, as if he hated having to admit any of this, as though he didn't want to have to tell me but couldn't stop himself.

And fuck, was he compelling. Maybe it was the pleading in his eyes, or the gentle tone of his voice, but something made me want to promise that I'd be fine. Maybe it was just me being stupid, me enjoying the idea of someone giving a damn about me.

However, I knew better than to give into that. My crow screeched in my head, telling me not to fall for it, knowing that trusting others, relying on them, was the end of everything. I couldn't trust anyone like that, knew it led to downfall.

Still, I couldn't get myself to push him away or reject him. He shifted his hand from my check to the back of my neck, then leaned in, pressing his lips to mine. They were soft and familiar, teasing and hot and comforting all at the same time. It was like he kissed me to tell me all the things he'd wanted me to understand, things he couldn't bring himself to say outright.

And me? I lost myself in the same passion. My hands moved as though on their own, sliding up his chest and around his shoulders, clinging to him, wanting to lose myself in his body. I might not have any answers—at least, none that he'd want to hear—but I could savor this. He tilted his head, deepening the kiss, sliding his agile tongue past my lips to tease my own.

I wrapped my leg around him, pulling him closer, ready to strip him down on the spot. I felt rushed suddenly, like we were teenagers who belonged in exactly this sort of situation, struggling against need while trying not to get caught.

I had no idea if it was him or me or both of us. Most likely, it was a combination, of the years we'd resisted this. It felt like we'd always headed this way, like it had been impossible for us to avoid arriving exactly here.

I wouldn't cock block the teenagers, so I sure as fuck wouldn't cock block myself, either.

"Is this really the place?" Harrison's voice broke the moment, bringing me back to reality.

And reality sucked, because reality didn't have me getting laid right then.

Galen released a growl that sent a shudder through me. It had me considering how that would feel if he made such a sound when he was between my thighs, if it would send a dangerous and pleasant vibration right through my cunt.

Talk about something to add to my bucket list…

Except I had a feeling that wouldn't happen right now, so I broke the kiss and dropped my forehead against Galen's solid chest, glad to at least find it rising and falling in rapid succession, showing he was just as affected as I was.

He extracted himself from my grip, then took a step backward. Something wild rested in his eyes, a hint at the beast that lived beneath his skin. And why the fuck did that do sinful things to me?

Galen turned a vicious look on Harrison, one that would make most sane men take one big fucking step backward. "If anything happens to her, I will hold you *personally* responsible."

That sounded like a pointless threat, but I knew better. Galen was in a position to make that Harrison's problem, to pose one hell of a danger to him. Not that

Harrison appeared all that worried. He didn't so much as flinch in response. "If you wish for her to remain safe, I would suggest you stay out of our business. Your presence only further complicates and endangers her."

Galen lifted his lip on one side, baring his teeth in a snarl, before he turned and stormed out of the room.

It left Harrison and me alone, and I suddenly felt like a kid caught with a boy. Which, I sort of had been.

"He is going to cause you problems," Harrison said.

"Of course he is—he's a man. In my experience, you all mostly cause problems in my life."

Harrison shook his head, but didn't argue my point. Instead, he gestured for me to follow.

It seemed day three of my drug dealer life had come to a close, and I hadn't even gotten an orgasm out of it.

Maybe I wasn't as good at being a criminal as I liked to think…

Chapter Nine

A whimper escaped me, the pain in my head having grown by the day. Tomorrow, Friday, marked five days of selling product—we'd even created another batch the day before. However, no matter how well my career as a dealer was going, my health had continued to deteriorate.

Something cool rested against my forehead, and I arched into the touch. It was heavenly, as though it pulled that heat right out of my body. Of course, I'd tumbled between freezing and overheating, bouncing back and forth like a fucking ping-pong ball.

"You're running a fever," Harrison said from beside me. Him there, in my bed, should have bothered me, but right now? I couldn't give less of a fuck. His palm against my head felt too fantastic to care where he was or what he was doing. Hell, he could have been masturbating beside me and so long as he didn't move his hand, I didn't care.

"It's probably your fault," I muttered, groaning at the end.

"My fault?"

"I don't think I've gotten sick since I turned into this. If I'm sick now, it's got to be because of you."

"I don't think that's the case." His words were calm and slow, and I got the sense he meant something more by them. I didn't know what it was, and I had a feeling he didn't intend to tell me, either. I also lacked the energy to care. "You should eat something."

"Why? Are you into cleaning up vomit, because I'm pretty sure that's what we'll get."

He sighed, then shifted, removing his hand. I whimpered, reaching out blindly, wanting nothing more than to feel him again.

"Easy," he whispered, his voice soft. His strong hands grasped my arms, pulling me closer. I forced my eyes open to find he'd removed his shirt, then tugged me against his now bare chest.

If I didn't feel like death warmed over, I might have enjoyed the sight more. It was worth drooling over, after all. His skin was impossibly pale, as though he never spent any time in the sun. He was lean, without a speck of fat on his body that I could see. Instead of his body feeling jagged, however, I molded against it, pressing my cheek to his left pec, his cool skin helping to cool the heat inside my body. He ran his fingers through my hair at the same time, easing me.

"This can't continue." His voice was so soft that I struggled to make it out at first. Was he even talking to me? Did I even care?

No, I really don't.

He shifted again, and his voice echoed in the quiet room. "Hello? Yes, trust me, I never intended to call you, either. She isn't doing well. Could it really be anything else?" His voice was soft and soothing, and I stopped trying to make sense of it. He wasn't talking to me after all. It went on, the back and forth, and I lost myself in the sound of it. "This is your fault. I don't care what the crystal said, you caused this—you need to resolve it. I expect to see you within the hour." Harrison moved again, but I just wrapped my arms around his torso, grasping him closer, clinging to him. He sighed, then went back to stroking his fingers through my hair. "I am not leaving, Grey. Just relax—you'll feel better soon."

I wanted to call him a liar, but even that felt like too much work. Maybe this was some weird drop from the attack? Maybe it was a reaction from being around Harrison so long? Whatever it was, his cool skin seemed to be the only thing that helped right now.

So, without another choice, I did as he said and let myself drift off, pressed against his skin, disappointed to waste this perfect opportunity. I'd always said I'd pick orgasms over rest, but fuck, maybe at my age, it wasn't as easy a choice as it used to be.

Voices roused me, but I lacked the energy to even open my eyes. It felt like far too much work. Fuck, I couldn't even tell who exactly spoke, only knowing that they'd made my headache somehow worse.

"What do you want me to do?"

"I want you to fix this."

"I can't—assuming it is due to the bond."

"You can't be serious. Just look at her. That is clearly withdrawal."

I squeezed my eyes tightly closed, trying to block out the noise. The movement must have caught the attention of the two, because their voices lowered more.

"You can't just let her suffer like this."

"I can't do what you're asking me to. After everything that happened? How can you even ask me to?"

"Trust me, I wouldn't ask this if I had another option. Do you think I enjoyed having to call you? This is the last thing I wanted, but I can't just allow her to suffer. Who knows what stress this could put on her, how much it could harm her?"

A loud sigh answered those words a moment before the bed shifted beneath me. A delicious scent reached my nose, something sweet and heady, like caramelized sugar. I wanted to bury my face in it and breathe it into my lungs. Something touched my forehead, more of the smell surrounding me. "Grey, can you look at me?" The words coaxed me, as though they promised me so much more than I could possibly imagine.

Fuck, they silenced my crow, made me want to believe anything they said, to follow them wherever they went. Even still, the idea of opening my eyes felt far too difficult.

"Look at me." A tempting darkness in those words drew me in, and without resisting this time, I opened my eyes to find familiar bright blue eyes staring back at me.

Kelvin. I had every reason to pull away, to reject him, but something in his voice and his eyes kept me from doing it.

Or maybe it was that mouthwatering smell that kept me docile.

He smiled, the look tense. "You're not doing so hot, are you?"

I shook my head, answering without thinking.

"Do you want me to help? I don't know if it will work, but I can try."

"Look at her—she's in no condition to refuse," the other voice said. It took a moment for me to recognize it as Harrison.

Kelvin turned his head the other way. "I've fucked this up once already. I'm not about to make it worse by doing anything else against her will."

"So you'll let her suffer?"

Kelvin had a pained expression, as though stuck between two equally horrible paths. I couldn't seem to keep up with what he meant, with what we should do, but I knew one thing. I *needed* Kelvin. Whatever was wrong with me, he was both the cause and the cure. It meant no matter what the risks, the consequences, I knew I needed him.

I grasped Kelvin's wrist, holding it tight, pleading with my expression.

It drew his attention back to me, his look softening. "You really aren't doing good, are you? Okay, Grey, I'll help." He turned his gaze on Harrison, then. "You know what this will do, right? You understand the reaction that will happen, and you're prepared for that?" Whatever Harrison said must have been enough, because Kelvin nodded.

He shifted on the bed, moving so his back was to the headboard. Before I even had to do anything, his firm hands moved me, pulling me against his chest, my back to him. His body was strong, his arms unyielding around me. It surrounded me with more of the amazing scent, made my head fuzzy and eased the pain between my temples, the soreness of my body. It felt like sliding into a hot bath.

He grasped my chin, tilting my head and exposing the side of my throat. My messy brain couldn't keep up with the actions, even now, so I gave in. "Don't hate me," came an agonized whisper from Kelvin, so close and quiet that I doubted anyone else could have heard it. It happened only a split second before a sharp pain ran through my neck. Just like that, I knew *exactly* what was going on.

He'd bitten me.

As quickly as I'd understood that, however, the same heat from before rushed through me. Just like the first and only time he'd bitten me, that heat burned, igniting something deep and primal inside me. It moved through my body, racing from my neck to my clit and hitting every erogenous area between the two.

I arched my back, even the brush of my shirt against my nipples too fucking much, as though someone held a vibrator against me. Was this how it had felt before? Maybe I'd just forgotten, maybe I'd blocked it out since I didn't want everything that went with it.

A low growl left Kelvin, and something familiar and hard pressed against my back. Even in my lust-addled brain, I knew *exactly* what that was. And fuck, because it was everything I wanted right now.

I reached for my own clothes, needing to strip out of them, to douse the fire inside me. Strong hands caught my wrists, holding me still. Even then, Kelvin didn't pull away, sucking gently at the wounds at my throat.

"Please," I begged, my pride gone, not giving a fuck if I sounded pathetic. "Just touch me, please. It hurts so much."

His ragged breath told me how close to the edge he walked. "I can't," he whispered, releasing my throat only long enough to get the words out. "Harrison?"

Jayce Carter

I didn't understand what he meant until the mattress moved, pulling my focus in front of me. There, kneeling on the bed between my thighs, was Harrison. He was shirtless, and from his pants—unbuttoned but on—I could tell he had every bit as much interest as I did.

Or, maybe not just as much, but his hard cock told me he wasn't sad about being there, either.

He leaned in, and I expected something soft, something gentle. Harrison was always careful, a man who held himself in control at all times. That wasn't how he touched me, though. Instead, he kissed me with a hunger that shocked me, one that felt every bit as deep as my own. He moved closer until he trapped my body between his and Kelvin's, sliding into the space between my thighs.

I hooked one leg around him, then rolled my hips, rubbing myself against him. Had I ever felt so much like some animal in heat? Had I ever needed something this badly? The first time Kelvin had bitten me, I recalled a similar rush, but it wasn't anything like this. Maybe because I'd gone so long without?

Whatever it was, I allowed Harrison to quench that desire with his kiss, with his hard body.

But I needed *more*. This was good, sure, but it wasn't enough. I felt empty, hollowed out by need. However, no matter how much I yanked at the hands that held me still, I couldn't get free, couldn't grab for Harrison, couldn't force him to give me more.

He must have known, though, because he grasped the front of my pajama top and yanked, the tearing of fabric loud in the room, even over my panting moans and the noisy sucking from Kelvin's lips at my throat. Harrison slid his hands over my bare skin, and I was so fucking thankful I'd forgone a bra. Hell, I'd burn every scrap if it meant getting what I needed sooner, if it meant enjoying this moment and quieting the noise in my head a little faster.

Harrison's fingers lacked callouses, nothing but cool, smooth skin. He didn't tease, didn't go slowly, instead cupping my breasts to thumb over the pointed tips of my nipples. I shuddered, desperate for more, for everything. I lifted my hips, grinding against his erection through the fabric of our pants.

Through all of it, Kelvin didn't let up, his tongue teasing the sensitive skin of my neck, each pull drawing that fire further through me. It was like I'd taken a bunch of shots, like the alcohol clouded my head, but I didn't give a fuck. All I knew was I needed more, that I was horribly empty.

"More," I begged. "Please, fuck me. I need it so bad." I spoke the words between the kisses, whispering them against Harrison's lips.

Harrison broke the kiss and groaned, pressing his forehead to my collarbone as though he had to collect himself, like he needed a moment to gather his wits.

But I didn't *want* him to do that. If he thought, he might say no. I wanted him as drunk as I felt, as out of control. I didn't think it mattered who was in front of me, I just needed to be filled. Kelvin, Harrison, fuck, I was pretty sure I'd take a stranger right then if they had a cock worth a damn.

"You said you were ready for this," Kelvin said, pulling away from my throat for a moment.

"I've never actually *felt* this from someone," Harrison snapped, his warm breath sliding along my bare chest. It made me arch my back, begging him with that action to put those lips to good use. "I can feel the

120

desire from you both. I can't normally feel her emotions, but I can right now. It's...overwhelming."

"Well, I warned you," Kelvin said, groaning when I tried to shift back, rubbing his hard cock trapped between us. "Now, you said you would do what needed to be done. I suggest you get to it. If any girl would make you pay for not living up to expectations, Grey would."

Kelvin's words should have embarrassed me. Fuck, I should have wanted to haul off and hit him for saying such things. Instead, however, I nodded, as though he needed someone to agree with him. It was obvious I was this far gone, the way his bite had stolen all my senses and enslaved me to the same lust he had.

And later, I could get mad about it. Later, I could hate him and myself for this moment, for letting him get this far, for allowing him to see me this way. For now? For now, I only knew I needed more of this.

Harrison lifted his head, his eyes hard and ravenous. In that look, I knew he wouldn't reject me. It wasn't possible, not when he wanted this as badly as I did.

The fact that this was a bad idea didn't matter to me either. Harrison and I were...well, we were something. Not romantic, that was for sure, but I'd be a liar if I said it was entirely platonic.

He reached down and slipped his long, agile fingers into the waist of my shorts, tugging them down my legs with no finesse. He didn't strip me slowly, carefully, teasingly. Instead, he rushed, like he needed to see me without a stitch of clothing as fast as possible. Once bare, I let my knees fall open, not giving a fuck about embarrassment or how I looked. A cunt was a cunt, and I'd bet mine wasn't the first or last he'd ever seen.

Really, so long as he touched me, he could look at whatever the fuck he wanted.

Harrison ran the flats of his large palms up my inner thighs, the touch forcing my legs wider. He brushed his thumbs up my slit when he reached the juncture of my legs, the touch not nearly enough for me.

"I swear, if you keep teasing me, I'll kill you." I barely recognized the darkness in my own voice, each word dripping with desperate need.

"Easy, Grey," Kelvin whispered into my ear before dragging the flat of his tongue along the side of my throat, the action causing that desire inside me to grow yet again. "You'll get what you want if you just be a good girl."

Good girl? I laughed at the words, at the stupidity of them. I was never a good girl, had no desire to be one, either.

It also seemed to wake my crow from its slumber, rousing it.

Before I knew what I'd done, before I could think about it or consider, I moved forward. Kelvin's hands slipped free of my arms—probably due to a mix of surprise and my crow's ability to keep me from being trapped. I shoved Harrison backward, crawling on top of him, feeling like a beast pushed too far.

I wasn't prey, even if it felt like that sometimes. I yanked at Harrison's pants, getting them down just enough to free his hard cock, then wrapped my hand around it. It was solid and thick and just as pale as the rest of his skin. The head was wet with pre-cum, and he twitched against my palm as I stroked him just because I couldn't not do it.

However, that wasn't enough. It wasn't what I really wanted. I rose, angling his cock so the thick head nestled against my drenched pussy, then lowered myself. He spread me, the burn enough to make me hiss in response even if it didn't stop or slow me at all. Instead, I took that burn, let it add to the fire that roared inside me, shivering until my body met his and not an inch of him remained outside of me.

I set my hands flat on his stomach, his muscles shifting beneath his skin under my touch.

Kelvin ran his hand up my spine, the action making my back arch. "That's good, sweet," he said. "You aren't the passive type, the sort to wait until you're given what you want. So go on, take him, fuck him exactly the way you need right now."

His words broke any leash I had on my actions, like the permission I'd really wanted, someone telling me it was okay to be selfish, to take, to *own*. So I rose until Harrison's cock was barely inside me before coming down again, riding Harrison hard, the action rough and fast but exactly what I needed. My fingers curled against Harrison's stomach, my nails biting into him, but if he cared, he said nothing.

A glance at his face showed his gaze locked on me, his focus absolute. I was pretty sure there could have been a fire roaring around us and he would have taken no notice. It could have burned us all to a crisp before any of us gave a fuck about it.

And burning was exactly how I felt, consumed entirely by the sensation of Harrison's hard cock filling me, the power as I rode him, the touch of Kelvin's hands on my back and the searing need from his venom inside me. It all melted together until it was bigger and stronger and more overwhelming than anything else.

Kelvin slid his hand from my back, around my ribcage, to cup my breast. "I told myself I wouldn't touch you like this, but how can I resist? I won't fuck you, not until you tell me you want me to when you're in your right mind, but this much?" He dragged his fingers along the curve of my breast, circling closer and closer to the pebbled tip like the worst sort of tease. "This much I think we can allow, don't you?"

The word no danced on my tongue, but instead, I nodded. It seemed, like often, my body and my brain were not anywhere on the same page.

Fuck, I doubted they read the same book.

And during it all, I didn't stop riding Harrison. I didn't slow, couldn't, not when the sensation of him filling me was so fucking perfect. Harrison reached up, grasping my thighs, then lifted his hips just as I lowered myself. It made him slam into me harder, and it didn't stop at just the one time. Harrison didn't look that strong, especially because I knew that, as a Mind, he wasn't physically much stronger than a human, but he proved he wasn't weak right then. He fucked me hard and fast, taking over so I leaned backward, falling against Kelvin's broad chest.

It should have been painful, even, so rough that I'd have slapped a man for even thinking about it. Instead, all I could do was accept the treatment, basking in the pleasure that bordered on pain, the wonderfully freeing feeling.

Kelvin slipped his hand down my front, over my stomach, to my cunt. He ran his fingers along my pussy, where Harrison's cock was buried. "I would ask if it feels good when he fucks you, but I don't need to ask, do I? I can tell from the sounds you're making, from just how wet you are. I remember how your cunt feels, how tight you squeeze down. Your pussy is heaven, Grey. Do you have any idea how much control it takes not to push you forward and push in beside him? Could you take that, sweet? Could your pretty little pussy handle that?" He ground his palm against my clit as he teased my cunt, pressing in at the edges, as if threatening to force his fingers inside along with Harrison's cock.

And somehow, Kelvin's words made me want that. I wanted to be used, to think of nothing, to be nothing but passion and feeling and *this*. It was like he weaved a spell with his words, his promises, and I wanted so badly to never stop this.

So I nodded, reached behind me, looping my arms behind Kelvin's neck to hold him tight.

He took his other hand, the one torturing my cunt, and moved it behind me. He traced my spine, following the curve of my lower back, then ran along my ass. "If that's too much, how about here? Do you think you would let me slide myself into you here? To claim something on you I doubt you've ever allowed another?" He swiped wetness up from my cunt before pressing his finger against my ass, not pushing enough to enter but enough to tease me.

He'd made a similar threat before, and just like that time, I didn't think I could resist. Once was a joke, but twice made for a kink.

A kink that I amazingly was all up for trying…

I pushed my ass backward, the action causing his finger to grind harder, to nearly enter me.

Kelvin groaned lowly, the sound going straight to my clit. "You are like a fucking drug, Grey," he growled into my ear. "No matter how much I think I can handle you, that I can resist anything you say or do, you are always proving me wrong."

The words felt like a strange win, like I knew he was right and I was rather proud of it. Kelvin, who was so much older and more powerful than me, felt like putty against me right then.

However, he didn't give me what I wanted, either. After one more teasing push, he removed that finger without entering me. "I told you — I won't fuck you, not until you can tell me you want me when you're not high off my venom. So for now, get your fill with Harrison." He pressed a kiss to my throat, then latched his lips on the bite mark. The blood had slowed but not fully stopped, which meant he was able to feast. One hand on my back shoved me forward, so I was on top of Harrison, my chest against his. He fucked up into me just as roughly as before, the actions wild.

Meanwhile, Kelvin moved behind us, and a glance gave me one hell of a sight that I hadn't expected. He moved Harrison's legs so they were together, trapped by Kelvin's knees, then undid his own pants. He stroked his hard cock a few times, then leaned forward and fit his cock between Harrison's thighs. His thrusts were rough and fast, as though he were fucking something other than just the crease of Harrison's legs, and the pre-cum from his dripping cock made Harrison's thighs shiny.

And Harrison, who must have been fully aware of what was happening, didn't seem to care. If anything, he groaned louder, his body tense as he kept his thighs tight to provide the best friction.

The orgasm that hit me came out of nowhere — probably both because of the sight and the venom. I gasped, trapped between the two of them, as we all strove for our own releases, all lost to our own pleasures that only grew between us. I cried out, my body tightening, my breath locked in my lungs when I couldn't even breathe. The orgasm seemed to go on forever, drowning me, dragging me into a darkness that I feared I might never escape from.

Harrison tightened his hands on my thighs so much that I knew I'd wear finger-shaped bruises there the next day, using the grip to yank me down and fill me as deeply as possible. The sound he released was low and angry as he came, and a similar sound escaped Kelvin as well.

It left the room silent other than the rough panting of the three of us, my body too exhausted to even hope to think straight. It didn't matter to me, nothing did. I was tired and sore and yet that nagging pain from before had disappeared. It meant that when my eyes slid closed, when the muscles needed to keep me upright became far too troublesome, I slid into a blessed, wonderful sleep.

Covered in cum and sweat, pinned between the bodies of two men who I shouldn't trust, none of that was worth thinking too deeply about. Instead, I let myself sleep.

Tomorrow me could deal with the mess I'd just made.

Tomorrow me had always been one unlucky bitch.

* * * *

I should have woken in pain. Fucking two Spirits was the sort of work out only the experienced should ever try, and even they might not survive it. That was why, when I did finally open my eyes later, I'd braced for pain.

I'd expected soreness in my stomach, for my muscles to complain, for bruises to cover me. Imagine my surprise to find myself actually feeling well.

In fact, I wasn't sure of the last time I'd felt quite this good. A glance down my body showed bruises — I guess those wouldn't go away as fast as anything else — but they were the only proof that the night before hadn't just been some filthy dream of mine.

I was clean, which was strange because I sure as hell hadn't been clean at the end of our little tryst. Did that mean either Kelvin or Harrison had wiped me down? My hair wasn't stuck to my previously sweat-soaked forehead, and I didn't have anything dried on my thighs. It meant someone had to have cleaned me.

My cheeks flushed at that, the fact somehow even more embarrassing than anything else I'd done. The idea of being entirely passed out and having one of those two clean me?

It was the sort of thing I hoped they forgot, or that we could all possibly pretend had never happened.

Whoever it was, they hadn't dressed me, though. The sheets felt clean, and the idea of dressing now felt like a lot of fucking work. However, it seemed clothing was a very small barrier when it came to interacting with two men I'd just had crazy, drugged sex with, so I forced myself to go to the closet and pick something out.

I could have dressed in a few of the cute items there — the sun dresses or the pretty skirts or even the hoochy-mama shorts where the pockets fell longer than the bottom of the shorts. Instead, I picked something that hopefully would help me keep my head on straight.

I headed down the hallway after braiding my hair back and tossing it over my shoulder. The scent of food drifted from the kitchen, and my stomach growled in response.

An appetite was a good sign, right? After how horribly I'd felt recently, wanting to eat showed improvement. I'd take what I could get.

"We should check on her," Harrison said.

"No need. She's fine."

"So you say. Forgive me for not taking your word on the matter."

"I'm the one with experience in this area—unless you have some expertise in dealing with thralls that I don't know."

It seemed a night of sex hadn't fixed the issues between Harrison and Kelvin, judging from them sniping at each other at—I glanced at the clock on the wall—one in the afternoon.

One? That meant I'd slept far longer than I'd realized, and it also meant we'd missed the last workday of the week. Not that I was all that sorry about it, especially since I felt like I wasn't half dead for the first time in a while.

I considered turning back around and leaving, but the scent of food drew me in. I could handle the awkwardness if it meant getting to taste whatever was cooking.

I expected to find Harrison in front of the stove, which was why my steps faltered for a moment when instead, I found Kelvin there, spatula in hand, his broad back in a white button-up shirt. Harrison stood to the side, watching over the actions like some supervisor.

They both turned my way when I entered the kitchen, and even if nothing else had clued me in, their pause showed last night had happened. No one acted *this* awkward unless they'd had sex. Nothing quite threw people off like sex.

"Morning," I said, forcing myself to sound cheery and unbothered. Fuck, maybe they'd let me pretend nothing had happened and we'd all move forward. That sounded like a fantastic idea to me, and any polite person would pick up on what I was putting down.

"Seems like orgies agree with you," Kelvin said, before turning back to his task, stirring whatever was in the large skillet on the stove.

"Really?" I asked. "You couldn't give me like ten minutes of pretending like nothing happened? You just had to blurt that out first thing?"

He shrugged. "Why pretend? We all remember last night. My venom might make you a bit drugged, but it doesn't take away your memories."

"Are you cold?" Harrison asked, his blond eyebrow lifted as he took in my outfit.

Kelvin snorted—loudly. "You really don't know her that well yet, do you? That little ensemble is called armor. What, Grey, you think a parka and boots will somehow make last night not happen?"

"No—I'm hoping it'll just keep it from happening *again*."

"Nice try, but one little tear and you'd be buck naked again. It's the benefit and downside to screwing with Spirits—clothing isn't much of a deterrent. If it makes you feel better to dress like you're going skiing, though, go for it." Kelvin took stack of plates from the cabinet, setting out three of them on the counter beside the stove. He lifted the skillet and scooped what he'd been cooking between the plates.

After putting the skillet back on the stove, he balanced two of the plates on one arm and held one in the other hand, moving past me and to the dining table.

And me, like an idiot, followed, because who wouldn't follow food that smelled that good? Kelvin set the plates down, then pulled one chair out for me, waiting until I sat. He sat across the table from me, and Harrison took the spot at the head of the table.

Talk about uncomfortable.

Just three fuck buddies eating eggs together like nothing had happened at all. I picked up my fork and plopped a bite into my mouth. If anyone could pretend—I could.

Of course, despite the fact I suspected the food was fantastic, I couldn't taste any of it. It might have as well been raw and unseasoned for all I enjoyed it. Still, I shoveled more into my mouth, playing the part.

"You look to be feeling better," Harrison said.

I nodded, swallowing the food in my mouth "Yeah, I guess I do."

"So that proves my suspicion."

I shifted my gaze over from Harrison to Kelvin, knowing exactly what he meant even if he didn't say it. Given how shitty I'd felt before, and the way Kelvin's bite had fixed it, it could only mean one thing—Kelvin had created a bond between us when he'd bitten me before.

"But the crystal…"

"You didn't seem to lose your old place, probably because of what you are, but the withdrawal you went through and how quickly you recovered after Kelvin bit you again shows that that was the problem. Denying it would be pointless, don't you think?" Harrison said.

131

I snapped my mouth shut because I couldn't argue with his reasoning. I still felt a connection to Kelvin, no matter my anger with him, how he'd betrayed me. Pretending it wasn't true wouldn't change what happened or where I was now. I liked to fight against the inevitable, but even I wasn't foolish enough to make myself suffer just to prove a point I knew was false.

"So I guess that means I'm your thrall."

Kelvin stared back at me, then nodded, his motions slow as though testing the ground. "Seems that way."

"That means I'll go through this again?" The idea of being tied to someone else, dependent on them every day, it chafed. I didn't like that idea in the least.

"You got so bad this time because you didn't realize you needed him," Harrison said, breaking into the conversation as though this weren't in the least uncomfortable. "Since you understand that now, you should be able to remain on top of it so this doesn't occur again."

"Meaning…" I sighed, setting my fork down when even the wonderful, mouthwatering scent wasn't enough to overcome my discomfort. "That I'm bound to you?"

Kelvin nodded. "I've never seen or heard of a bond like this, but we know that you're different because of what you are. It seems like you're my thrall, that you've got a bond with me, but it didn't shift your clan to mine. Still, clearly you need my bite."

"How often?"

"That I can't tell you. When did you start feeling unwell?"

"Two weeks ago," Harrison said when I didn't answer. At my look, he shrugged. "You started rubbing your temples at that point."

"Two weeks ago means you went three weeks without serious symptoms. You could probably go two weeks then, but I'd suggest you try not to go more than a one."

"That often?" I shuddered at the idea of being trapped like that, as though a noose tightened around my throat. "Why one week instead of two?"

"Just because you don't tell the effects right away doesn't mean they aren't there. You'll start feeling sick by week two, but your body will struggle before then. To feel your best, you'll need more venom each week."

"More venom, huh?" I laughed at the way he phrased it, how innocent it sounded. He made it seem so simple, like we weren't talking about him sinking his fangs into my neck.

And I tried *very* hard not to think about what would happen after that, because I sure as fuck couldn't imagine resisting the way his venom made me feel. It meant that every single time we had to do this — weekly it sounded, like some fucked-up therapy session — I'd end up in this same position?

It took me back to when he'd bit me, to the way I'd felt strangled by it.

"I'll give you a moment." Harrison rose from his seat, walking toward the backdoor. He headed outside, leaving Kelvin and me alone.

Fuck, that wasn't what I'd wanted. If anything, it made the tension between us even more overwhelming, more obvious. Every moment that passed, my heart pounded harder against my ribcage, so loud that I would have sworn Kelvin could easily hear it.

"I'm sorry," he said, his voice soft. It was a far cry from the memory of last night, the filthy things he'd whispered into my ear. In the daylight, he seemed like a different person.

I leaned forward, resting my forehead against the table, trying to slow my breathing.

"What can I do?"

I shook my head, unsure of what to say. What I wanted was for him to fix this, to make it so it never happened, so I wasn't trapped. However, I knew better than most that there were some bells that couldn't get unrung. This was one of them. "It's funny—I didn't think this possible before. Even after you bit me, when I was waiting for the trial, I didn't think you could really form a bond."

"I'm not trying to cause you pain," he said. "I want to make this as easy as possible, but I don't know how to do that."

I snorted, my eyes closed, hating the way him speaking—even from across the table—still somehow sounded like him whispering right into my ear. It felt intimate, even more so since I wasn't looking at him. "How did we end up here?"

"Maybe we were always headed here. I'm not a man who believes in fate, but maybe there is something to be said about paths intertwining." He paused, then let out a soft sigh. "I met with a Nature Spirit one time, and they claimed that the entire world was formed out of a tree, that we were all just roots and branches and leaves on the same tree, bound together like vines. I thought he was an idiot back then, but when I look at you? I wonder if there wasn't some truth to that theory, because I've felt a pull toward you all the years that I've known you."

"Fate is bullshit."

"The fact you believe that doesn't surprise me. You aren't the type to want to believe in anything having control of your life."

"And yet here I am, bound to you. If there is such a thing as fate, she's a fucking bitch." I turned my head on the table so I could look over at him, resting my cheek against the smooth wood. I expected at first for him to argue, for him to tell me all about how I was wrong, that I should accept my place, that it wasn't so bad.

Whether Kelvin just knew better than to try to sell me that shit or if he truly understood how hollow those words would be, he didn't do it. Instead, he nodded. "Yeah, well, we're in agreement about that. She really is one mean bitch, and all we can try to do is survive her."

* * * *

I had needed the weekend to recover, but that didn't mean my brain was any less frazzled come Monday. Still, I forced myself to get up, get dressed, and drag my ass to school along with Harrison.

The man who, by the way, had failed to even mention what had happened with Kelvin. Whether he did that because he regretted it or he was just trying to be nice, I had no idea. Whatever the reasoning, I appreciated it. I didn't want to discuss that mess — even if the reality was that it had replayed in my head over and over again.

And yet again when I'd taken a leisurely bath. As it turned out, I was exceedingly good at remembering details at moments like that. I rather enjoyed the memory of the time, even if I'd never admit that to anyone.

So here we were, back and school, another pocket full of drugs to pawn off on other kids. I just had to hope that we'd find our supplier soon, because I had no idea how long I could keep this up. It wasn't the selling, or even the guilt, but more the eight in the morning start time and snotty kids.

And the slang. *No cap?* I still had no fucking idea what that meant, but I knew that by saying it, I annoyed the little fuckers here which was exactly why I said it so often.

I took a sip of the coffee, wondering just how a school could have a café on campus. The reasoning didn't matter that much—I planned to take full advantage of it. And I had. This was my third cup of the day. Even without the sexy memories from last week, my heart rate was in peak condition from all the caffeine I'd poured down my throat.

I'd sold a few bags thus far, mostly to regulars who had come to me the week before. It seemed that Harrison had done what he'd said, managing to create a product that people wanted to try again. It worked well enough for me.

Except…

I'd yet to spot Trey.

My phone rang, so I pulled it from my pocket and glanced at the screen.

Ignis?

"Hello," I answered, holding the cell between my ear and my shoulder.

"Hey—where have you been?"

"Working."

"Really?" Her voice held an edge of suspicion. I couldn't blame her for that. I'd done plenty of deliveries in the past, but I rarely called them work and sure as fuck had never treated it as a job.

"Yes, really. I do work, you know?"

"Uh-huh. And here I'd started to believe the rumor I heard about people seeing you around with Harrison." The sly tone of her voice sounded like one hell of a gotcha. The bitch knew the truth to that, then, and she just wanted to catch me in the lie.

"Trust me – dealing with your brother *is* work." I sat on the edge of a planter, ignoring the dirty looks from a teacher as she walked by. "And who told you that? I swear, you Spirits are no better than teenage girls – and I know a lot more about teenagers than I did before, so I can say that."

Ignis chuckled. "Well, to be fair, no one sees other people with Harrison. If he even got a dog, I think it would start up the rumor mill. It's why hearing he was seen with some blue-haired girl was enough for me to take notice. What's that all about? Are you two besties now?"

A flash from the other night hit me, the sensation of Harrison's lips, the way his cock had sunk into me. *No, not friends.* Thankfully, our conversation occurring over the phone meant Ignis couldn't read my expression, the nosy bitch. "Not exactly," I hedged. "I'm helping him with a problem."

And there it was, the silence that screamed of disapproval. Why was it that no one seemed to believe that? Was it that they didn't think I could be helpful or just that they thought I must have caused the problem? "Please tell me this isn't about the Cloud…"

"How did you know about that?"

"I'm a Mind, Grey. I may stay out of clan business, but that doesn't mean I don't hear what's going on. Harrison has been tracking Cloud for months now. I just didn't think he'd be stupid enough to get you caught up in that mess."

"He didn't. I found my way into it all by myself. Trust me, I don't need any help to find trouble."

"Well, I can't deny that. At least tell me that you're safe."

"I'm as safe as I ever am," I answered. "And Harrison is keeping an eye out for me."

"That's the only reason I'm going to let this be. If it were anyone else, I'd try to haul you back by the nape of your neck. If there's anyone who can keep an eye on you, though, it would be Harrison."

"Really? He doesn't strike me as a real caretaker type." I thought about the cold way Harrison spoke, the way he seemed uninterested in the entire world around him.

"Yeah, that's how he wants to look. I've known him my entire life, though."

"Who's older?"

I could almost see Ignis smirking at the question, at the fact that I was curious about them — and because of that, curious about him. Still, I couldn't help it. Harrison was so tight-lipped, I felt like I knew almost nothing about him.

Well, I knew what his cock looked like — and felt like — but that wasn't something I planned to tell his sister.

"I am," she said. "I was five when he was born."

"Why is he the way he is, then, but not you?"

"Ouch. Are you really asking me why my brother is so much more powerful than I am? Don't you think that's a sort of rude question?"

"You know I don't mean it like that. It's just that you're normal, and he is very much not. Is it just random?"

Papers shuffled on the other side of the line, suggesting she was in her office, still working. Not that it shocked me—Ignis was one hell of a hard worker, after all. I could picture her at her desk, reviewing files while she made a call between clients. "The power that Minds hold follow bloodlines, but like anything, there's a lot that seems like random chance. Think of it like having good genes, but the mixture of those genes determine exactly how useful. Our parents are powerful, which set us up for being powerful as well. Believe it or not, I'm not considered weak. It's just that my skills are less obvious."

"But Harrison is on a whole different level."

She sighed, and I got the sense that the conversation wasn't all that pleasant for her. I got it, though. We were talking about her brother, after all, and I could imagine how she'd be compared to him at every turn.

I'd gone through that with my siblings as well. I was the fuck-up, and I couldn't have attended a single gathering without someone looking at me and treating me exactly that way.

"He is different," she admitted. "When his powers started to show, when the clan realized just how strong his powers were, they separated him. They even took him out of our household to be raised by the previous clan head."

"So he wasn't raised with you?"

"Nope. They didn't want anything to risk his powers or change his mind. They wanted to mold him into the perfect leader. I saw him every few months when he got to come home for a weekend, but it was different. He'd always been trying to live up to that standard, to the things that everyone expects from him. I don't think he's had a single real friend in all these years."

"And no one knows why he became the way he is?"

"Not exactly." She said the words slowly, giving me a sense that there was more to the story than she told me. Then again, I sure as fuck knew how that was. No one ever told the entire story, because it was usually far too painful.

Part of me wanted to ask, to know more. It felt like craving pieces of his past that he held close to him, like the little bits of information were shiny baubles my crow wanted to collect. However, in the same way, I really didn't think I wanted to know. Knowing would mean making it my problem, would mean seeing Harrison differently, and that was the sort of thing I couldn't put back afterward.

So I let it go, not pushing her. If I needed to know, later, I'd find out. Until then, I might as well ignore it and respect Harrison's right to privacy.

"The thing about Harrison," she said, her voice quiet as though she weren't sure she really wanted to say this next part. "He's never had anyone to take care of him, anyone who was there for him because of who he is, not because of *what* he is. Even his family handed him over to strangers to raise. Then, because of his powers, he's been isolated most of his life. He's used to people using him, to them not giving a damn about him, and I don't think he knows how to accept help. Even though he has no idea what it's like to have people behind him, people willing to help, he's always putting himself out to do that for others. He's pushing himself, working ungodly hours, ignoring anything for himself to take the load off of others. Maybe you staying with him isn't so bad, not for either of you…"

I swung my feet, tapping my heels against the brick of the planter. "Yeah, well, don't start planning the wedding just yet. I'm fun to have around for a few days—especially if someone has a reason to deal with me—but it gets old fast." That took me back to all the people who had walked away from me.

I'd learned one important lesson throughout my life, over and over again. A small amount of time with me was one thing, but once anyone stuck around for long, they ran in the other fucking direction. A little of me was fine, but more than that?

Too much.

Sure, I'd had fun the other night, and given that Harrison had come, I had to assume he had as well, but fun like that didn't mean much in the long run. It meant I needed to get this shit settled and out of here as soon as possible. The longer I stayed, the closer I got to Harrison walking away, and I had a feeling that would hurt. That strange fondness he had for me morphing into annoyance then hatred?

I didn't want to see it.

"Grey."

I jerked my gaze up, startled to find the same voice speaking to me that I'd just been thinking of. Harrison stood there, looking rather professional in the sports coat. Sure, he looked more like a model playing a teacher than an actual teacher, but I'd bet it helped keep the girls in line in his classes.

"Sorry, I've gotta go," I said to Ignis, not waiting for a response before ending the call. If I told Harrison who I'd spoken to, I felt like he'd figure out the content, too. He was far too observant to give him any additional chances at guessing my thoughts and feelings. If anything, I really needed a handicap. "What's up? Is it time to go already?"

"It's ten in the morning, Grey."

"Boring," I muttered and crossed my arms after sliding the phone into my pocket. "So what are you doing here now?"

He glanced toward my pocket, the curiosity obvious in his expression. Still, he didn't ask about who I'd been on the phone with. Maybe he didn't want to know, not really. I mean, I had fucked him with another man there, so maybe he knew better than to ask too many questions. "Trey didn't come to school today."

"Trey is a drug dealer. I don't think skipping school is really that crazy a thing for him."

Harrison shook his head. "I called his home, and I was told he never came home over the weekend."

"And his parents didn't call anyone?"

"He doesn't have parents anymore, Grey. He is a Were, infected young."

"So call Galen."

"He isn't a wolf—not all Weres have such pack structure. He is a Werebear, and they are solitary Spirits. Besides, it isn't the first time he's run off. I don't think the people he stays with are that concerned about him."

I frowned, a tension inside my chest. Could something have happened to him?

Could it be my fault? What if the supplier we were searching for found out I'd stolen his dealers and wanted to make an example out of Trey? What if he were suffering all because of what I'd asked him to do?

"It might be nothing," Harrison said, but even I could read the lie in his words. The timing was far too suspicious for it to be meaningless, for it to just be a coincidence.

I'd done this for the supplier to target me, but what if Trey paid the price? What if all I'd done was put a target on his back?

I silently cursed my crow, the source of all this mess, the magnet that drew trouble to me and made those around me suffer.

Why was it that I never got a chance to just live my life?

Because you have a cosmic debt that you're never gonna be finished paying…

Chapter Ten

Two days later and Trey still hadn't shown up at school. Harrison and I had gone to his house, trying to find some information, but just as Harrison had said, the family didn't seem all the concerned. Or, perhaps it was better to say they saw him as a nuisance, as a penance they had to pay.

Spirits were often expected to take in young from the clan, since the types who were infected couldn't remain in the human world, with their human parents. They often didn't get any choice about it, and this was one such case.

Seeing the disinterest in the two Weres' faces made me want to punch them, but Harrison had hauled me out before I got the chance. *Rude.*

"Do you think he's okay?" I asked Harrison as we sat in his classroom during lunch, food spread out on his desk between us.

Harrison didn't pretend to not understand, but neither did he lie to me. He probably knew that wouldn't work, that I'd see straight through it. "I don't know. He's skipped out on school before, but never for this long."

Which again suggested this was a serious problem. Each morning, I scoured through the local groups, searching for any sign of Trey. It was the worst thirty minutes of my day, hands down, fear beating at me as I checked out any article that could have to do with Trey. A body found, an accident, a missing person report, anything. Each time, no matter how much I looked, I found nothing.

"So what now?"

"We wait. The supplier has taken notice—he must have. I haven't seen any evidence of Cloud made by him here. I suspect the dealers here have moved over to getting from you instead of him, which would prove a large loss in profit for him. Trey is probably hiding right now, waiting for this all to blow over. If he just stays out of sight, he should be able to return when we have finished."

I nodded, the food not tasting so great despite the five-star café on campus that we'd gotten it from. It seemed I didn't care for the seasoning of guilt when it came to food. I hated the idea of just waiting, but really, what other options were there? Trey had vanished off the face of the earth, and it didn't seem like he had any friends that we could find, any leads to where he might have gone.

All I could do was hope that he was just hiding, that once we handled this shit ourselves, he'd show back up and go back to his weird little life. I never would have figured I'd sit here hoping a kid got back to dealing drugs, but given the alternative, that sounded like a happy ending to me.

My phone vibrated on the desk, so I grabbed it and looked at the screen. It showed a number I didn't recognize, though that wasn't all that uncommon. I'd added a number to the phone for my current side hustle, which meant I'd have both buyers and dealers calling me for product.

"Hello?" I answered.

"You have proven yourself quite the problem for me," came a voice I didn't recognize, one that tugged the corners of my lips down.

"You're going to need to narrow that down a whole hell of a lot," I said. "I cause problems for way too many people for me to even hope to know who you are or what you want." I moved the phone from my ear and hit the speaker button, the caller's voice filling the empty classroom.

"I had a rather nice thing going until you showed up. I have to admit, your product *is* impressive, but I don't sit back while people ruin what I have created. So, how should we handle this?"

"Handle what? From where I'm sitting, I don't have a problem. Business is booming for me."

"If this is going to be a problem for me, trust me, I'll make it a problem for you, too. I'm not mean, though. You're new to this scene, so it shouldn't be too big an issue for you to take off and start back up somewhere else. That'd fix this for both of us."

"See, the thing is, I'm pretty happy here. I'm making plenty of easy money. Restarting somewhere else would take time and effort and at the end of the day, I'm pretty fucking lazy."

"Yeah, well, lazy or not, it's gonna to be better and less painful to start over."

"And if I refuse?"

"Then I've got no problem getting mean. Your product will be bad by Friday. If I see your symbol after that, you'll see what happens." The call went dead, so I set the phone down on the desk, the threat lingering in the air. He sure as fuck sounded serious…

I could usually tell the difference between a bluff and a person ready to follow through, and this asshole seemed the type to do exactly as he said. Or, fuck, maybe I was just being paranoid?

My phone rang again, and I let out a sigh as I picked it back up. People didn't call me much, then did it all at once. When it rained, it poured. It wasn't the same number as before, so it wasn't that asshole trying to get a last word. Instead, Galen's name showed.

"Long time no hear," I said as I answered.

"You need to come over."

"I'm working. Can I come later?"

Galen paused, as though he really didn't want to keep talking, didn't want to tell me whatever perched at the end of his tongue. He sighed, his voice softening in a way that suggested this was serious. "No, you can't come later. It's Trey."

The phone fell from my hand, all the fears that had swamped me earlier rising again. I knew without hearing another word this was bad fucking news.

Just like I'd thought earlier — the moment I got close to anyone, I fucked their lives right up.

* * * *

I didn't bother knocking on Galen's door, twisting the handle and barreling inside like it was my own place. Then again, I'd broken in here often enough, and this time, he'd at least called me.

Harrison was on my heels, but he paused at the threshold.

Galen walked down the stairs, and the fact he didn't look annoyed by my entry told me how serious the situation must have been. He glanced behind me, then nodded at Harrison, giving him permission to enter.

Later, I'd probably get myself a lecture about how, as a council seat, I needed to remember things like decorum more. However, if I caused a war with a little breaking and entering, it was only my problem. Plus, we were talking about Galen here—he was used to things like this.

"Where is he?" I rushed out, not waiting before heading toward the stairs. The bedrooms were all upstairs, so I had to guess that's where they'd put an injured guest.

Galen caught my arm before I got past him, pulling me to a stop halfway up the staircase. "He's resting."

"So? I want to see him."

"You need to calm down first. Do you really think he you'll help anything half-cocked right now?"

I opened my mouth to tell him that he was welcome to kiss the whole of my ass, but snapped it shut before the insults went flying. He wasn't wrong. This was my fault, and the last thing Trey needed was me making this all about me. I took a deep breath, trying to pull the scraps of my temper together into a patchwork version of self-control, to ignore the energy that soared around inside me, the desire to get up there and make sure Trey was alive.

Galen hadn't given me much information, telling me to come and see for myself. All I knew for sure was that Trey had been brought here, and that wouldn't have happened unless he'd gotten seriously hurt.

"Okay," I admitted, trying to keep my voice steady. "See, I'm fine. Not acting crazy at all."

Galen lifted one of his dark eyebrows from behind his glasses, the look saying he didn't trust me a bit. I couldn't really blame him for that, though. I could make the trip from sane to bat-shit-crazy in one little hop. It was the only cardio I ever did. Finally, he nodded and released me. "Third room on the left."

I bolted past him, taking the steps two at a time, until I arrived at the door to the room he'd indicated. I didn't bother knocking—if I wasn't going to at the front door, I wouldn't inside the house, either. I opened it, finding the room brighter than it ought to be. I'd expected some old Victorian room, something dim with stone walls and some wasting away sickly child. Maybe that was just the stupid part of my brain focusing on foolishness to make the situation less dire.

Instead, I found a brightly lit room, sun streaming in through the open window, and Trey stretched out on the bed. His eyes were closed, but I didn't see any injuries on him. No black eyes, no broken bones, nothing like that.

"What's wrong with him?" I asked, keeping my voice low. "I thought he'd gotten hurt, but he looks fine."

"He's a Werebear," Galen said from just behind me. "And a strong one at that. There aren't a lot of Spirits who could tangle with him physically."

"So what's wrong with him?"

"Cloud." Harrison stood at the doorway, staring at the boy's still body on the bed. "I can feel it from here. Someone used Cloud and invaded his mind."

"That's what I figured. He hasn't regained consciousness, not since he was found on the side of a road."

"The side of a road?" I drew my hands into tight fists. "You're telling me someone just dropped him like trash?"

"Seems that way. A nurse at the hospital realized what he was, so she called me. I had him brought here because I have no idea what this might do to a Were, and the last thing we need is a crazed Werebear running amok. Seemed safer to have him here. We made sure the police weren't involved and we already contacted his foster family to let them know."

I turned back toward Harrison. "You saved me when I got attacked. Can't you do something?"

Harrison pressed his lips together—a pretty obvious no—but moved past Galen and me to the side of the bed. He held his hand over Trey's face, then set it against his forehead. A rush of power filled the room, but it wasn't violent. Rather than a quick moving river that might sweep a person away, it felt like the ebb and flow of the waves in the ocean—undeniably powerful but not as volatile.

It again reminded me that while Harrison's power might not be as obvious as other types of spirits, it was no less impressive.

He closed his eyes, his focus entirely on whatever he felt through the touch to Trey's head. Trey's expression shifted as though in pain.

Before I could think twice, I moved the few steps closer and took Trey's hand in my own, squeezing tightly, hoping he might somehow sense that and that it might soothe him in some small way. His expression didn't suggest it had, but with nothing else to offer, I kept hold of his hand.

After what felt like minutes without ends, Harrison took his hand back, his face appearing exhausted. "Someone dug through his mind. They didn't just view it, they tore it apart. He has burned out neurons everywhere." He shook his head, as though looking at something tragic.

"What does that mean? How long until he wakes up?"

"He may not wake. The damage is severe. If he were anything other than a Were, I'd say there was no chance of him recovering, but Weres have exceptional healing abilities. Plus, because of their animal spirit, they can come back from injuries others couldn't. Even if he does wake, though, there is no telling what condition he would be in. He might prove uncontrollable and beyond repair."

"Beyond repair?" I repeated the words, hating how heavy they felt on my tongue. That was the sort of thing someone said about a car whose engine knocked, not a *person.* "What do you mean by that?"

Harrison didn't respond, and at least he had the decency to turn his face away, to look out of the window instead of at me. It was a good choice because I was fighting hard against the desire to slap him across his stupidly perfect face.

"Weres are not like other spirits," Galen said. "They have to be able to control their beast. If they can't, they are a danger to everyone and everything else around them."

"So what happens if he's a little testier when he wakes up? So what? I'm around and I sure as fuck have a temper."

"A Werebear like him could slaughter people, Grey. If he wakes and can't control himself, I will have no choice but to deal with it and make sure he doesn't endanger anyone."

I sat up straight at Galen's words, as though they were a knife he'd just waved in my direction. The meaning was obvious even if he tried to use cute little euphemisms to say it. Even if Trey somehow survived the attack, if he woke up against all odds, but he couldn't control his beast? Galen would kill him. I rejected the idea before my brain even fully formed it, clenching my molars together to keep from saying all the shit I really wanted to say.

Instead, I kept my voice quiet. "Get out."

"Grey…" Galen said, his voice gentle enough to piss me off. It wasn't *me* that required gentleness right now. Not only was this all bad, but it was all my fault.

"Give her time," Harrison said.

"We can't just leave her in here with him." Galen kept his voice low as he responded, as though I couldn't hear them despite only being a few feet away.

"It's fine. He won't wake, not in the next day or two at least."

With that, the two left, the door shutting quietly behind them.

I squeezed Trey's hand again, trying to ignore the burning in my eyes. Tears didn't help anyone. It was something I knew better than most. Tears were cheap and easy and ultimately useless. People cried because they thought suffering made them special, but who wanted the tears of someone else? They were just dressing people put on their own selfishness—nothing more.

"You know, you really should wake up," I said, my voice trembling. "If you do, I'll owe you something nice. What do you want? I'll get off your ass about selling anything, and I'll bribe your teachers to pass you whether or not you show up. Fuck, you want a car? I can steal you just about anything." I laughed, the sound hollow and broken as I pictured pulling up to his school with a freshly pilfered sports car. I'd do it, too.

I just didn't want to lose someone else, didn't want to carry the weight of another life ruined on my shoulders. I didn't know if I could carry it, not anymore.

But no matter what I promised to him, what I offered up, Trey didn't move. He didn't respond, didn't wake, didn't squeeze my hand back. Nothing worked.

I had no idea how long I sat there, how long I waited for any sign that he heard me, that he was still there. Harrison and Galen left me be, even after the sun had set, when the sky outside the window was bathed in pinks and oranges. Eventually, the tightness in my back and the silence in the room overcame my desire to stay there.

I released his hand and rose, staring down at him, the difference startling. When awake, he'd been bigger than life. I recalled the way he'd faced off against me, the way he'd accepted changes and surprises so easily. Now, however, he lay there lifeless. He seemed like an empty shell now, and that hurt more than anything else.

"Wake up and I'll make this up to you. I'll make this right." I glanced out of the window, swallowing hard enough that my throat hurt. "And if you don't wake up? I'll make damn sure that the fucker who did this to you lives just long enough to regret it."

With that, I walked away from the bed, leaving Trey there. Something ugly and painful grew inside me, gnawing at my stomach, swiping at me. I would have called it anger, normally. I was pissed that this had happened, that a kid had gotten targeted, that some asshole had decided to tear Trey's mind apart and for what? For nothing. I wasn't stupid enough to think it was really anger, though.

No doubt when I sat alone later, when I closed my eyes to rest and couldn't avoid or ignore the feeling anymore, I'd know the truth. Anger was just an easy costume for me to put on something far worse.

What really hurt was guilt, because I knew this was all my fault.

Chapter Eleven

Somehow, coming back to the council headquarters felt strangely like coming home. It made me laugh, since I'd always hated coming here. It had always felt like just the building where I had to work, which made it one of my least favorite places.

Maybe because of my time living with Harrison, and with Kelvin before that, I realized just how much I'd missed this stuffy, vast building.

And somehow, I'd even missed Ruben with that severe expression.

"And you *will* remain here?" Harrison asked from my left.

"You know, I'm not a kid who's going to get lost. You don't have to act like I have babysitters."

Harrison glanced to the side, at Ruben and Beth—a Mind there to ensure my lovely little stalker couldn't get access while Harrison was gone.

"They're not my babysitters," I muttered under my breath, pouting.

"I will ensure she is fine," Ruben said, like a date reassuring my father before taking me out.

If only this was a date. It would be just as awkward, but at least a date had the chance at sex at the end. Beth was pretty good looking, and I could go for a threesome.

Harrison narrowed his eyes, the look telling me he'd guessed what I'd thought, then shook his head. I only smiled back widely. At least he didn't push the conversation — probably because he knew it wouldn't do either of us any good, and I could argue all fucking day if I wanted to. He turned and walked out, leaving me there with Ruben and Beth in Ruben's office.

Somehow, having Harrison gone let me breathe a little easier. It wasn't fun spending all my time with a man who could read my mind if he really wanted to, who seemed to tell my thoughts and feelings with just a glance. It made me feel constantly on edge, and I hadn't fully realized the toll it took until it was gone.

Harrison had needed to attend a meeting today. He'd put off most of his official responsibilities to focus instead on me and our investigation. However, as the head of the Mind Clan, a lot of people relied on him, and it seemed this task couldn't be put off any longer. He'd spent the morning hemming and hawing over leaving me, but eventually, his job won out and he'd agreed to go only if he left me in Ruben's care.

The task would take all day — possibly until tomorrow morning — and I was rather looking forward to a little time away.

Ruben took his seat, behind his desk, and started to flip through the papers there. I'd seen this from him plenty of times, the way he could drown out the rest of the world in favor of whatever work needed doing.

"You're the worst entertainment," I complained before I plopped down on the couch in his office.

"I'm busy. You said yourself I wasn't your babysitter, didn't you?"

I rolled my eyes, then turned my attention to Beth, who looked more than a little uncomfortable. She appeared to be in her twenties — younger than I would have expected Harrison to leave me with. Then again, age had little to do with power for Spirits. If she was here to keep an eye on me, she must have been rather powerful. She hadn't said a word to me, and barely responded to Harrison when they'd seen each other. Not that he'd spoken to her either, treating her like an underling, the way he did to most people.

"So your name is Beth, right?" I asked, then patted the couch beside me.

She turned her gaze to Ruben, as though asking for permission.

He looked over at us, his expression tinged with annoyance. "I would tell you to be careful around her, but what is the point? Grey does as she wishes, so just make sure to keep your wallet close by."

"That was *one* time."

Ruben lifted his eyebrow.

I crossed my arms, slouching. "Fine, it might have been more than once, but if I'm stealing your wallet, you clearly don't pay me enough. Besides, I only steal from people I like. Or I really dislike."

"Imagine my distress as I wonder which I am." He waved his hand, like shooing us away. "This floor is fully warded, so as long as you don't leave this floor, you are safe here. Perhaps if you take her on a walk, she'll behave."

I stuck my tongue out at the fact Ruben spoke about me like I was a pet. Somehow, I'd moved from a child needing a babysitter to a puppy needing a pet sitter. I was always moving downward in life, wasn't I?

Still, no reason to look a gift horse in the ass or whatever the saying was, so I hopped back to my feet. "Come on, Beth. Let's have coffee."

"I said *this floor*," Ruben reiterated.

"Yeah, yeah. We won't leave."

"Then where are you getting coffee?"

I smiled, then took Beth's hand as though we were five-year-old BFFs and headed out of Ruben's office, Beth in tow. I made a point of slamming the door much harder than needed, smirking at the idea of how Ruben would be glaring at the now closed door.

"Is this your first time here?" I asked.

"At the council headquarters? No. I've attended meetings with Harrison in the past."

Which again showed that Beth must have been pretty highly skilled and trusted. Given that leadership wasn't passed down by bloodline, was she next in line for that position? Were they getting her ready to take over for Harrison one day? It didn't seem possible, not with how young and sweet she seemed. She was sure a far cry from the current leader.

I stopped at a door down the hallway. Beth raised her hand, as though to knock, but before she could, I twisted the handle and opened it. "Don't worry—no one's here."

She paused at the threshold, as though the idea of going in without an invitation bothered her. *She really is sweet, isn't she?* "Whose office is this?"

I hiked a thumb at the nameplate on the desk. "Terry O'Campus."

Her eyes widened as she took a step back. "We probably aren't supposed to be in here then, right? I mean, the head of security for the Justice Department isn't the sort of person who would want people just coming into his office."

I strolled in as though it were my own office — mostly because I'd done this many times. "Like I said — coffee." I drew my hand into a fist and hit it against the door of a cabinet against the wall, the action releasing the magnetic closure on the door so it swung open. Sure enough, inside sat a number of one-cup coffee makers, including lattes and espresso. A sink was on the main level, and a mini fridge sat below it. All in all? It was like a wet bar but for people who needed caffeine. "I found out about this little treasure my first week here."

"How did you find it?"

"I was getting lectured, and Terry had to step out for a moment to get his temper back under control. What can I say? I get curious when I'm bored. As soon as I saw his set up, though, I knew exactly where I was getting my cup of joe."

"And he's okay with that?"

"Well, people are mostly okay with things they don't know about." I smiled, then opened the fridge to pull out the milk. *Ah, whole milk, the good stuff.* "You have a problem with caffeine?"

She shook her head, the gesture slower than normal, as though she really didn't want to get caught in here.

"Stop worrying so much. Terry doesn't come to his office often." I poured the milk into the clear pitcher, then pushed it into its place. I picked out a small capsule, plopped it into the machine and pressed start. The thick scent of the espresso filled the office and made my mouth water, and the sound of the steamer heating the milk felt familiar and pleasant.

The first cup finished, so I poured the milk into the mug over the espresso, then handed it all over to Beth before restarting the process for my own. Once finished, I rinsed the milk pitcher and closed up the cabinet. If I made it too obvious that I stole coffee from him, it might not be here one day.

I sat at Terry's desk, then waited for Beth to sit across from me.

"This is good," she admitted after her first sip.

"Told you. You want to know the truth, though? It's not just the coffee. Things that are stolen always taste better. It's like a perfect seasoning for making anything tastier." I took another slow drink, savoring the sweetness of the milk. After spending what felt like forever surrounded by men, it was rather nice to sit here with another woman, with someone who lacked most of the weirdness that existed in my relationships. "Did Harrison say why I needed a Mind here?"

She nodded. "He said that someone using Cloud had targeted you."

"And you can stop that from happening?"

"I don't know for sure. Harrison is much stronger than I am, but if nothing else, I can buy some time and make it more difficult."

"You know, I appreciate that you don't just say yes. That's kind of reassuring. I'm used to people telling me they can do anything. Truth is a nice change."

"Well, I'm just honest. I've never tried to stop someone on Cloud before, so I don't know if it's possible."

"Harrison must think it's possible if you're here, though."

"Minds are ranked by power. I'm considered a top tier Mind."

"So you're on par with Harrison?"

She set her cup down on the desk, shifting in her chair. "Technically, sure, but it's like saying that two humans are both ranked equally in speed when compared to sloths. Even if they seem equal, it doesn't change that there is a vast difference between the speed of a toddler and that of an Olympic athlete." She let out a soft, quiet laugh. "In this case, I'm the toddler."

"Is Harrison really *that* much more powerful?"

"You don't know?"

"I don't like to stick my nose into clan business. In fact, I've worked really fucking hard to stay as far out of it as possible. I know people have talked about Harrison being powerful, and he's mentioned it himself, but I don't know why he is or if it's all just propaganda. Maybe it's like those dictatorships, where someone claims the leader is a god and everyone else is just too afraid to argue about it."

Beth shook her head and leaned forward. "It's not propaganda. The elders for the Mind Clan, I spent time with them. All top tier minds do, to learn and receive training. They said that they have no records to show any Mind has ever been as powerful as Harrison." She slouched forward. "Right now, I'm set to take over for him one day, but how am I supposed to follow someone like that?"

"Well, how did he become that way? Maybe there's something you can do?"

"Yeah, I don't think so." The way she said it suggested it wasn't anywhere close to a good story.

"I thought he was just born that way?"

Beth pressed her lips together into a tight line, and I could spot the fight on her face between telling me the truth and keeping their secrets. Finally, she looked away as she responded. "He's always been powerful — more power than should exist in any single person. Some people say he stole that power."

"Stole it? I didn't think that was possible. Granted, my knowledge of Minds is pretty fucking limited, but I thought people had the power they had and that was it?"

Beth fidgeted, running her finger along the edge of the desk. "Usually, yeah, that's the case. Harrison, though? Nothing else explains how he could be that much more powerful. There are rumors, you know? About what might have caused it. Some people say that's why he seems so empty, because he takes his power from others. Doing that would hurt the person, don't you think? It would explain why he seems so closed off."

I thought back to how hard Harrison worked, how often I'd found him up late, going over papers, trying to deal with the never-ending problems for his clan. Sure, I didn't disagree that he was closed off, that he was hard to understand, but Beth spoke about him like he was a monster. *That* didn't match what I knew about him.

Was he stubborn? And difficult to read? Sure, but he wasn't some other species, something so unhuman-like that others needed to stare at him like some freak.

The fact that Beth, someone who was part of his clan, a person who was in many ways the most similar to him, would view him in that way bothered me. He didn't need me sticking up for him, but I couldn't shake the desire to do just that.

"You know the problem with rumors? They're never fucking true. Even worse, the things that sound the best, that are the juiciest, are always the most untrue. Be careful listening to shit like that—it'll bite you in the ass."

Beth looked down at her lap, as though she didn't want to meet my gaze. Then again, I had just lectured her about someone she'd likely known longer. Who cared, though? I felt like I understood Harrison at least somewhat, and I hated the idea of people talking shit behind his back, especially given how much he did for his clan.

Well, so much for a nice, relaxing conversation.

* * * *

A few hours later, I found myself back in Ruben's office. I was stretched out on his couch, my feet up on the armrest. I yawned loudly, not bothering to cover my mouth as I did it.

"Why do you insist on staying in my office, then complaining about it?" Ruben didn't look up from his paperwork as he spoke. "If you are that bored, why did you send that girl away?"

"She was a shitty conversationalist." I folded my hands behind my head, staring up at the ceiling. "Besides, she's only one room over, so close enough to still be a wonderful shield for me without me having to listen to her."

"I once saw you have a full conversation with a parking meter. Somehow, I doubt she could be worse than that."

"That was a three-way conversation, and vodka kept up a good portion of the talking in that case. Sober? I'm not a fan of Little Miss Judgey over there."

"Judgey?"

"Yep. Can you believe she tried to imply Harrison had stolen his power?"

Ruben didn't answer, causing me to twist and look over at him. He'd paused his work and was looking across the office at me. His expression suggested he knew *exactly* what I was talking about.

"Come on, out with it," I asked.

"There have been rumors about that since he was young. It is not uncommon for such things when someone appears who is an outlier, someone who breaks the bounds of what we understand as normal. Harrison did that, and since then, Spirits—both in his clan and not—have tried to come up with a reason it happened."

"That's just jealousy. It's people mad that they can't do something so they demonize the person who can." I huffed out a harsh breath as I thought back to the times people had done that to me. It hadn't been because I was fantastic, like Harrison, but because I was different. I didn't fit into their idea of who and what I should be, so the only way to bring order back to their world was by turning me into the bad guy.

"Perhaps it is," Ruben acknowledged. "Or perhaps they have a point. I've been alive a long time, and Harrison is something entirely different. I've seen many Sprits that are stronger than others, that are unique, but Harrison's power on a different level all together. If I heard that he had done something—or something had been done to him—to turn him into what he is, I would have no reason to doubt it. Besides, even if we should not take rumors at face value, neither should we ignore them entirely. They always spawn from some bit of truth."

Jayce Carter

"Yeah, well, I don't think the truth is that he's some boogeyman going around and ripping the power out of other people."

Ruben shook his head, then set his pen down as though admitting he was done trying to focus on his own work. Really, he'd managed to ignore me a lot longer than I'd expected him to. "You know, I've heard some strange stories about what you and Harrison have been up to."

"If you ever didn't get strange stories about me, you'd come looking for me to see if I was still alive," I pointed out.

He let out a soft laugh, one full of equal parts annoyance and affection. "That's true. I recall your first week working here. Do you have any idea how many complaints I received?"

I thought back to that week, to how I'd had to work my way through an entire world I'd known nothing about. Sure, I'd had someone train me, but that was a far cry different from actually dealing with people.

And people fucking sucked.

"It's not my fault people are stupid."

"That's exactly what you said when your supervisor spoke to you about it. I had so many meetings that week and every person who interacted with you said the same thing—*fire her now*. They all said you would cause far too many problems, that it wasn't worth having you there."

"And you didn't immediately kick me out?" I chuckled at the idea of five years ago, of big, stern Ruben dealing with problems caused by little ol' me. It probably wasn't as funny as it felt right then, but I couldn't help laughing about it. "Your life would have probably been a lot easier if you had. I mean, no one

165

would blame you for not sticking up for the little weird crow girl who didn't fit in."

Ruben didn't answer right away. In fact, it took so long that I sat up so I could look straight over at him. He stared at me, the same expression I'd seen from time to time on his face. Normally, he was difficult to read. I recalled the way people said Justices lacked emotions, that they weren't human anymore, but neither were they Sprit. They were something twisted between the two, lacking the soul of a human, driven only to obey and uphold their code. Nothing else mattered to them.

I might have believed that as well, except I'd seen this glimpse too many times from him. I'd watched his expression soften, something deeper inside him peering out through those eyes of his. That look said he felt *far more* that anyone thought. Maybe it was buried deeper or maybe it was an echo of his old, human life, but he wasn't as hollow as others thought.

Finally, Ruben laughed softly again, as though he had no idea how he'd gotten here. "Maybe I thought that, but I can't bring myself to regret it. When I first saw you in the council room, when the crystal turned blue, you were so confused about...everything. I recalled when I woke after being turned into a Justice — well, after the process for it to happen. It was difficult to adjust, to find my place, but at least I had a place, a spot to fill. You lacked even that."

I sorted through his words, trying to make sense of them. "So you wanted to give me a place?"

He paused, then sighed. "That sounds far too sentimental, but I can't deny it, either. I couldn't do anything about you not fitting in, but I could ensure you always had a place to come back to. I've done that for the past five years, kept a place for you here no matter how you tested every limit set before you, no matter how many enemies you made, how you rebelled against every rule—I did the only thing I could and made sure you had a home here no matter what."

I took my bottom lip between my teeth, the slight ache telling me I probably chewed it a bit hard, but what did that matter? Ruben's words sounded suspiciously like some weird declaration of love, but I knew better than that. Whatever he felt toward me—probably mostly pity—wasn't anything nearly as sweet as love. Maybe he just connected with that feeling of isolation and offered me something to help. It was him taking care of me as a way of soothing his own past.

Ruben twisted his arm and looked down at his watch, then cut off anything else I might have said. "It's getting late. I don't know how long Harrison will take, but you might as well close your eyes and get a little sleep."

I wanted to argue with him, but if I remained awake, I'd keep talking, and I wasn't sure I really wanted to keep this conversation going. It seemed too close to finding out or saying something neither of us wanted to deal with. Our relationship was uncomplicated and slightly antagonistic—just the way I liked it. However, if we kept talking, if either of us uttered something we shouldn't, then my happy place here would become strained.

Just like it had with Kelvin, with Harrison, with Galen.

So I twisted and lay back down again, this time closing my eyes. I didn't expect to fall asleep, but pretending would pass the time if nothing else. However, before I knew it, I'd been lulled to sleep by the rustling of papers and scratching of a pen against the paperwork.

Hours later, I woke, blinking slowly. I was still on the couch, but when I shifted, I found a thin blanket thrown over me. It hadn't been there before. Did that mean Ruben had put it on me? I peered at the desk, and the sight startled me.

Ruben was seated there, just like he had been before, but his head leaned back against the headrest of his chair and his eyes were closed. It made him look oddly young and innocent. The hard lines of his face were relaxed in sleep, and I found myself drawn closer to him. Why was it that seeing people sleeping made me view them in a different way? They lost the masks they wore in their regular life, like the weight of the people we were supposed to be was lifted.

I picked up my blanket and crept closer, the sun starting to rise from behind the mountains. I paused beside him, staring down at him. "You know," I whispered softly, keeping my voice low so I didn't wake him. "You talked about creating a place for me, wanting to make sure that I had somewhere I belonged. I know I've never made things easy on you, that I've caused you a lot more trouble and stress than anything else. Still, thank you. You did make a place for me here. Even when I didn't think I wanted a place, it was good that I knew I always had somewhere I could go back to." I pulled the blanket around him, leaning closer as I did it.

It put my face just before his, letting me study him. He wasn't all that young. He had to have been in his forties when changed, and it didn't seem like it had been an easy human life. Somehow, it seemed fitting on him, though. His face showed the years he'd lived, the weight he'd carried all that time. Not near the bottom of that list was me, of course. I didn't know if I'd even have survived this long in this world if he hadn't taken me in, if he hadn't given me a job as a courier, something that created a safety net for me.

At the start, his meddling had felt like a leash placed on me, but now? It felt more like a safe place, somewhere I always knew I could retreat to, and I owed that to this stubborn, difficult man.

Before I could think twice about how bad an idea it was, or how complicated it would make things, I leaned forward and brushed my lips against his like a test. Would I feel something? Nothing?

As fast as if happened, I pulled away, terrified of his eyes opening and catching me in the act. *What the hell is wrong with me?*

When I knew I couldn't answer that, I retreated from the office, shutting the door quietly behind me as though fleeing from the scene of a crime. Harrison would return soon, and I'd wait elsewhere on the floor for that.

Clearly, I couldn't be trusted on my own—hot men beware…

* * * *

Seeing Harrison drive still felt strange. He often used drivers, and he sure as fuck fit in the back of a town car. Him driving himself was like seeing him do dishes or clean the toilet. He had the look of a spoiled, rich model, and that didn't fit with him doing anything for himself.

"I am sorry it took so long," he said as he drove toward his house. "I had hoped I would be back before it got so late, but that failed to happen."

"What were you doing?"

"I told you—a meeting."

"Sure, but a meeting with who? Was it really just a booty call and you're too embarrassed to tell me? Was she, like, a four?" I snorted at my own stupid joke. I couldn't imagine Harrison out on the prowl like that. Sure, I'd slept with him, so I knew he was good in bed, but the game to get someone into that bed that I couldn't picture him playing.

And the side-eye he gave me said he hadn't been picking up chicks and he couldn't believe I'd suggest something that stupid.

You clearly don't know just how stupid I can be.

"Of course it wasn't personal. Do you really believe that I would leave your safety to someone else if I had another option?"

"You're always so serious. Maybe you *do* need a booty call."

"Are you offering?"

"Sorry, but you know the whole hot to crazy ratio? Mine is *way* too far on the crazy side to be a good bet for one-night stands."

"Good thing I have no interest in one-night stands, then."

I went to answer, to snap out a snarky little comeback, but then his words settled. Was he suggesting that our time hadn't been a one-time thing? He couldn't be implying he wanted something more than a little fun, right?

Again, the words of so many others hit me. Beth claiming that Harrison might have stolen someone's power, the rumors that he'd hurt others to gain his position. Ignis talking about how isolated and lonely he had been his entire life. All these people thought they knew him, wanted to classify him and put him in some neat little box where they could feel empowered.

And I'd done the same exact thing, hadn't I? I'd decided who and what he was based on what made me the most comfortable, assuming that a man like him just participated in our little fling because it was easy and available. Never, anywhere in my mind, had I even thought that it might be something more, something deeper.

A rumbling in my stomach that had nothing to do with food kept me quiet, when I had no fucking idea how to respond or deal with that idea.

Why was it that people couldn't keep things nice and casual?

These men were worse than women…

Chapter Twelve

"I should go see Ignis soon," I said as I sat in the living room of Harrison's house. I had stretched out on the couch, my heels up on the table. Harrison used to try to get me not to sit like this, but I must have worn him down enough that he no longer cared.

"Why?"

I shrugged. "I'm used to seeing her every week. It's part of my routine."

"Her powers don't work well on you, do they? How can she make you feel better, then?"

"Well, no, they don't really work. At least, I don't think they do. She says she doesn't really feel emotions from me, but I'm not sure if she can affect my moods or not. Still, talking to her makes me feel better."

Harrison closed the book that had been open in his lap, looking across at me. "I am capable of doing anything she does — typically better."

"Are you being jealous?" I lifted my eyebrow, amused by the thought.

"It isn't jealousy." He paused, then let out a rush of air. "Even if it were, why would you leave where you are safe in order to have Ignis help you, when I could do so here? If you have a headache, if you have anxiety, if you need sleep, I can help with any of that. I dislike that you still don't trust me."

I nearly told him I did trust him, but I knew better than to utter that. The fact was... I didn't, not fully. Even if I didn't think he was the monster others seemed to think, I also knew he wasn't entirely honest with me. "It's not like that," I said, the words true but softer than the full truth. "I just don't like the idea of letting anyone dig through my brain. I went through that already — remember? Turns out, it is not my kink."

"What you went through was the equivalent of a mental vivisection. That is not what I am suggesting. Even if I didn't use my powers, you could still speak to me. We have spent weeks together at this point and you say so little to me. You still talk to me as though we are strangers, even after everything we have been through. You are the first person I have allowed into my home, who can stand being near me, and yet you keep up these walls."

I dropped my head back so I stared up at the high ceilings instead of at him. "You're no better. Last I checked, you aren't telling me shit about your life. You don't tell me who you met with the other day, you don't tell me anything unless you've got no choice. So you'd better be careful because you might topple right off your high horse up there."

"What do you want to know? What piece of information would make you feel better around me? If I tell you about my childhood, will you trust me? If I tell you the weight placed on me by my position in my clan, will that allow you to rely on me?"

And the fact was, he wasn't wrong. There was no one specific piece of information that would suddenly make it so that I believed in him. People were too complicated, too deep for me to take one little bit of background as the end all to them.

"Exactly," he said, then sighed and got to his feet. "Nothing I could tell you would fix this. You look at me with distrust, and there's no way that one little story will get you to let go of that. I doubt it is even about me, at the end of the day. I saw how you acted around Kelvin, heard you rejected Galen's offer to become his mate. You refuse to allow anyone close. Even Ignis, who you claim to miss, you do not tell the truth to. Perhaps I need to simply recognize that there is a line between you and everyone else, and to stop trying to force a relationship that won't ever occur."

Fuck, the boy could guilt trip better than my mom. I actually felt bad about it, all of a sudden. Looking back, logically, he hadn't fucked me over. Instead, he'd helped me, again and again. Even still, even with that, something about him just made me untrusting.

Or maybe it wasn't him at all—maybe it was just about me.

I thought back over the past years—fuck, over my whole life. Had there really been a single person I'd let close to me? Someone I didn't hide from? I didn't push away?

Even with my own family, who I loved endlessly, I never let myself relax. I still played a part, still hid away everything painful and real inside me. Suddenly, my future felt much longer than it had been before. Was this what I was forced to expect for the rest of my life? This same isolation? The loneliness?

"Wait," I whispered as Harrison walked toward the hallway that would take him to his room.

He paused, but didn't speak. Instead, he gave me the chance to gather my thoughts and figure out what I wanted to say.

"If you just want to explain to me how fucked up I am, you're wasting your breath if you think I don't already know. I'm well aware of how screwed up I am, but knowing what's wrong is a lot different from knowing how to fix it. How am I supposed to be different?"

He turned, facing me for a moment before coming over and kneeling in front of me. It was strange to see him like that. Harrison, a man feared by so many, was there before me in such a position. And damn it, my filthy brain rather liked the sight. He set his hands on the tops of my knees and looked up into my face. "People don't change at all once. Instead, you can only decide in each moment what you want to do, who you want to be, and take it one step at a time."

"And what does that mean right now?"

"Tell me what's wrong, and let me help."

I blew out one long, centering breath, before nodding. "I can feel myself getting closer to needing Kelvin's bite, and that terrifies me. I'm stuck here, knowing I can't leave, and that offends every part of my crow. I feel like I'm in the middle of something I can hardly understand, but I'm somehow expected to help. I just feel…" My voice trailed off when I couldn't come up with something that truly fit, with an explanation that would tell him just how out of sorts I felt.

Harrison didn't flinch, didn't pull away. He listened to each word, seeming to weigh them, to take them in, to consider them as though they mattered. Finally, he offered just one word. "Overwhelmed?"

And yeah, that fit. "Yeah, that's it. It's just all too much."

"Do you know why it is too much? Because you hold it all yourself, because you try to be everything and do everything yourself. No one is meant to hold so much all on their own."

"Including you?" I threw back.

He smiled, though it held hints of pain, as though he knew damned well I was right. "Fair enough. So what if we both tried to let someone else help…just a little. Let me help you, and that will ease my burden as well."

Fear beat at me, as though I stood on a cliff. I didn't know what help meant, but I knew I had to make a choice. Would I open myself up to this man? Would I trust that I knew him better than what others said? That I understood him well enough to know he wouldn't turn on me?

I nodded when the words felt too thick in my throat.

Harrison moved his hands from my knees, up to my cheeks. His palms were warm against my skin as he straightened his back, still on his knees but at his full height. It brought his face up to where mine was, and he pressed his forehead against mine.

The brush of his mind to mine was gentle, even it made me jerk away. It didn't hurt, not like it had before, when I'd gotten attacked. This felt like the difference between someone biting my lip hard and someone coaxing a kiss from me. Harrison coaxed, with soft touches and careful movement, and damn him, but it worked.

He slipped into my mind, the sensation strange and uncomfortable and oddly familiar. It felt warm, like sitting before a roaring fire, but I recalled how many times I'd ended up with red skin because I'd ventured too close. Would this burn me, too?

"Your mind is a mess," he whispered, his voice in my head. *"You really carry too many worries, all of them rushing through you."*

"I don't do that," I argued out loud. "Anyone who knows me would say my brain is empty more than it's got any thoughts in it."

"That's what you want people to think, but it isn't true. I can see it, feel it all. Just try to relax, let it all go."

As he said that, my mind felt...lighter. It seemed as though he'd removed some of the heavier items, shifting things until it didn't feel nearly as crushing as it had before. Perhaps it was better to say he shored up the fears inside me, balancing them, making them easier to carry myself. It didn't feel like it did before, during my attack, where that other mind had forced me to relive whatever he wanted, where he tore through my barriers and my thoughts. That had been someone breaking in and ransacking my house, where Harrison behaved as though I'd invited him in and he was careful to not get mud on the carpets.

It felt as though he hummed, a melody playing inside my head, calming and quiet. Was that him? It was funny, as I didn't think he had much peace in him, yet he somehow shared what little he had with me. And for the first time—possibly ever—I let him. I gave in, giving my mind over to him.

Still, the sensation of him there in my head was oddly familiar. I tried to work out why, even though it was hard to hold on to any thoughts of my own. I recalled what Ignis had said before, the fact that each Mind had a feeling of their own. It was like any other Spirit, each on its own wavelength, like a DNA to identify them. I knew how Ignis felt because of all the time I'd spent with her—she was like mint, something clean and fresh.

The Mind who had attacked me had reminded me of cinnamon—spicy and almost sweet. It had felt overwhelming at the time of the attack, but looking back, I could best identify it as cinnamon.

"Whatever you are thinking about, don't. Just sleep." Harrison's whispered command in my head was too strong for me to resist, to even want to resist. He made it so the worries, the fears in my head didn't feel so close, so unbearable.

So I didn't fight his command. My eyes slid closed as I gave in, as I leaned against him, allowing him to hold me up. He lifted me into his strong arms, and the steady beat of his heart further lured me into that placid place inside me where nothing bothered me, where nothing worried me.

He carried me with such care, as though I were precious to him. Just as he'd slipped into my mind, I also moved through his. I didn't understand any of it, only got a general, vague sense of *mine*, but he didn't resist my presence. It made me recognize that no matter what I thought of him, whether or not I trusted him, he felt some connection to me.

Still, none of that stuck with me. As he settled me into a bed—his bed—with him beside me, only one tiny detail remained in my head, something I couldn't shake away.

It was the scent of cinnamon from his mind, the same one I'd felt during my attack.

178

* * * *

I guided the car along the road with absolutely no idea where I was headed.

Okay, so maybe running away wasn't the best idea. Still, when I'd woken beside Harrison, the tension inside me had reached a breaking point. Staring at his sleeping face while the memory of how his power had felt like it was mocking me had become too much. Before I'd thought too much about it, I'd swiped the keys to his car and taken off, unable to stay there another fucking minute.

The power felt exactly the same. Or, maybe it was better to say it felt like the same power, just used differently. It had been rough the first time, gentle this time, but I couldn't ignore that they still felt like the same power.

The cinnamon I'd tasted from my attacker was the same I'd felt with Harrison.

I came to a stop sign, still not sure where to go. Left? Right? To Galen? To Kelvin? Maybe I just needed to take off east, to drive until this stupid car and the few credit cards I'd swiped ran out. Maybe it all had become too much and I just needed to nope out of it all.

I rested my forehead against the steering wheel when my body refused to move, to pick a direction. Every damned time I thought I got a handle on the mess that my life was, I ended up losing it all.

It seemed my lot in life, but fuck was I sick of it.

A horn blared from behind me, making me jerk myself upright and drive forward. I pulled off the road, just beside a park, then grabbed my phone. My fingers moved almost on their own, hitting the button for the only person I thought could really understand what I was going through, who might have any real advice.

Ignis answered on the third ring. "You calling me at three in the morning is a bad sign. Please tell me I don't have to bail you out."

"No bail needed, at least not yet."

"Small miracles, huh?" She yawned, and I could almost picture her sitting up in bed. I really didn't deserve a friend that good. "So, what's going on?"

"You said before that all Minds have power that feels different, right?"

"Yep, that's right. It's like a fingerprint. It can't be faked or changed."

"Can two Minds have power similar enough that they're confused for each other?"

"Not really. They can feel similar, sure, but it'll always feel different enough to know. Though, if someone waits long enough, they might not remember what a power felt like, if years have passed." She paused for a moment, her voice shifting as though she realized this might be a more serious question than she'd expected. "Why?"

"No reason," I lied. Somehow, trying to tell Ignis that I thought my attacker might be her brother didn't seem like something that would go over all that well. I could already hear Ignis defending her brother, not because she didn't care, but because she'd never believe he could do that.

Then again, we were all blind in our own way when it came to those around us. Hadn't I thought the same thing when Beth had said plenty about Harrison? Yet here I was, doubting him just as she had.

"Where are you?" Her tone suggested she knew damn well I wasn't where I was supposed to be, though that was usually a pretty easy guess to make.

"Just out for a little drive."

"Meaning you stole Harrison's car, right?"

"Well, I mean, if you want to get super specific, sure."

"Which means you're out without anyone making sure you don't get attacked? Of course you are—why does that not shock me?" She paused, the sound of a long, slow breath telling me that she'd had to pull her temper back under control. I wasn't sure if it was a sign of her maturity or just her professional training in dealing with fucked-up people, but when she spoke again, she was calm. "Why did you run away from Harrison? You must have run away, because if he knew you had left, he would have called me already. What happened?"

"How do you know you can trust someone? People talk about it like it's so simple, so easy, but how do you know? In my experience, even the people I thought I could trust, they just needed the right reason to betray me. They're never what you think they are, never what they pretend to be."

"You can't ever be sure. I mean, I can sense people's emotions and even I get fooled."

"So, what's the point of trying, then? If even *you* can't do a damn thing about it, then what hopes do any of us regular folks have?"

"You think life is about coming up with the right answer, but that's not it. It's about the journey, the process. You might find out at the end that you picked wrong, but that's not as important as the path to get there."

"Sounds like some psychobabble to me."

"Well, that is my job. Come on—why don't you come over to my place? Then Harrison won't need to have a heart attack once he realizes you're gone. We'll talk about whatever's bothering you."

The desire to drive off again hit me, the temptation to just nope the fuck out of this entire mess. However, cutting and running wasn't an option, so I nodded. "Okay. I'm over by Lucky Park—I'll get to your place in like, twenty minutes."

"I'll put on some coffee—looks like we'll have an early morning."

I put Ignis on speaker, then tossed the phone onto the passenger seat. I slid the car into drive, then pulled from the side onto the dark road. "I'll pick up donuts, too."

Ignis laughed, but before I could understand her next words, a sudden pain raced through my temples. It was familiar, the same feeling I'd gotten during the other attacks. This time I recognized it better, and fear swamped me.

"Grey?" Ignis' voice came from a million miles away, like we were both drowning and the water distorted her voice. It became more frantic as I hit the brakes of the car. I could see nothing, the pain in my head taking every bit of attention, but the last thing I wanted was to come to later finding out I'd run over some kid.

Though, if a kid is out at this hour, they probably had it coming.

The crunch of metal shook me back to my right mind, the pain letting up just enough for me to pull the parking brake, then open the door. I stumbled out of the car, gripping my head as though I could hold it together with my hands alone.

"You were so careful up until now." The voice floated through the darkness, reverberating somehow between

something physical and something in my head. Still, I recognized it as the one I'd heard during the attacks.

I wanted to bury my face in my hands and pretend anything else was true, but I couldn't. I'd survived too much already to give in now. Instead, I lifted my head toward that voice, peering through the darkness to find the person behind it standing there.

Blond, wavy hair, blue eyes, and a face I would never forget.

Harrison stood above me, his lips twisted into a smirk he had somehow hidden from me. *How could I have been this horribly wrong?*

Chapter Thirteen

The pain let up, the absence of it making me collapse forward like some puppet without strings. I gasped in shaky breaths, my chest burning, my muscles weak.

Harrison crouched down in front of me, dressed in jeans and a T-shirt. It was strange to see him in such casual clothes, but he must have left soon after I had. He must have rushed to get here. "What are you doing out here all alone?"

"I got a little stir-crazy," I forced myself to say, wishing I'd come across as smooth and in control. I doubted that was the case, though. Instead, I sounded just about off the deep end, hanging onto my sanity by the thinnest of strings.

"Well, that was pretty fucking stupid, right?" His words made me frown, but my brain still felt scraped raw. I couldn't make it through enough to really know what bothered me, what didn't sound quite right. "Did you really think I wouldn't find you? That you could ever escape me? Because that was a bad choice. All I had to do was wait."

"And now what?"

"Now? I don't think we'll get interrupted, so I'll enjoy pulling apart your brain. You're not like anyone I've ever tasted before and I just can't get enough. It doesn't matter what you do, where you go, you'll never escape me." He caught my shirt and pulled me closer.

A sheen rested on his lips, and it made my stomach clench in something that wasn't even close to pleasure. I thought about the kisses we'd shared, the feeling of his body, all of it. Just yesterday I'd been so sure that there was something between us, but now? The idea that he might press those deceitful lips against mine made me promise to bite them the fuck off if he tried — consequences be damned.

"You're much prettier than I realized at first. This hair is like a lure. Is it how you draw men in? It's like feathers on a pretty bird."

"More like the red hourglass on a black widow," I spat back.

He smiled, the look nothing like the man I'd gotten to know. It was so wide, so open. "I've always liked easy women, but fuck, maybe you're able to show me the benefits of one that takes some work. Fuck knows you've been more fun than I've had in a while. I can't wait to see what else you've got hiding in the thick skull of yours." He leaned in closer, his breath smelling of something sweet enough to make me nauseous.

"Well, that's really too bad." I wrapped my fingers in the soil beneath me, then twisted, tossing it right into his stupid eyes.

He must not have expected it, because he didn't have time to even close his eyes. Instead, he yanked backward in surprise, a yelp funny enough I almost laughed in response. That would have been a waste, though, so I took off instead, rushing toward the park. At this hour, there were no cars on the road, no businesses open in the area. Help wasn't something I was likely to get, which meant my better chance was to break line of sight. Without that, he was unlikely to be able to affect me with his powers, and since I couldn't be tracked in any way other than visually, I'd be safe if I could just get away.

My foot hit an uneven bit of ground, sinking into where something had burrowed beneath, pitching me to the side. I caught my balance, somehow, and kept moving away from Harrison's angry shouts. I knew damn well that moving away from angry yelling was usually in my best interests, especially when the angry yelling including cursing my name.

If Harrison had been pissed before, I had a feeling that getting dirt thrown in his eyes wasn't going to make him any happier to see me.

If I could just get a little distance, I could change into my crow form. Sure, he'd spotted it easily before, but the smaller footprint would allow me to hide in places my stupid human body couldn't. I glanced around the trees, the darkness, looking for anywhere that might work. Nothing looked promising, though.

Instead, I leaned down as I tripped and wrapped my fingers around a thick branch, one about a foot and a half long. It wasn't the best weapon, but it was better than nothing. When running didn't seem possible, the only other options were fighting or giving in—and I'd never been the type to give in.

I moved behind a tree, pressing my back to it, trying to slow my breath. If I could just stay out of sight for a little bit, I had a shot. Harrison was powerful, sure, but he was as fallible as any other living creature.

The bark of the tree dug into my back, but I ignored it, straining for sounds of him following me. I had no idea how long I waited. I didn't dare to try to open a portal to get a phone, didn't even dare to breathe deeply. No sounds echoed through the park, nothing to tell me where he'd gone, to let me know when it was safe to try to take off. One wrong move and all I'd do was hand myself right over to him.

A snap behind the tree made me press my lips together to silence the noise of surprise. I reminded myself he couldn't track me, which meant he had to be looking blindly for me.

I held the wood tighter, my arm crossed over my chest, holding myself as still as possible. Another snap, another groan of the dirt beneath shoes, and it was obvious. Harrison was headed this way, just on the other side of the large tree I hid behind.

I sent up some prayer, one I didn't expect to be answered, then twisted out from behind the tree, aiming based on my hearing. The branch sailed through the air, and a sickening thud came when it made contact. I'd swung it so hard, even my shoulder hurt, the vibration from the hit running up the wood and into my arm. Not that I gave a fuck about that—I wish I could have hit him harder.

Harrison looked back at me, his eyes wide, as though he couldn't figure out what I'd done or why. Blood streamed down his face, appearing black in the darkness. I'd struck him on the temple, aiming high because if I was going to hurt someone, I'd do as much damage as possible. Half-assing was for diets and workouts—not battles for survival.

The thing that took me by surprise, however, was the shock on his face, as if he couldn't figure out what had just happened. The blood streamed from a gash at his temple down his face, over his throat, dripping onto the collar of his white coat.

A coat?

Something struck me as strange about that, but I couldn't figure it out as I backed away, stumbling and catching myself against another tree. "Stay back," I warned him, holding the branch up in threat.

"What do you think you are doing?" he asked, lifting his hand to hold it against the wound. "Why did you disappear?"

"Why? How about because you've been behind this all!" I couldn't believe how hysterical I sounded, but fuck if that wasn't exactly how I felt. "You tricked me. Why? Did you just find it hilarious to see me struggling so bad, to hurt me then pretend to help me? Was this some fucking game for you? I heard that you were fucked up, that you were twisted, but I never would have thought you could do something like this."

Harrison frowned, deep lines in his forehead, as though I were speaking a language he no longer understood. *Did I really hit him that hard?*

Bushes to my left moved, the leaves rustling just as someone burst through the area. Was someone drawn by my yelling? I didn't want to think about what Harrison could do to an innocent bystander, but I couldn't deny a thrill at the idea of not facing this entirely alone. I turned, but what I saw made no more sense than anything else in my life.

Harrison, in jeans and a T-shirt.

I did a double take, back and forth between the one in a coat with a bloody gash on his face and the one to my left, a sneer on his lips.

There are two of them?

Suddenly I was a hell of a lot less sure than I'd been before. They looked identical at first glance, but all those little things that had bothered me came back.

The way casual way the one in jeans had spoken to me, totally unlike the way Harrison normally spoke. His clothing, his smile, none of them were what I'd come to expect from Harrison. It could mean only one thing—somehow, Harrison had a doppelganger of some sort.

Oh, right, and I'd also just hit Harrison in the head with a stick...

I really hope he doesn't hold grudges.

I twisted, pointing the stick at the fake Harrison. I wasn't sure I could trust Harrison, but I knew for sure I couldn't trust this asshole.

He turned his gaze from me to Harrison, and a rage unlike anything I'd ever seen flashed across his expression. "*You,*" he all but growled out. "Why am I not shocked that I'd find you here, ruining everything again?"

"Ryder," the real Harrison said, his voice saturated in pain.

At least I have a name for the asshole now...

"Don't you use my name," Ryder snapped back. "And don't you think this is anywhere close to over. You took *everything* from me—I won't let you get her, too." Ryder spared one more at me, one that seemed more like a promise than anything else, before he took off at a run.

I took a step to follow, hating the idea of him getting away. Leaves crunched behind me, along with a pained groan. I turned to find Harrison had collapsed to his knees, his hand on the tree beside him to keep him somewhat upright.

It meant I either had to give chase or help Harrison. *I'm really not up to the weight class of Ryder, clearly.*

I kicked the leaves on the ground before dropping my stick and going to Harrison's side. I'd done the damage — that made it my job to take care of it, right? It was like after a bar fight. If you knock a fucker out, you gotta wait in the hospital until they wake up.

"I'm okay," Harrison argued, but the slur of his words told me that wasn't true.

I took his weight as I helped him back toward the car, listening carefully for signs of Ryder. I didn't expect anything, because he hadn't seemed interested in tangling with Harrison, even when he wasn't up to snuff. "Yeah, you look real okay. Just shut up — we need to get your head looked at." I helped him into the passenger side of his car, then went around it to the driver's.

"No," he muttered like a petulant kid before his eyes slid shut.

That was probably not a great sign.

And it meant I needed to get him looked at. I could have tried to contact someone I knew, but that didn't sit right. I didn't trust that Kelvin, Ruben or Galen might not take advantage of the situation for their own benefits, and I didn't know who among the Minds I could trust.

However, I did know one doctor who would do as I asked no matter how much he bitched, and I sure as fuck trusted him not to screw me over.

I turned the engine on and pulled the car into the dark road, headed for the clinic where I knew he could get treatment.

"Hope you're ready to meet my family — if you think I'm a handful, you really have no idea."

Chapter Fourteen

I never felt like I had that much in common with my siblings. They'd grown up in such a different world than I had, and we didn't share fifty percent of our DNA. On top of that, they'd both turned out so fucking perfect that I felt like the only one in the family who really didn't fit in.

However, the glare my brother, Joshua, gave me was so damned familiar that no one would mistake us for anything other than siblings. He looked half asleep and more than a little annoyed at getting pulled from his bed and brought into work.

"You are the worst older sister," he muttered as he walked into the exam room. "I expected to find you waiting outside. How did you get in?"

"The same way I got into your room for years. Lock picking is a very useful skill."

Joshua lifted his hand to cover his mouth as he yawned, then peered around the room.

Harrison had woken, which meant he was at least sitting upright on the exam table. Still, the blood that escaped his temple and ran down his face showed he wasn't up at his best.

And Joshua proved ever the professional he was when he spotted the injury and didn't so much as lift his eyebrow. Instead, he slid right into his doctor mode, the sleep seeming to leave him in an instant.

"My name is Dr. Joshua Reynolds," he said as he approached Harrison. "What happened?"

"He got hit with a stick."

"*You* hit me with a stick, you mean," Harrison pointed out.

"Oh, that was like fifteen minutes ago. How long are you going to keep complaining about that?"

"How about until I at least stop bleeding?"

I sat in the chair beside the exam table and crossed my arms, getting out of Joshua's way. It wasn't like I could really argue with Harrison right now, in front of my brother. Besides, was an argument really needed? Joshua had so easily accepted the idea that I'd been the one to hit Harrison, I was almost insulted.

Joshua went about his work, first using prewet towelettes to clean Harrison's face. It made me realize…I really had hit him hard.

Then again, in my defense, I'd had every reason to believe that he was about to kill me. I valued my life too much to fuck around.

Still, I couldn't help the bit of guilt that assuaged me as Joshua wiped off the blood.

"Headache? Vision issues?" Joshua went about asking questions to judge just how much damage had occurred, then added two butterfly bandages to hold the skin together. "I don't think you have a concussion or any severe damage, but I'd like to do an MRI just to be safe."

Harrison managed to give me one hell of a glare, as though pointing out yet again this was all my fault. I'd thought him so pointlessly serious before, but that face showed he just hid his feelings behind a good mask. "Very well," he said, pulling his focus back to Joshua.

Joshua turned toward me, looking just as pleased with me as Harrison was. "Stay here. I'll take your friend for the MRI, then I'll have to review the results. I'll come back in when I have them."

"Sure. Sit, stay, I get it." I waved them off, telling them with that gesture that I was fine and wouldn't cause any problems.

Joshua and Harrison wore almost identical looks as they left the room.

The door remained closed for only a few moments before a familiar voice floated through it and it opened.

"Grey!" Ignis threw her arms around me, her face bathed in worry.

Right, I probably should have talked to her and told her I was fine. It reminded me that she'd been on the phone when I'd first gotten attacked.

"Wait, did you call Harrison?"

"Obviously," she snapped as she pulled back. "You were on the phone, then you cried out and the line went dead. When you wouldn't answer, I called him and told him where you were."

Which meant I owed a lot to both Ignis and Harrison. He must have come running the moment she'd called him, even after I'd taken off like that.

"Sorry for worrying you. How are you even here, though?"

She held up her phone. "I track Harrison's phone. He used to get lost a lot when he was younger, so I like knowing where he goes. When I saw it here, I was terrified you'd gotten hurt."

"Nope, I'm okay."

"Which means..."

"Someone hit Harrison with a stick."

"You mean you did, right?"

"How does everyone know that? I'll have you know that I've hit very few people with sticks in my life."

"More people than the average, I'd bet."

"I wonder what the average is." I tapped my finger against my bottom lip, grateful for the distraction.

Ignis sat in the chair beside me, then took my hand in hers. "What really happened?"

I could sense the gentle waves of her power, as clean as they always were. I could have fought them, but I didn't really want to, not right then. Instead, I allowed it to ease me as I told her the events of the night. My realizing that the power felt the same, me running away from Harrison, me getting attacked near the park, the appearance of a man who looked exactly like Harrison. I spilled every detail, holding none of it back. If anyone could understand it all, it would be Ignis.

"Ryder," she said, her voice soft and knowing.

"That's what Harrison called him. Who is he?"

Ignis released my hand, and the loss of warmth bothered me. I knew better than to think of it as some rejection, rather than her not wanting to transfer any of her feelings to me by accident. "Harrison was not a single birth. Twins are rather common for Spirits, but identical can be troublesome. Harrison and Ryder are a good example of it."

I frowned as I pieced all the tiny bits of information together into a coherent thought process. "I heard a rumor that Harrison had stolen his power from someone else."

Ignis let out an annoyed, sharp breath, as though she'd dealt with this pesky rumor enough times already. "People like to talk when they don't know the specifics. Harrison didn't steal Ryder's power."

"Didn't I?"

Ignis and I both turned toward the door, where Harrison stood, his eyes locked on the floor instead of at either of us.

"No, you didn't," Ignis pressed.

Harrison came into the room and shut the door, then sat on the exam table again. "You have always said that, but the facts fail to support it. I have power that no others have wielded, more than any one Mind should have. On the other side, my twin, Ryder, was somehow born with no power, something unheard of when a Spirit has two powerful parents. It leads to a single obvious conclusion, does it not?" His words had that flat quality, as though they didn't bother him, but the fact he hadn't met my gaze yet suggested otherwise.

"You can't blame yourself for something like that. You didn't *choose* to be born the way you were any more than Ryder did. And you've always done everything you can to help him, no matter how much he screws it up."

"Did you know Ryder was behind this all?" I asked Harrison. He had to, right? If he knew about his brother, he had to have suspected him.

Harrison waited a long moment before he answered, and that told me the truth. "I suspected it, but I wasn't sure. Ryder, see, he is…different. He doesn't have any powers." He sighed, slowly, then added softly, "I created Cloud about a decade ago to help him. I felt so guilty over having powers and the idea that I'd stolen his that I wanted him to feel normal, to feel accepted, so I figured out a way to create Cloud as a way for him to have powers."

Ignis didn't show any surprise at that. She must have known that little tidbit already.

It also told me something else. "That's why his power felt just like yours, because he used your blood to create it…"

Harrison nodded. "When we were first creating it, I emptied a lot of power into a crystal so he could make it on his own. He has been making it from that ever since. Others have backwards engineered from our version, to replicate it, but this all is my fault. I was the one who brought it into the world." He slumped his shoulders, looking worse than he had even after getting whacked by a stick.

It went to show just how heavy this burden was, and how he struggled to hold it himself. He still failed to meet my gaze.

"I'm going to step outside and check with the doctor," Ignis said, her tone gentle, as though she really didn't want to be part of this conversation.

When she left, Harrison sighed and leaned forward, placing his elbows on his knees, appearing to sink even more, like without Ignis there he couldn't keep up the appearance of nothing bothering him. It seemed he even kept that up around his own sister, which was crazy given he was closer to her than anyone else that I'd seen.

Did that mean he showed me a side of him no one else ever got to see?

"Are you okay?" he asked, his voice so quiet, it was difficult to hear above the buzzing of the florescent overhead light. "Did Ryder harm you?"

I shook my head until I recalled he *still* hadn't looked up at me. "Not really. I stopped the car when he first attacked my mind, then he let off. I think he wanted to talk to me or something."

"How did you get away?"

"The old dirt in the eyes trick. Turns out that works with anyone."

He laughed. "Well, I'm glad you did that even if you did think he was me. It is good to know you'll defend yourself against anyone—myself included. Still, you were in that position because of me, because of my actions, and because I didn't admit the full truth to you. For that, I am sorry. I have tried to control Ryder, to keep him from harming others, but he has been unhinged his entire life. Then again, he was truly cheated."

"Maybe he was cheated," I said, "but he wasn't cheated by *you*. Sometimes life sucks—I know that better than most people. Trying to find someone to blame for it doesn't help at all—it just makes you angry. You have to put on your big girl panties and deal with the shitty parts of life sometimes."

Finally, he lifted his gaze to look right at me. Surprise rested there like he hadn't expected me to say that.

That look got me to keep going. "You can't blame yourself for the actions of others. It's a long road you just don't want to go down. It's too hard, too painful, and there's no way to win that battle. No matter what you do, no matter how you try to fix it, you'll always come up short because you can't take responsibility for what others do."

"You blame yourself for Trey," he pointed out.

"Look here—I give excellent advice but I don't always take it as well. Besides, Trey got hurt because I used him to get the supplier's attention. That's different from you and Ryder."

"Is it? You didn't hurt him, but you still carry the weight of that action. Perhaps we both need to learn to put blame on the person who deserves it rather than holding it ourselves."

I knew he wanted me to agree, but I couldn't quite do that, not when Trey had yet to wake. Instead, I changed the subject. "So, do you actually know where Ryder is?"

"No. When I went to that meeting, it was to try to locate him."

"But you couldn't find him?"

"Ryder was not just born without powers—he is like a negative space when it comes to Mind powers. In other words, I cannot read anything from him. He creates a void, so I have no way to locate him. I wasn't sure that he was the one who had attacked you, but I knew he was behind selling the Cloud locally. I recognized the formula as soon as he sold it here."

"Why would he come here, though? Why come back to where you were if he knew you could stop him?"

"Because he has always wanted to take what I have back. He feels cheated by life, by me, feeling as though I'd stolen everything that he should have had. I think the idea that I would rule here bothers him, because he doesn't want me to live peacefully if he can't. He has shown back up to throw my life into chaos more times than I can count. In fact, I fear him realizing I know you might actually make him obsess over you even more."

His words suddenly helped everything make so much more sense. The way Harrison had swooped in so fast, seeming to take responsibility for everything. The fact he'd seemed one step ahead when it came to investigation was because he'd already known about much of it. The way he'd kept me close also made more sense — he blamed himself for what had happened.

"I never wanted you hurt because of this. Ryder is my problem, my shadow. It is my job to deal with him, and I hate the idea that you suffered because of it."

I got up from my seat and moved over to stand before Harrison, waiting until he lifted his gaze and looked into my eyes. "This isn't your fault. You weren't the one who hurt me, but you were the one who has saved me more than a few times."

"But—"

I poked his temple, just away from the cut. "Besides, I did this. I feel like that makes us about even."

He blew out a long breath, then offered me the barest hint of a smile. Even subtle, it felt real. "Fine. I still think you should be far angrier with me than you are, but you have never struck me as someone with much sense. Also, you brought me here, so even if you did hit me, I suppose you took responsibility for it. And, I can hardly blame you for running. I didn't expect you to be quite so attuned to notice the same power between me and Ryder, so I never thought you would catch that. It seems I underestimated you."

"Story of my life," I said with a laugh, trying to ease some of the tension. Sure, I could easily blame Harrison for a lot of this, but the pain in his expression made me not want to. Instead, I found myself wanting to remove some of that weight, to reassure him that was fine.

"What will you do now?"

"Now? A coffee of an entirely unhealthy amount. Like, I want to bring in an empty pitcher and just hand over a credit card—tell them to pour until we hit the credit limit."

"I'm serious. Now that you know the person after you is my brother, now that you know I knew about it, are you going to leave?"

"Would you let me?"

"I've never forced you to stay. I truly believe you are safest by my side, but I can understand why you might not agree. For that reason, you could choose to go elsewhere. I would continue to track Ryder even in your absence." He spoke quietly, and I could tell how much he didn't want to say any of that. The truth was obvious—he wanted me to stay.

"It's funny, because for a while, all I really wanted was to leave. I don't like feeling trapped, and I miss being on my own, however…" I paused, trying to figure out how to phrase the rest of my statement so it wasn't misconstrued. "Now that I've got the option, I don't really want to take it."

A line appeared between his eyebrows, as though those were the last words he'd expected me to say. After a breath, he reached out and wrapped his arms around me, pulling me against his chest. The action was so quick and unexpected, I let out an embarrassingly loud yelp.

"Sorry," he whispered, despite not releasing me. "I just never expected you to say that, to willingly remain after you knew everything. Every day that you have been with me, I have feared you discovering the truth and what would happen at that point. I was certain that you would walk out the moment you understood my past, that you realized it was my flesh and blood who had caused you harm. I never thought you would choose to stay." His breath warmed the side of my neck, and as much as I felt as though I should hate the way he held me…I didn't.

In fact, I actually rather enjoyed it. What the fuck was wrong with me? Maybe it was just good old-fashioned Stockholm syndrome — I'd been with him so long that I thought we had a connection we didn't really have. Whatever it was, I let myself savor it, the way his fingers clutched around me, the way he held me so tight, the fact it chased away the chill inside me after my fight with Ryder.

A knock on the door came a moment before it opened, and it happened so fast that despite me jumping backward, I didn't quite clear the crime scene.

Ignis seeing it would have been embarrassing enough, but it was *nothing* compared to the heat that rose on my cheeks at the sight of my brother standing there, a clipboard in his arms, his eyes narrowed like he'd just caught me with some boy's hand down my pants in high school.

Ignis broke the uncomfortable moment by barging in past Joshua, a smile on her face. "Looks like you'll live," she said before slapping Harrison on the arm. Seeing her with her brother was a bit strange for me, since she treated him as any sibling would, rather than the reverence others treated him with.

Joshua tore his gaze away from me, then looked down at the clipboard. He opened a file on it and started to read the information printed out. It was one of those times I found myself impressed by him and his whole doctor thing. It was a far cry from the kid who had nearly broken his arm when he fell out of a tree, then hid it from our parents because he didn't want to get in trouble. It was weird to think of him as an adult.

Hell, I often still thought about making him sit in the backseat if we drove anywhere together.

"If you experience any lingering headaches, if you lose consciousness or if you have any signs of infection, you should go to the hospital immediately. Otherwise, you are welcome to return here in a week and I will check it once more."

Harrison nodded. "Thank you. I appreciate you spending the time on this—I know it isn't your normal hours."

"Yeah, well, that's what happens with sisters, I guess. Speaking of…" Joshua gave me a look loaded with a lot of annoyance, then nodded toward the door. "I think I need to have a moment with my sister. If you can excuse us."

"Of course. We'll wait here," Harrison said.

And just like that, I knew I'd get one hell of a lecture.

A few minutes later I sat across the desk from Joshua. Despite me being the older sibling, I sure as fuck felt like the little sister waiting for my older brother to tell me off.

Though I wasn't entirely sure what I'd done. Yeah, I'd woken him up in the middle of the night so he could tend to my buddy for free, but that was hardly something out of the ordinary for me. Maybe it was what he'd walked in on?

"How do you know that person?" Joshua asked.

So yeah, it's about what he walked in on.

"He's a friend," I hedged.

"And just how did you meet him? What do you know about him?"

I furrowed my brows. "You've never given a damn about my friends before. What's this sudden brotherly concern you're showing?"

He pressed his lips together, signs of stress all over his face. He wasn't foolish enough to think I was some blushing maiden who needed his protection, so what the fuck was with this attitude? When he spoke again, he did so slower, like he grappled with his temper. "You should be careful around him."

"Do you know Harrison or something?"

"So you at least know his name? That's something, I suppose. I'm serious, though, Grey. I've never put my nose into your business before. I've always known you were a free spirit and were going to do whatever you want, but this is different. This is serious. For once, just listen to me, please."

I waved him off, slouching in the chair. "Please. This is hardly the worst thing I've done, and out of all the people in my life, Harrison is probably the least likely to be a problem. I mean, come on, I hit him in the temple with a stick and he wasn't even mad at me! At least, not that mad."

Joshua pinched the bridge of his nose for a moment, then folded his hands on the desk. "You don't understand. The man in there, he isn't what he appears to be. Even if he makes you feel a certain way, you can't trust that."

His words made my eyebrow lift. "Wait…are you telling me you know what he is?"

Joshua's eyes widened. Guess that answered it, right? I'd worked so hard to keep my family out of the Spirit world, away from dangers, but from Joshua's comments, he had to know about it. "How do you know?"

I pointed my finger at him. "That isn't the point. How the hell do you know about any of that?"

Joshua waved his hands around his office. "How do you think? I run a well-known urgent care clinic here — you really think we wouldn't get our fair share of Spirits in here? That I wouldn't figure that out? Spirits have people everywhere to keep their truth a secret, so people like me, we're made aware of the truth and expected to keep it secret."

"How long have you known?"

"Since my second year working as a doctor. We had a patient come in from a car accident. I stabilized him, but almost before my eyes, the injuries started to heal faster than was possible. I called my attending, and they told me not to report it. He called someone else who came to pick the patient up and we removed all the records. At the end of the shift, he took me out to a diner and explained how things worked."

I did the math in my head, thinking about when Joshua had worked as a resident, when he'd opened his clinic, all of it. "So you've known about Spirits for eight years?"

Which meant three more years than I'd known. Part of me felt rather annoyed by the idea that I'd thought myself some sort of expert, only to discover my brother had been a step ahead of me.

Annoying.

"A better question is how *you* know. Please tell me you aren't some sort of groupie…" The muscle in his cheek twitched, as though he were thinking about seeing Harrison and I so close together.

"Trust me, I'm no groupie. In fact, I'm pretty sure I hate most Spirits I've dealt with. Somehow, the more powerful, the more frustrating."

"I'm not liking the plurals you keep using. Just how many Spirits do you know?"

"Know is such an iffy word. What does it really mean? Do we ever really know anyone?"

"Grey!" Joshua snapped, stopping my rambling.

"If we're being technical, you know how I work as a courier?"

"Dear god, please don't tell me…"

"Yeah, I work for the Justice Department and do deliveries for Spirits."

"And that's how you met Harrison?"

"Not exactly. Technically, I'm friends with his sister. Also, we're sort of both on the Council."

Wow, it looks like that vein in Joshua's head might just burst…

"The Council? Please tell me you didn't just admit to not only knowing those on the council, but to having your own seat there? Wait, I heard a few weeks ago about a new seat being created."

I smiled, and no doubt it had way too much teeth and too little joy. "Surprise! That's me."

Joshua dropped his head forward so he leaned against his folded arms. Sure, I'd seen him do this sort of thing when he'd been a kid and I'd been a teenager doing stupid, teenage things that he was far too smart to do. It had been a while since I'd exasperated him this badly, though. His voice came out muffled from his position. "I knew you find trouble, but even I didn't think you could work yourself this far into danger. And the fact that you *know* who Harrison is, what he is capable of, and you still hit him with a stick? He could have fried every synapse in your foolish mind. Of course, even if he did, what would it matter? Clearly you don't use the brain you were gifted anyway."

"Harsh," I pointed out. "Fair, but still, ouch. Look, Harrison is fine. I've been working with him for a few weeks to deal with a Cloud issue."

"And you're involved with drugs, too. It just keeps getting better and better."

"Are you going to just keep complaining, or are you going to listen?"

He lifted his head just enough to look across the desk at me. "Both, I'm thinking. I have a feeling that as I listen, I'm going to need to complain. Come on, start at the beginning."

I blew out a long breath as I went back in my head to where it all started. Fuck, it felt like a lifetime ago. After a moment, I jumped in on the day I'd been changed, then gave him the outline version of the years that had come after. I left out some parts—my bond with Kelvin, the fact I'd slept with Harrison, Galen asking me to be his mate. I didn't think my brother needed any details about my sex life, after all.

I glanced at my watch when I hit the end of the story, impressed that I'd gotten it out in a matter of about seven minutes. *My life summed up in seven minutes.* When I thought about it like that, it was rather insulting, really.

Joshua hadn't interrupted during the story. His expression hadn't remained nearly so quiet, though. Neither of us had good inside voices when it came to our faces.

Silence hung between us, the story there, my past suddenly exposed, my secrets I'd expected to take to my grave, at least from my family. How would he react? His reaction to Harrison told me he wasn't a fan of Spirits, so would he see me the same?

What if he distanced himself from me? What if he somehow got my mother to do the same? What if I ended up losing my family because of this?

The idea terrified me, but all I could do was sit and wait and see how he'd react.

After what had to be the longest moments of my life, Joshua finally responded.

By *laughing*.

He started with a chuckle, but it grew quickly until it was loud enough that Harrison and Ignis *must* have heard it. I stared at him until the moment suddenly struck me as equally hilarious. All our years together and brother and sister and we'd both hidden so much.

"I don't know why I'm surprised by this," he said, breathless from the laughter. "If anyone was going to end up in the middle of something as messy as the Spirit Council, of course it would have been you. And after so many years of me being terrified that someone would find out about my family and use it against me, it turns out my sister has a Council seat." He shook his head. "I bet Mom would be laughing if she knew about this."

"Somehow it seems fitting that her kids would be here, doesn't it?"

"Yeah, it does," he agreed, sitting back after catching his breath. "Are you really okay, though? I know you better than most people, and you look exhausted. You like to hide things, to keep it all to yourself, but I can see it wearing on you. I might not be a Spirit, but I'm always here to help you however I can."

"Why do you think I'm here?"

"Because I'm the only doctor you know who would answer the phone at three in the morning?"

"That's why you're the best brother."

"You won't be saying that after you see my bill."

"If I didn't pay you when I lost your bike, I'm not paying for this, either. It's called a sibling tax."

"Lucky me." He moved his gaze to the wall, toward where Harrison and Ignis were, as though he could see them there. "I'm serious, though. You need to be careful. I've seen what happens when people get mixed up in Spirit affairs. You might sort of be one of them, but that doesn't mean you're on the same level. It's still *their* world. Don't ever forget that, because I don't want the next call I get in the middle of the night to be identifying your body." The conversation felt far too personal, too serious. Joshua must have felt it as well, because he softened his expression and smiled. "If that happened, what would happen at the next family dinner? Who would we make fun of if you're not there?"

And just like that, he eased the pressure in my chest, the fear that I'd lost my family.

He might be right that I didn't really belong in the Spirit world, but he'd always reminded me of an important truth. No matter what happened, I had family and a place with them.

Chapter Fifteen

Kelvin didn't seem to fit in at Harrison's house. The last time he'd been here, I'd hardly noticed since I'd been so sick. The next morning it had been awkward, but I'd worked hard to pretend it hadn't been.

Somehow, this time, it was all the more obvious.

He'd shown up as soon as the sun had set, just after I'd forced myself out of bed. After being out until the sun had risen the night before, Harrison and I had managed food and a shower before sleeping the entire day away. I hadn't even gotten dressed yet, since somehow sleeping all day never made me feel quite rested enough.

"Where's Harrison?" Kelvin asked as he peered around the living room. "He's normally hanging all over you."

I hiked my thumb toward the hallway. "Sleeping. We had a sort of long night."

One corner of Kelvin's lips curled up into a suggestive smirk. "Oh really?"

"Not like that."

"Pity. That would have been more amusing. So if that wasn't the case, why did you not get enough sleep? I can see by those dark circles you should probably be napping as well."

"Well, we got a bit closer to the guy stalking me."

"That's good. Do you need help?"

Yes. Despite me wanting to say yes, I didn't know what he could really do. Worse, I had no idea what Ryder might do to a vampire if he set his sights on him. The memory of Trey, who still had failed to wake, kept me from asking Kelvin. "No," I said. "We're getting closer—don't worry."

"So all you need is my bite?"

"Do you have to come right out and say that?"

He shrugged, somehow acting as if he were at home, as though he belonged here even when I knew damn well he didn't. "I like the idea that we're bound. It's also nice to know that you have to deal with me. You can't just ignore and avoid me anymore. It might not be what you wanted, but now that we can't change it, I might as well enjoy it." He sat on the couch, then put his feet up on the table the same way I often did. "Now, I told you last time, I won't fuck you until you ask me when you're still in your right mind. That means right now is the time you get to tell me if you want that or not."

"Talk about being pushy."

"It's not pushy. Pushy would be to bite you, then listen to your venom-addled mind when you beg me. I'm being a gentleman, though, and letting you make the choice before I bite you. So the deal is, you have to tell me you want me to fuck you, out loud, before we start. Until you do that, I won't do it."

"Well, you better get used to disappointment, because I am *never* going to say that. I don't have a choice about accepting your bite — because of you — but that doesn't mean I'm ever going to trust you any further."

"I guess we'll see about that," Kelvin said with a shrug, as though my rejection didn't bother him at all. "Until then, I'll do everything short of putting my dick in you."

I rolled my eyes at the way he acted like that was something chivalrous.

"Let's get on with this," I muttered before sitting down beside Kelvin and moving my hair off the side of my neck.

"You don't want to wait for Harrison?"

"I'm not afraid of you. Besides, he's sleeping — because I hit him with a branch — so I should let him rest. Let's just get this over with." Despite my big, confident words, the moment Kelvin set his hand on my arm, I flinched.

It was a reaction I couldn't help, proof of how tightly strung my nerves were. Maybe I should have waited for Harrison, because him being there might at the very least break some of the tension between Kelvin and me, the issues between us we'd failed to work through.

"Relax," he said, his voice low and compelling. Fuck, had it always been that tempting?

No, I was pretty sure this was new. Was it because of our bond? Did that make me want to please him more? Did it make me trust his words in a way I hadn't before? I had to believe it was something like that because the other option was that I had fallen for him, and I refused to accept that.

I tried to do as he said, partly so he wouldn't speak so close to my ear again. I forced myself to relax, to slow my breathing, to tell myself that being this close to him meant nothing. That would have been much better than the truth, which was that even without his bite, my body had already started to heat and react.

He pressed his warm lips to my throat, and even that light touch had a moan escaping me. How could such an innocent touch feel *that* good? It really wasn't fucking fair. His words ran circles in my head, the mocking way he'd known that I'd beg for him, and the fact I knew better than to deny it anymore. It was good that he wouldn't change his mind, that he'd wait, because I knew damn well I'd plead for his cock pretty soon.

At least hold off until he bites you – then you can pretend it was all due to that.

"Just get on with it," I said.

"I always knew you had no patience." Kelvin paired the jab with a chuckle, but he neither moved away nor gave me what I wanted. Instead, he brushed his lips over my bare flesh again, eliciting the same reaction from me. "I prefer taking my time. If something's worth doing, it's worth savoring. Besides, this is the only time I get with you—I have to make the most of it."

I drew my elbow back, into his stomach. Unfortunately, given he was a vampire and not human, he hardly seemed to notice the hit. *Stupid abs…*

He laughed then, dragging the tips of his fangs against my neck. It stung, making me suspect he'd left two long, red lines in their wake. As if the scars I wore weren't bad enough, weren't proof enough of our connection—and his power over me.

The idea annoyed me, but I didn't have long to think about it. Instead, Kelvin pulled back for a heartbeat, followed by that familiar pain yet again when he sank his fangs into my neck, somehow finding the same place as before.

And just like before, lava seemed to pour through me from that place, lighting up every part of my body. I reached out blindly, needing to hold something, feeling adrift and lost in the feelings that swarmed me. My left hand found the couch, but my right landed on Kelvin's knee. I gripped tightly, not caring if I drew blood, if I dug my nails into his skin. That felt like a fair thing for him to bear, given he'd caused this all.

He didn't pull back, no matter how hard I dug into his leg. Instead, he let out a low growl that I felt through where he'd bitten me, then clamped down tighter as though I were prey and he wanted to ensure I couldn't escape.

Not that I had any plans of escaping. In fact, he should probably be more worried about me jumping him at this point. My entire body felt supercharged, so even the sensation of air against my skin had me gasping and shuddering. My nipples had hardened, and them brushing against my nightgown had me almost ready to explode. *Just a little more…*

He wouldn't, though. He didn't touch me, didn't do anything to help cure the fire searing through me. *Worthless bastard.* Then again, I'd never been the sort of girl who had to wait for a man to take care of me and my needs. I was a strong, independent woman who could get myself off.

With that little burst of confidence, I moved the hand that was on the couch, slipping it beneath the hemline of my dress. Given it was nighttime, I hadn't put on any underwear, but the sensation of just how hot and wet my cunt was surprised even me. The first brush of my fingers against my slit forced an embarrassingly needy moan from me.

Kelvin released his bite, then dragged the flat of his tongue over my neck. "You really are a do for herself sort of woman, aren't you?"

"Well, you aren't helping."

"Is that what you wanted?"

I refused to admit that I needed him, so instead, I gritted my teeth together and kept the words inside. I stroked two of my fingers along my cunt, dragging them forward until I slid them across my waiting clit. The feeling overwhelmed me, so much more powerful than it should have been. That's what Kelvin's bite did, though. It cranked up the power on everything, electrifying all my nerves so everything felt like so much *more*.

"Did we wake you?" Kelvin's question confused me for a moment, but all too quickly I realized he wasn't talking to me when Harrison responded.

"Do you really think I could sleep when I felt all this?" Harrison stood there, in his sweats and a T-shirt, his hair messier than usual to show he'd come straight from bed.

I probably *should* have felt bad for waking him—especially since the side of his head appeared worse than before, the bruise having darkened. I blamed my lack of guilt on Kelvin and his fucking venom, however. Who could blame me for reacting this way?

"Consider it one fucking nice wake up call, then," Kelvin said before reaching around me and setting his hands on the insides of my thighs. He pulled, spreading my legs, and despite the sudden exposure, I couldn't stop myself from stroking my clit as I had been doing already.

The weight of Harrison's gaze was unbearably sexy. Those icy gray eyes of his locked onto my cunt, as though nothing existed outside of that. The thin sweats he wore failed to hide his physical reaction, either, and fuck if the sight of his hardening cock didn't make my mouth water. I reached out with my free hand and wrapped my fingers in the waist of his sweats, using the grasp to pull him closer. He took each step as though dazed, not even reacting when I tugged the fabric down to expose him.

I hadn't had the chance to play with him much the last time, and I didn't intend to repeat that mistake. I leaned in and dragged my tongue up the length of his cock, savoring the way it twitched in response. Fuck did that make me feel oddly powerful.

Kelvin latched his lips onto the bite and sucked, the action causing me to cry out, trying to pull in enough oxygen. Meanwhile, he released my thighs and moved his hands up my body. He grasped my chin with one of them, then reached out and wrapped his hand around Harrison's cock with the other. He stroked his length with a slow, teasing touch. Kelvin pressed one finger to my lips, his meaning clear enough that I obeyed without a second thought, opening my mouth.

Kelvin held tight—to me and to Harrison—to force Harrison one step closer, guiding Harrison's cock past my parted lips. I accepted it, using my tongue against the bottom of his dick, savoring the salty taste of him. He groaned, the sound low and pleased, his gaze locked on my face.

Kelvin didn't release either of us. He kept his fist around the base of Harrison's cock and his other hand still grasped my jaw, his thumb stroking over my bottom lip even as it was stretched wide. Why was this so hot? Somehow, having sex with Kelvin or Harrison was one thing, but the way Kelvin touched me, almost seeming to use both Harrison and I like toys he could pose at will, was such a turn on that it made his venom seem impotent.

Kelvin took his lips from the bite, and I didn't have time to prepare myself for that low rumble of his voice. "Is this better, little bird? Does his cock make you feel better? Does it quell that need inside you?"

I nodded, despite the action being little more than a tiny incline of my head between Kelvin's grip and Harrison's cock. Somehow, that made it hotter, though. The way Kelvin held me still, the way Harrison thrust shallowly, the bump of Kelvin's fist against my lips, it all added to the lust inside me. I stroked my clit again, harder, and that was all it took to send me right over the edge.

I kept my mouth open, careful not to get Harrison with my teeth as I came hard, as the tension rolled through my body in heady waves. Despite that, neither Harrison nor Kelvin let up. The stroking of Harrison's cock against the inside of my cheek and tongue, the way Kelvin's breath warmed my throat, it all mixed together to prolong my orgasm.

"Good girl," Kelvin whispered, then teased my earlobe with his sharp fangs, leaving a sting behind. Even still, after the orgasm started to fade, I knew it wasn't enough.

Not even close.

The fire inside me burned brighter and hotter than ever, as though my release had only spread it, had only tossed more fuel on it. That made me pull against

Kelvin's grasp to take Harrison deeper, wanting to drown in him, in his scent, in his taste.

Kelvin laughed, though the sound was far darker than usual. He let me go, the action not separating Harrison and me. Instead, it let me lean forward, giving me back control as far as speed and depth. And fuck if this wasn't the only place in my life where I wanted to be an overachiever. Kelvin moved from beside me, but he wasn't opting out. That became clear when he set a hand on Harrison's arm and pressed him forward.

Harrison moved as though he'd already been thinking this, but the touch of Kelvin's hand was all the prompting he needed. He withdrew from my mouth, then moved over me, forcing me to lie back as he crowded me. It ended with me stretched out on the couch and him over me, in the space between my thighs. He didn't wait, leaning in and taking my lips in a kiss that already felt familiar. I slid my arms around his shoulders, clinging to him as I lifted my hips in a blatant plea.

"I can't hold back anymore," Harrison said.

"Who's asking you to?" I nipped his full bottom lip, the action meant to get him moving. I wanted him as crazy as I felt. He might not be drugged on Kelvin's venom, but that didn't matter. I still wanted him lost to the same feeling that raged through me.

He braced his weight on one arm, then used his other hand to reach between us. If I had any doubts about his experience, they were wiped away when he so easily fit his cock against my cunt then plunged into me. The sudden fullness had me setting my foot on the couch and pushing—not to get away, but rather due to the overwhelming sensation. He didn't pause, instead setting a brutal pace right from jump. It went to show that he really wasn't thinking fully.

I had one moment of wondering if this was good for him, if my brother would have yelled at me if he'd known that this was what his patient was up to so soon after leaving? He'd said to rest, and while we were horizontal, I had a feeling this wasn't what Joshua had meant.

But fuck if I felt bad about it in the least. Instead, I gave myself over to it.

"You two are better than the best porn," Kelvin said, his fingers appearing on top of Harrison's shoulder, his skin standing out since it was darker. I peered around Harrison to find Kelvin staring at his back just as he drew his hand down, over Harrison's spine, the touch slow and undoubtably sensual.

And Harrison shuddered at it, thrusting harder into me. That showed he wasn't all that unopposed.

"Your skin is so pale," Kelvin went on. "It's so perfect and soft. Don't get me wrong, I find myself rather jealous that you're a stand-in for me, but I don't think I mind this all that much, either." Kelvin gripped Harrison's waist. Meanwhile, he leaned in and ground his still clothed crotch against Harrison's ass.

Harrison parted his lips on a groan, his eyes closed.

"What do you say? I've covered your thighs in cum once already — why not again?"

"Don't…" Harrison said, but paused after that one word, as though unsure how to finish the though.

Kelvin leaned forward, his thicker build dwarfing Harrison, especially because of the way he was dressed and Harrison nude. He pressed a kiss to Harrison's shoulder, then dragged his fangs over Harrison's pale skin. "I won't fuck you. I'm a pretty despicable person, but I don't pressure people into things they don't want. I promise not to enter you."

If I had been in my right mind, I'd have laughed. Who the fuck would be stupid enough to trust any promise Kelvin made? However, in this, I found myself believing him.

Even when he'd made me his thrall, he'd resisted doing anything else out of his own guilt, because I couldn't consent. It seemed a sticking point for him, an odd little moral hiccup in his otherwise amoral life.

"Okay," Harrison said, hesitation in his voice.

Fuck did I recognize that hesitation, though. It wasn't one born of not knowing if he wanted to do something, but rather an internal battle between what he wanted and what he *thought* he should want. It was like the times I'd seen someone hot who I wanted to sleep with, but didn't want anyone calling me a whore because of it.

"Good answer," Kelvin said, moving his hands farther back. He cupped Harrison's ass, then spread his checks. "It's a damn pity, because this sight tells me you would feel amazingly good." He shifted his hands, seeming to run his thumbs down, over his ass. "However, you set that boundary, and I'll respect it. Tighten your thighs for me."

Harrison shifted, bringing his knees tighter together. He didn't pull out of me as far, instead thrusting hard and grinding deep into my cunt. The action allowed his body to tease my clit at the same time, since he was pressed snuggly against me.

Kelvin moved—I had to guess he was undoing his pants, though I couldn't see past Harrison's body— then moved closer behind Harrison. Kelvin pressed a knee onto the couch, beside my thigh, and braced his other foot on the floor. He let out a low, feral sound that screamed pleasure, and Harrison's shiver suggested he'd just fit his cock between Harrison's thighs.

And suddenly I hated my spot. I wanted to be farther away, to watch this, to see Harrison come undone as Kelvin thrusted against him. However, the sensation of Harrison's cock buried deep inside me was a pretty good consolation prize, all things considered.

I wrapped one arm up and around Harrison's shoulder, holding him tight. I rolled my hips up, wanting as much of him as I could get. Nothing would ever be enough, though.

Or maybe that's some weird, kinky death wish of mine…

Considering all I'd been through, though, and all the ways I'd nearly gotten myself killed, I had to admit death by sex was probably one of the better options.

Kelvin grasped Harrison by the hips, his fingers digging into Harrison's soft skin, then thrust forward. The action forced Harrison to plunge into me, his body caught between mine and Kelvin's. When he moved forward he sank deeper into me and away caused Kelvin to rub against his thighs.

It also made me wonder just how it would feel if he ever said yes to Kelvin for real. The idea of Harrison being fucked at the same time he took me was far hotter than anything had the right to be. It made me wrap my leg around Harrison, holding tight to him, letting him and Kelvin set the pace.

"Fuck," Kelvin muttered, his voice so low it was difficult to even figure out what he said. The passion in it, however, clued me in enough to make some guesses. "You both make me crazy, you know that? No one else tastes like this, no one else makes me so damn hungry. I haven't been able to so much as look at anyone else, not since the last time. You are both like the worst drug, one I didn't realize I was getting addicted to. I feel like you ought to take some responsibility for that."

"Harrison is too nice to say it, so I will. Pretty sure 'fuck off', is the right response," I said, the words cut off with a whimper when Kelvin thrust especially hard, the action grinding Harrison's pelvis against my needy clit.

"This feels like 'fucking off', doesn't it? Or am I not quite living up to your expectation?" Kelvin's words felt like a joke, as though he were getting off as much on the banter as he was on the soft tightness of Harrison's thighs. "I could always try harder, if you needed me to."

Fuck did *that* sound like a threat more than some nice offer.

Part of me wanted to mock him more, to push him into it, but I snapped my mouth shut instead. He'd always proven the sort of man who would keep going just to win, someone with few if any real limits beyond consent. Given how I already felt, I really didn't need him bringing his A game anywhere.

Kelvin laughed, but the sound came out more strained than before. It went to show that he was far from unaffected by our little tryst. That also struck me as a petty win.

Harrison slid his hand behind my neck and pulled me toward his lips, the kiss aggressive and passionate. The moment his tongue entwined with mine, he fucked deep into me then paused, his breath heavy as he came. The twitch of his cock inside me broke my own resolve, leading me down the same path, allowing a second orgasm to rush through me.

Harrison sagged against me after pulling out, his chest rising and falling in heavy panting, his face in the crook of my neck. It allowed me to look over his shoulder, to meet Kelvin's gaze.

And damn did Kelvin look good like that… He was still dressed, with only his pants undone, lowered just enough to access his cock. His eyes, normally a startling blue, seemed to glow in the dim room. He appeared every bit the monster I'd thought he was before. Even still, I didn't reject him, didn't try to pull away. I accepted every bit of him, at least in this moment—the need for control, the desire for more, the doubts he held—I saw them all and didn't push him away.

His lip curled up at the corner before he leaned forward and placed one hand to the center of Harrison's back, pressing him forward and arching his back. He grasped Harrison's hip with his other hand, lifting his hips and pinning him in place. The action had pulled him back slightly, so Harrison's face was in my lap, and he rested his cheek against me. Kelvin replaced his cock between Harrison's thighs, his gaze locked on me the entire time. The position allowed me a *much* better view than the last time, and I realized just how much I'd missed before.

Because of how he had Harrison, Kelvin could fit his cock higher, so when he thrust in, he rubbed against Harrison's dick. The sound Harrison released said the sensation was at the very least overwhelming. Even when he shifted, Kelvin held him still, fucking his thighs with passion that bordered on violence. He took him hard, as though he really were inside someone, like he lost himself to the pleasure and need. Part of me worried that Harrison would wear marks from it, but when he didn't appear bothered, I saw no reason for me to worry much about it.

If Harrison hated it, if he wanted it to stop, I had no doubts he could stop Kelvin. And somehow, that was even hotter, the fact that Harrison accepted the treatment — no, not just accepted but got off on it.

Kelvin leaned forward slightly, driving hard against Harrison, his thrusts losing their rhythm. He appeared unhinged, as though he'd lost himself entirely to the moment. The ability to see him like this excited me, made me wish I'd consented to whatever he'd wanted from the start.

He thrust forward once more, stilling with a deep groan, his eyes fluttering closed. He had some blood on his cheek, a reminder that he'd feasted on my blood. It felt like some strange cycle between the three of us, all of us giving and taking from the others.

Kelvin leaned forward, over Harrison, until he could get my lips in a kiss that made my heart race yet again.

This was one fucked-up situation, but I couldn't deny how it made me feel. Nothing else was normal in my life — why would I ever think my love life could be?

So instead of fighting it, instead of arguing with myself about it, I returned the kiss.

Fucked up as it might be, maybe weird wasn't so terrible.

Chapter Sixteen

I'd gotten more used to meeting *him,* the man who had made me, the one who had told me to call him Knot, in my dreams, though it seemed more awkward now. I spotted him across a busy shop, the people around me speaking a language I couldn't understand. A glance at the menus as I passed identified it as Korean.

He didn't lift his gaze at first, staring down at a plate with a mixture of rice and veggies and sprouts, a small container of kimchi to the side. He poked at the food with the end of his chopstick, as though it hadn't quite hit the spot he'd hoped.

I approached his table, surprised at the idea that I might sneak up on him. After...well...everything, I wouldn't have thought that possible. He proved that guess right when he lifted his head as soon as I reached the table. He gestured toward the seat across from him. It made me wonder if he'd known I was coming somehow, if he'd sensed it. He'd said before that he could feel when I was upset, and fuck, who knew what else he could have felt from me. The idea that he might have caught what I'd been doing with Kelvin and Harrison made me sit and stare at the food instead of the man across from me.

"So you're still alive," he said before taking another bite of the rice mixture in his bowl.

"You already knew that, didn't you?"

"Yeah, I guess I did. Still, I was wondering how long you'd make it. You know, I don't usually step into human problems. I find them tedious and never worth the effort."

"So why did you for me?"

"I wonder." His words made me lift my gaze to find him smiling at me, the fondness in that look easing the sting of his words earlier. He could say whatever he wanted, but the truth was that he'd come forward and risked himself just to help me. It was hard not to feel at least a little charmed by that.

"Where are you now?" I asked, despite being pretty sure I knew the answer.

"Korea," he acknowledged. "I like it here. It's busy in the cities and the countryside is pretty. Besides, it's hard to get good kimchi anywhere else." His words sounded like the sort of things he always said, but they held an edge that worried me. It was in the way he glanced to the side, past me, as though looking for something.

Or someone.

"Is something wrong?" I asked.

He brought his gaze back to mine before laughing and shaking his head. "You really were the right choice, you know that? Anyone else would know better than to come right out and ask but you? You just do whatever you want. I like that about you—at least, when you aren't using it against me."

"That's a lot of words just to avoid answering what I'm asking."

He blew out a breath, then set his chopsticks down on the napkin. "Let's just say that I'm a bit more popular than I was before."

I frowned as I thought about the meaning behind that. Knot tended to prefer staying vague and forcing me to figure it out myself. It started to come together, though, and I didn't care for the picture it made. "You're talking about the council, right? Are you saying you're in trouble because of that?"

"I'm never *in* trouble, little crow, I *am* trouble. Also, yeah, I'm in a little trouble. I've kept my head down for a long time so no one bothered me. Now, though, the others are taking notice of me again."

"The others?"

"You've already figured that much out—the other Old Gods. The ones who made the Spirits of your world. I've never been well liked, but since I kept my nose out of their business, they ignored me—if they even remembered me anymore. They probably figured I was dead."

"But now they realize you aren't?"

"Pretty much."

"Has anything happened?"

"Not yet. I think they're still just playing games. I can *feel* them around sometimes, so I keep moving." He reached across the table and ran his thumb across my forehead, as though to smooth the lines out from there. "You look way too worried. This won't fall on you, so don't worry."

"I'm not worried about it falling on me."

He tilted his head, as though my words confused him, but didn't remove his thumb from my forehead. "You are such a strange little human. You always do things I don't predict. Are you telling me you're worried about *me*? After I changed your life so much, after everything I've screwed up for you?"

"Of course I'm worried about you. We're..." I paused when I had no idea how to finish that thought. What were we? Undeniably intertwined, sure, but beyond that?

I really had no fucking idea.

Knot chuckled, then stroked his fingers across my cheek before sitting back in his chair. "We are that. Don't worry your pretty little head over me, though. I've lived a long time avoiding the others — I can avoid them longer. No one's better at it than I am."

"I was surprised that I didn't hear from you after the council meeting. It's been weeks."

"Sorry. Each time we meet like this, though, it forms a connection. That's risky."

"So they could find you because of me?" I peered around as though I might catch the people following him in the shadows around us.

And do what exactly? We were talking about *Gods.* I was a big fan of knowing one's own limitations, and that included me recognizing that I was far from equipped to deal with Gods. I was hardly equipped to deal with toddlers who missed their naps!

I turned back toward the man to find him staring at me with that same look from before, one full of confusion. "I didn't not meet you because I was worried about them finding *me*."

"Then why?"

He lifted an eyebrow as though telling me to work that out myself.

Before I could, however, he turned his head toward the front door and narrowed his eyes. His expression was different from any I'd ever seen from him before. It wasn't playful or amused, it was downright threatening. He stared as though fully ready to fuck up whoever had come in.

I turned to look at the door, but somehow my eyes couldn't make sense of what I saw. It was too bright, too different, as though something I wasn't meant to see at all.

Knot reached across and caught my chin, forcing my face back to his. "Go back. I'll talk to you when it's safe."

I didn't have time to ask him what he meant before I felt myself thrown back into my body with a force that made me bolt upright in bed. Normally returning to myself felt like waking from a dream, something simple and not stressful. There was no doubt that this time was different, however. I had a feeling it was Knot's fault, as though he'd physically tossed me back into my own body.

But why? He'd never done that before.

His words swirled in my head, and the meaning hit me all at once. He hadn't met with me not because he was afraid of drawing attention to himself, but because he didn't want attention drawn to *me*.

When the fuck did he get all noble?

I sighed and rubbed my face, since it seemed unlikely I'd get back to sleep. My bed was empty, something I found oddly disappointing. Sure, I didn't expect to find Kelvin or Harrison, but a part of me thought it might not be so bad to wake up and not be alone. Fuck, it might have even been sort of nice...

My phone buzzed on the nightstand, vibrating against the wood. I reached out and grabbed it, then brought it closer, squinting against the bright light in the dark room. I'd gotten a text message, and a few taps and swipes later, I'd brought it up.

If my heart wasn't already going a mile a minute, it sure as fuck was now.

The words were short and to the point, as expected from a man like Galen, but they got across what I needed to know.

Trey is awake.

* * * *

Galen's expression dampened my excitement when I arrived at his place. After his first text message, I'd gotten a second telling me to come over in the morning. I could have called him—was almost tempted to do so—but something held me back.

It was the fear of bad news. I didn't want to call and find out things were worse than I thought, to find out it was bad news. Instead, I allowed myself the giddy few moments of believing everything would be okay.

The look on Galen's face told me I'd been naïve.

Harrison got out of the passenger seat, having let me drive—I had stolen the car just a few days prior, so clearly he could trust me. He walked behind me, something I appreciated. Too often the men in my life liked to take the lead, liked to act as though I needed them to guide and protect me. Harrison never behaved that way. He always remained behind me, willing to step in if he thought I needed it, but quick to allow me to handle myself the rest of the time.

"You're here early," Galen said.

"You said to come at nine."

"Sure, but you're *always* late. You getting here at nine is unheard of."

"So, you're funny in the mornings, huh?" I paused at the front door, waiting for the first time before going in. Usually, I barged in—often completely uninvited. Things like social rules and expectations weren't things I cared much about. However, this time, I hesitated at the threshold.

I didn't *want* to go in. Up until now, I'd thought that Trey would wake up eventually, that he was just taking his sweet ass time. Now, though? Now that he had, I had no idea what exactly that meant. What if he wasn't him anymore? What if Galen had to kill him?

Over my dead fucking body.

Harrison stopped a few steps back, as though giving me a moment of privacy. That was fair, though. This might be an issue with the Minds, but the victim was a Were. That put it strictly in Galen's jurisdiction.

"You don't have to do this," Galen said, his voice low. "You don't need to see him."

"Guess that means I don't need to ask how he is."

"Harrison warned you that if he did wake up, it might not be good news."

I nodded, trying to force myself to smile even if I didn't feel like it at all. "Yeah, I guess he did. Still, I have to see him."

"Why?"

"He ended up on Ryder's bad side because of me. He's in whatever state he's in because of me. The least

I can do is see it. Besides, who knows, maybe there's something I can do…"

I could tell from Galen's look that he didn't agree, that he'd already written Trey off. Even so, he said nothing, only nodding.

I moved past him, headed for the stairs.

"Downstairs," Galen said, drawing me to a stop. When I turned to face him, he hadn't moved at all. "He's uncontrollable, Grey. We had to put him downstairs where we can keep him from escaping or hurting anyone."

"Is Grey safe there?" Harrison broke in.

"Yeah, she will be. He's bound and in a cell."

Each word felt like a fresh slap, and I couldn't seem to get a break from any of it. Still, I wouldn't run away. I'd do what I came to do—face Trey and at least apologize for what had happened. I forced myself to walk toward the door I'd never gone through, the one that headed down to the basement. The door had no lock, and opened for me with only a loud creaking of the hinges.

The stairs were wooden, and the interior or the basement appeared lit by a warm bulb somewhere beyond the staircase. I took one more deep breath, then headed down them. From the basement, a deep, dark sound echoed up the concrete walls. It sounded almost like the vibrating of a phone on silent. Still, I walked down the stairs, toward the sound, toward darkness.

At the bottom, I was finally able to look at the full basement. I could see why Galen never invited me down here…

Cells lined the far wall—five, it seemed like. A single bare light bulb hung from the center of the ceiling, casting dim light over the gray room. It had a certain terrorist-chic aesthetic. The doors to four of the cells were cracked open, but one sat closed at the far-left corner.

That sound came from that direction, though I couldn't see anything in the cell. My steps were quiet as I approached, as if I might be able to sneak up on whatever made that noise. I stopped when I was just before the door, the thick iron bars on the cells a sure sign they weren't just for some kinky roleplaying. I doubted a rhino could break through this thing.

Which told me I probably didn't much want to play with whatever was locked inside.

Just as soon as I thought that, the darkness inside the cell moved. Something dark and shadowed rushed forward, and I couldn't stop myself from jerking backward, startled by how fast and how aggressive the thing was.

It got to the cell door, then reached through, a black, clawed hand swiping inches from my face. My eyes were open wide, my breath caught in my throat as the light finally illuminated the thing.

It was a bear — large enough I had to crane my neck to see the golden eyes that bore into me from its massive face.

A bear locked down here could only mean one thing, right?

I swallowed hard, then spoke with as calming a voice as I could. "Trey?"

The bear tilted its head as though confused by the name. Had that reached beneath his beast Spirit? Gotten to the man beneath? It must have, because a moment later, a shadow wrapped around the bear and when it dissipated, Trey stood there, nude and clinging to the bars. He breathed hard, sweat on his brow, his gaze down.

"Trey?" I repeated.

He slumped down, sinking to the floor, his forehead hitting the bars as though he lacked the energy to hold it up anymore. That had me rushing forward, not caring about the risk. Sure, the memory of those huge claws remained in my mind, but I didn't plan on worrying about it right now. I could ignore a risk if I had reason to. I dropped down beside the door, reaching through the bars to check his head.

"How do you feel?"

"My head hurts," he said, but it wasn't the voice I knew from him. I recalled how playful he'd sounded at the school, how full of life. He sounded nothing like that. Now exhaustion and pain filled his voice.

"That happens. Still, you look better."

He shook his head, but didn't pull back, as though he enjoyed the touch of my cool skin against him. "*Everything* hurts. It's like each thought in my head is made of razors, slicing my brain apart as I think." He shuddered, that growling occurring again, the same one I'd heard when I'd entered.

"You'll get better," I swore to him, trying to make myself sound confident. Sure, I had no idea how to make that happen, but I couldn't just not offer help. I couldn't not try when he was here and it was my fault.

"He won't." Harrison's voice made me twist my head to look back and find him at the base of the steps along with Galen. They both wore nearly identical expressions — pity. Clearly, they both were in agreement over Trey's odds.

"You don't know that," I snapped. "You can't."

Harrison came closer, not bothering to crouch. "Of course I do. I know the sort of damage done, and there aren't many ways to fix it."

"Many ways doesn't mean no ways. In fact, it's the opposite."

Harrison sighed, as though dealing with me was tedious. "It took a very specific power to cause the wounds in his mind. The only way to reverse any of it — and it wouldn't be all of it — would be for the person who created them to resolve them." He moved his gaze from me to Trey. "And that sort of thing is extremely hard on the Mind who has to do so. I know Ryder well enough to assure you, he wouldn't do anything so selfless."

That wasn't what I'd wanted to hear, and worse, I had no idea how to argue. After my small amounts of time with Ryder…yeah, I couldn't see him going out of his way to help some kid he'd used as a dealer.

But what other option did I have? What else could I do but try?

I opened my mouth to tell him that I'd find a way, that it didn't matter how difficult or how remote the chance, I still would do it. Except, before the words escaped me, something large and furry wrapped around my throat, trapping me against the cell, my back to the bars, facing Galen and Harrison. That deep rumble from Trey hadn't stopped — in fact, it was louder and so low I feared it might just vibrate the bars apart.

"Stay back," a voice I didn't recognize came from behind me. It was feral and primal and not even close to Trey's. It reminded me that Weres were not one but two beings. One, the human, and the other?

The Spirit of the beast that resided inside them, the animal that took them over from time to time. It was easy to ignore or forget that fact, but given the hand wrapped around my throat, the claws that dug into my flesh, I lacked the luxury of forgetting or ignoring it right now.

Harrison lifted his hands as if to placate the bear, even taking a step back. Then again, Harrison wasn't someone all that dangerous up close. He could bring someone to their knees from across the room with ease. Of course…the claws said the bear didn't need much to fuck me up, either.

"Release her." Galen's voice filled the basement, somehow even more terrifying than the claws at my throat. He was alpha for a reason, and while I rarely saw this side of him, it was impossible to forget it.

"Release *me*," Trey shot back.

"I can't. You're too dangerous. You have to recognize that." Galen came closer, each step against the concrete like a crack of thunder. "You *know* you aren't in your right mind, not either of you."

"I'm fine."

"You aren't. You are half of the same whole, and your human has been hurt."

"Then I will care for him, but not here, not trapped like some performing animal. Weres die in captivity — you know this!" Trey's words were so low that they were hard to understand, hard to make out, but I couldn't deny the truth in them. Weres craved freedom, like most spirits, and they didn't do well when trapped.

"You can't care for him," Harrison said. "You may feel fine right now, but your mind was shredded just as his was. You share a mind, so you were damaged as well. You simply don't use some of the higher functions like he does, so you don't notice it as much."

"I'll kill her," Trey threatened, digging his claws into my throat. "I'll slit her throat right now."

"Do *not* threaten my mate," Galen said, his voice having somehow grown even more violent than before. Before he was pissed—now he sounded outright feral. In fact, his tone turned me silent, even allowed me to pretend I hadn't heard his proclamation about being his mate.

Which I sure as fuck was not.

My life was complicated enough without *that* bullshit.

"She isn't," Trey answered. I couldn't see him, but fuck if I didn't *feel* the heat of his breath as he sniffed the top of my head. And I sure as hell tried to ignore how that position would put his teeth much closer than I felt comfortable with. Not that I could do shit about it. "She doesn't carry your scent, so no, she isn't yours. Still, you dare to speak as if she were."

"He gets confused in his old age," I said with a strained laugh. "It happens to everyone, right? Let's all calm down."

"You will remove your hands from her," Galen said as though I hadn't spoken. "Or I will remove *your* hands."

By this point, Galen stood just before me, so closer I could have reached out and touched him. Not that I'd dare—I had a feeling that would make this all worse.

Galen stared—not at me, but at Trey. He had to stare up and into Trey's face, given he was in his bear form. I would have cowered at that, but Galen somehow didn't. He faced off against Trey as though he were a pup in need of discipline rather than the full-grown bear he was. It made me unwillingly impressed by Galen. He appeared so young, like a college kid, that I sometimes forgot the power and position he held.

"I won't let her go," Trey swore, "not until you open this door."

"Even if I open it, you won't leave."

"Want to bet?"

I swear, if a dick measuring contest gets me killed, I am going to haunt someone's ass for all eternity.

Galen reached out and grabbed the door to the cell, placing his palm over the keyhole. The lock inside the door ground as though it had unlocked, the tension of the door let up, swinging freely and causing me to fall back slightly toward Trey, the bars still between us. "Door is open. Now, let her go."

Trey seemed to hesitate, making me suspect he'd never thought the door would open, that he didn't think he'd get what he'd wanted. If that was the case, though, why try it?

Galen shook his head, the action so fast it reminded me more of a wolf. Was he that close to losing his control?

This was, in all, a very bad situation to be in— especially because physically, I was nowhere close to the weight level of these two. If they started to take swings, it would only take one to really fuck me up.

Though, hey, at least I'd found something that was too far and I could easily say wasn't my kink. That was good, right?

Trey still hadn't released me. His hand trembled, the action causing the claws to rake lightly against my exposed skin. If I could ignore the size of the man behind me, the fact that he was evidently stark-raving nuts, if I only paid attention to his actions, it all came back to one thing.

He was doing this for a reason, but that reason wasn't about escaping. He was terrified.

Galen rolled his shoulders, narrowing his glowing eyes. "This is your last chance. I've held back my wolf as well as I can, but he doesn't take it well when people threaten his mate. If I lose control of him — you will be torn to pieces. So, let. Her. Go." With the last word, Galen snapped his teeth together.

Still, Trey didn't let go. He tightened his grip, pressing the sharp tips of his claws harder against my throat. He could have cut me so easily, but he didn't.

Galen spread his arms just as a dark mist started to consume him, the sign of the start of his change and the start of a lot of fucking questions.

"Stop!" I rushed out, putting my hands up.

"Stop? He's going to kill you," Galen said, his voice having returned more to normal. Maybe my stupidity had shaken some sense into him.

"No, he isn't — right, Trey? If you wanted to kill me, you could have from the start. You were just trying to get Galen to attack you."

A noisy chuff said Trey wasn't a fan of my theory, and Galen's expression suggested he thought I was an idiot.

The thing was, even an idiot was right occasionally, and today felt like my lucky day.

"Think about it, Galen. He could have killed me already. He had to know you wouldn't just let him go, especially with Harrison right here as well. He knows you're stronger, so why would he do this?" I gave Galen a moment to think it over, to recognize I wasn't wrong.

After a second, Galen let out a soft curse under his breath, the realization washing over his face. Clearly, he'd come to the same conclusion I had.

Trey must have realized it too, because he released me. Despite the fact that he hadn't been restricting my airway, I felt like I could breathe more easily. "You're an idiot," Trey snapped. "You *all* are idiots."

I turned to find him there, still in his bear form, having moved away until he was against the wall, as though trying to be considerate. Funny how quickly he could move from 'I'm going to tear her throat out' to 'I don't want to startle her from standing too close!'

"You don't need to die," I said.

"Of course I do. You really don't think I can feel the wounds in my mind? The way someone went in there and carved it all out, leaving gashes behind that will never heal. I'm nothing more than a rabid beast like this. Death is a far better fate." He lowered himself from his back legs to the ground, then lay flat. He set his head on top of his front paws, his face turned away as though he didn't want to see any of us. He really did look the part of a wounded animal right there, didn't he?

Galen closed the door to the cell, relocking it with his palm against the door. It must have been some magic lock, something connected with his wolf. Whatever it was, Trey didn't resist the action, didn't try to get away. It went to prove even more than he'd never intended to escape, not really.

"You should have killed me," Trey said as the rest of us headed for the stairs.

I turned back to face Trey, but he still didn't look my way. In fact, for a moment I wondered if I'd heard him at all. He cleared that up when he went on, "You'll see that I'm right. You'll come to regret not doing what I wanted and ending me here, and what happens next? All the blood that gets shed? Well, you'll have to live with that yourself, because it'll be on your hands."

That doesn't sound good at all…

Chapter Seventeen

Harrison had gone to meet with Ignis, leaving me there with Galen. Then again, I was pretty safe here, all things considered.

"I'm surprised you haven't done anything to me yet," Galen said as he walked into the living room with a glass of water that he handed over to me.

"Not sure what you think about me, but I'm not the type to jump people in their own homes." As soon as I said it, I wonder if I'd get struck by lightning for that particular lie.

Galen shook his head and sat on the end of the couch, leaving space between us. "You're not the type to let people run their mouths. I said something you would have normally made my life a living hell for, but you haven't even brought it up. Is it possible that you've softened recently?"

"Let's hope not," I answered, then took a sip of the cool water. "I didn't say anything because you didn't seem fully in control there. Fuck knows I've said some weird shit when drunk. If that got held against me, well, it would suck. I can give you the same understanding, can't I?"

Galen stared at me, the weight of his gaze feeling like an elephant sitting on my chest. "I wasn't fully in control, but I still meant it."

I sighed, making a show of letting my head fall backward. "I was giving you a perfectly good out and you just refuse to take it, huh? What, do you enjoy rejection? Do you get off on humiliation? If so, I don't kink shame. I'll play along, but at least be honest with me. I don't Domme for free, you know."

"You haven't rejected me," Galen pointed out.

"Pretty sure I have."

"No, you haven't. You say it isn't right, you tell me we aren't mates, but you have never told me that you don't *want* to be my mate. That's different."

"Pretty tricky line you're trying to walk. I feel like lots of people have said that right before they find themselves with a stalking charge."

"I'm serious. If you honestly told me you didn't want me, I'd give it up. You never have, though. You always come back here, no matter what happens, so I know you're not entirely against the idea. You might have reasons that you don't think it'll work, that you're afraid, but that's not the same as rejection."

"And just how long do you plan to wait around hoping I see the light?"

Galen shrugged, then pushed his glasses back up his nose. "As long as it takes, I guess. I've been here since you became a Spirit. My life is long, and I'm fine with spending it waiting for you."

"Sounds like a cuckhold thing," I muttered.

"Maybe, or maybe you're just worth waiting for. You don't realize how amazing you are, but that doesn't make it any less true."

I gave him one hell of a side-eye. "If you think being all romantic is going to get you anything, you really don't know me."

"What, are you trying to tell me your heart doesn't beat a little faster when I say things like that?"

I could only pray he couldn't actually hear my heart or he'd know just how right he was. It was harder to lie when the truth was right there in the person's face. Still, I'd give it a try. "Please. That works on teenage girls and middle-aged virgins who read romance novels. I'm not that kind of girl."

"You say that because you don't want to be that kind of girl," Galen said. "You don't want to ask for things you don't think you'll get, so you tell yourself you don't need any of it. That's different from saying you really don't want it. So, we'll see, but I plan to do whatever I think I need to."

"What is this, a warning? Are we adversaries now? Thanks, but I have enough enemies."

"Enemies to lovers is a thing, isn't it?" He smiled, the expression bothersome. He almost looked like some eager kid ready to take on some big challenge. "But, that's not a problem for today. Like I said, I've waited years—I'll wait longer. For now, why don't you take a shower, borrow some clothes from the guest room, then we'll eat."

Was that one of the things that Galen did that won me over? Instead of pushing, he just remained steady, unwilling to get scared off or dissuaded by repeated failures. If he'd chased, I'd have run, but instead he just waited. It made me think of how a person tamed a

Jayce Carter

fearful dog, by just sitting there near them until they got used to it.

So I got up, off the couch, then thanked Galen for the suggestion.

I doubted that a shower — no matter how hot — was going to wash off the things that bothered me. My problems were far too messy to be washed off with a bit of water.

* * * *

After a shower, a change of clothing and the food Galen had left on the counter for me, I found myself sitting on Galen's porch. He'd stepped into his office to deal with pack problems, which gave me a moment to myself. Every now and then, I'd hear roars from the basement. Once, the entire house shook, but Galen had assured me that even Trey couldn't break out of those cells. They could hold anything — including a rabid Werebear.

Not that it helped my conscience at all. Him escaping wasn't my bigger problem — it was helping him.

However, I saw no path to that. Instead, I had items that Trey owned spread out before me. Given that he wasn't expected to return to his old him, the family that had fostered him had sent his personal belongings to Galen's. They'd done so so quickly, it further showed how little they gave a damn about him.

An entire life, broken down to this…

It was weird to see it all, to know that if Trey didn't get better, this was all that would be left of him. Would that be the case with me, too? When I went — which I knew could happen at any time—what would still be here for those left behind?

A house full of shiny baubles and things I'd stolen? A pretty fantastic sex toy collection? A lot of stories many people wouldn't quite believe? It was almost terrifying how little really remained at the end of one's life.

And fuck did I hate thinking that as I looked over the items from Trey. There were yearbooks, sketchbooks full of scantily clad girls—he was a pretty good artist—and random electronics. It all fit into a large box, telling me he didn't have a lot of clothes, either. Then again, he struck me as the type who never really settled in anywhere. He might have been nineteen, but he'd still lived the life of a kid who had both grown up too fast and not at all.

I picked up a backpack, opening the pockets. He hadn't had it with him during the attack, but I had no idea why he would have left it behind at his house. We weren't even entirely sure *when* he'd gotten attacked. It seemed he had left his house in the middle of the night, then was found on the side of a road. What happened between those two points only Trey and his attacker could answer.

I had no idea what I was looking for, as though some answer might come to me just by riffling through his belongings. Or maybe it was just my attempt to feel like I was doing something.

Or, fuck, maybe I was just torturing myself over this all.

In one pocket of the bag, I found a few baggies full of Cloud, both ones from Ryder and myself. The crystals had turned brown, telling me they'd passed the time they'd be good. I set them aside to dispose of later.

Below that, I found a sweater and a pair of leather gloves—never a good sign when dealing with a delinquent. At the bottom of the bag, my fingers wrapped around something hard. I pulled it out, frowning at the burner phone.

I recalled back when these brick-like prepaid phones were all a teenager could get, but now they worked to keep a person's identity a secret. In fact, they were almost exclusively used by people up to no good.

I pressed the power button on the side of the phone, and the screen lit up. Once it turned on fully, it vibrated as waiting texts came in. I scrolled through them, moving past the ones from kids looking for their fix. This wasn't the phone he'd used when talking to me…

Judging from the date of the earlier text messages, this had to be the phone he used to contact Ryder with. *Which makes it my only true line to him…*

Harrison's words came back to me, the fact he'd said the person who caused the damage could potentially repair it—at least some of it. He didn't think Ryder would do it, but what other choice did I have?

My hands trembled as I worked through the notes in the phone until I found the number I was looking for. It had no name, but instead said Sparrow. I pressed it to call the number.

"Who is this?" came a voice that made my stomach clench with a fear I hated but couldn't deny. It showed what a number Ryder had done on my mind that he could make me this fearful with his voice.

I took one deep breath to center myself, demanding my voice come out strong. "I think you know."

Silence met me for a moment before a dark chuckle came through the line. "I never expected to have *you* reach out to me."

"Well, after what you did to Trey, I couldn't help it."

"Trey? Oh, is that the bear?"

The fucker didn't even know his name? The complete lack of care had me tightening my hand around the phone in anger. He'd damaged and possibly killed a kid and he didn't even think his name important enough to take notice of?

"So you admit it?"

"I had a seller who got out of line. He was selling other's product in my territory. He knew the risks and did it anyway. Really, if this is anyone's fault, it's yours."

"I didn't attack him."

"No, but you sent him into the lion's den. You got him involved, fed him lies about how you were going to help somehow, then left him out to dry. If you hadn't come around, it never would have happened. Fuck, to think that the girl I've been looking for is the same one causing me so many problems."

I hated that he was right, that his words mirrored the fears and guilt already inside me. Still, breaking down wouldn't get what I wanted.

"That isn't what we're talking about, though, is it? I mean, you didn't call just to yell at me about some kid."

"How do you know that?"

"Well, that'd be stupid. You have enough reason to hate me all on your own. Don't you want to cry and complain to me? Tell me to leave you alone, that I'm a horrible person? Wouldn't be the first fucking time I'd heard that in my life."

"So why do you want me to say it? Why do you care?"

He paused, then let out a soft laugh that sounded far too much like Harrison. "What first drew me to you was your mind. It was different than others, like a maze I could get lost in forever. After that, I had to know more about you. I asked around, gathered information, and found out you were far more unique than I would have thought. It's funny, because what I wanted more than anything was to overthrow Harrison, to get back what was mine, and to think that you did it. It makes sense that we're bound together, doesn't it?"

"Not really. One of us is a psychopath, and even with my questionable choices, I'm pretty sure it's not me."

"Ah, I love that bite of yours. Too many people just cower for me, but not you." He said nothing else for so long, I moved the phone from my ear to look at the screen and make sure he was still there. Finally, he went on. "It started with your mind, then your background, but you know what really made me settle on having you?"

"My charming personality?"

"Harrison. I saw him arrive to pick you up when you were drunk. Do you know how he looked at you? I've seen him get everything in his life, just given the things taken from me. He took all of our power, stole it to become the head of our clan while I got left with nothing. Not a Mind but not a human, either. Stuck between worlds with no one there to save me. I planned to take everything from him—I always want to do that—but when I saw him pick you up that day, when I saw the panic on his face, I realized *you'd* leave a deeper wound than anything else."

"So all this damage, all the hurt people, the dead ones, it's all because you have a weird brother complex?"

"Everything comes back to some petty hatred," Ryder said. "But you focus on that instead of the fact that I *will* have you? I'd figure you'd worry more about yourself. You really are fucking weird."

"Not the first time someone said that, won't be the last. I'm not worried about it because I already knew that."

"So why did you call me?"

"I heard that when someone damages a person's mind like you did, that the person who did it can repair at least some of the damage."

Ryder was quiet for nearly a full moment before he responded. "That's true. It still isn't a sure thing, and the process to repair the damage isn't a pleasant or easy one, but yeah, it's true. I'm guessing this means you're going to beg me to save your little bear friend?"

"He has a name," I shoved out between gritted teeth.

"Does he anymore? Didn't think vegetables needed names."

And just like that, I regretted my choice. I hated the idea of this asshole winning anything, and the thought of sacrificing myself to *him* burned. However, I calmed myself with the fact that Trey was far more important than my hatred of Ryder.

"I want you to fix him."

"And why would I do that? His punishment's pretty fitting for going rogue."

I took one more deep breath before forcing out words that I really didn't want to say. I could hear everyone in my life yelling at me over it, telling me this was stupid, that I was making yet another dumb choice, that if I just talked to them first, we'd find another way.

The problem was that this was my fault. No one else seemed to care about Trey, writing him off as unimportant. They saw his injury and death as unfortunate but ultimately just part of life. They all saw me as more important, as though we could trade his life for mine.

I wasn't okay with that, though, since I'd put him in the position that had ended up harming him. I *had* to take responsibility and do whatever I could to make this right, no matter what that meant as far as my safety or life. Sure, I wanted to have my normal, happy life. I wanted to keep annoying people, to live my life as I wanted, but I refused to trade Trey's future for my own.

So I stopped hesitating, stopped procrastinating, and uttered the words that I knew from the start I'd say. "If you agree to fix Trey, I'll trade myself for him."

Chapter Eighteen

"This is fucking stupid," Trey said, his voice dark, a mixture of the one from him and the one from his bear. I'd noticed so far that if they were both in there, they weren't entirely separate—or sane.

"Hey, I'm not arguing."

"So *why* are we doing this? You shouldn't have me out of that cell."

"For someone who came trotting like a pup out of a crate, I really think you don't have a place to complain."

"I don't *trot*." Trey tucked his hands into his front pocket, his gaze darting around in a way that would make anyone uncomfortable. Still, the fact he'd remained in control for this long was a good sign, right? It went to show he wasn't quite as far gone as everyone thought.

At least, I'd think that, then one look at him twitchy, his hands drawn into fists would show that he wasn't nearly as in control as he might at first appear. I'd grabbed him some clothes from the supply in the guest room, since walking him around naked would probably get us arrested.

"So how'd you get him to agree to help me?" Trey asked.

"I'm very persuasive."

"Not from my experience. What, you annoy him until he agreed if it meant getting away from you?"

"Something like that." I shuffled my feet against the ground as we walked, having left Galen's car about a mile back. I'd learned that stealing modern cars wasn't that helpful since many of them could be located quickly or even disabled remotely. So even though I couldn't be tracked when driving it, the GPS could give them hints far earlier. Better to ditch the car as soon as possible. Also, given how often I'd used my sticky fingers on cars lately, I'd bet I wouldn't get much of a head start.

I'd popped the lock using my powers—ultimate lock pick extraordinaire!—then gotten Trey to follow me by telling him I had a plan. It seemed some promise of a plan could get people to agree to almost anything, at least when faced with the opposite.

We'd driven about twenty minutes away, out toward Indio, then left the car at a large outdoor mall. The walk across the street, into the less crowded area of the city had taken another twenty minutes or so.

The sun was up high, and it made me realize how little time I really spent outside. Why did I notice it now? Because I knew what was coming, because it was sort of my last outing? People got nostalgic when remembering the things they were losing out on. I guess that couldn't be helped, but I kept it to myself.

Trey had no idea the price I'd agreed to pay—would have never agreed if he'd known. That was fine, though. I wasn't doing this for approval, to make him feel obligated to me. I was doing it because it was right.

Trey had a lot of years ahead of him, and he deserved the chance to actually live them.

"How far are we going?" Trey asked.

"Not that much further. See the bright light up ahead at the end of the street? That's where we're headed." I elbowed him. "You can't be tired yet. Come on, you're young! And also a bear."

"Yeah, well, I'm not exactly at my best right now."

"You will be soon."

"And what's keeping the asshole from just killing us both?"

"Don't worry so much—I'll keep you safe."

He stopped walking and caught my arm, pulling me to a stop. It made me turn, forced to look up and into his face. The lines of stress rested there, proving he wasn't anywhere close to himself but trying to hold it all together. "I'm serious. If he finishes me off, who the fuck cares? You're putting yourself in danger, though, and for what?"

I stared back at him, refusing to look away. "Because this is all my fault."

"It's hardly your fault."

"You were selling my product because I pushed you into it. Ryder attacked you because of that. That makes it pretty clear that I'm at fault."

He shook his head. "I was doing stupid shit that would eventually catch up with me. I always knew it, was ready for the consequences of my shitty actions. I was a two-bit drug dealer playing with people who wouldn't hesitate to put me six feet under. The fact it finally caught up with me doesn't make it your fault."

I sighed, not sure how to respond. He seemed to believe what he said, that he didn't blame me, but that didn't mean I held no responsibility for it. I knew damn well I couldn't sit back and let him suffer, not if I could do something about it.

"So I don't give a fuck if he finishes me off. If it wasn't him, it'd be Galen. At least this way, that arrogant wolf doesn't get to be the one to do it. My problem is that you're putting yourself in this problem and right in Ryder's crosshairs."

"She's doing more than that." The new voice chilled me, since it was easy to recognize.

I turned to find Ryder there, at the doorway of the building he'd told me to meet him at. His lips had curled up into a smirk that turned my stomach, one that was far too perverted to be meaningless.

Trey must have recognized it as well, because he shifted himself so he stood between Ryder and me. *What a stupid, chivalrous move.* The reality was that I'd come to protect *him.* I didn't need some barely adult standing between me and anything, thank you very much.

"What are you talking about?" Trey asked, his voice low and threatening. It was funny because from first glance, it appeared that Ryder would be no threat at all to Trey.

Too bad I knew the reality.

"She didn't tell you?" Ryder laughed, the sound unnerving. "Of course she didn't. You probably wouldn't have come if she had, right?"

"She said that you agreed to try to fix what you did."

"Yeah, I did, but did she tell you *why* I'd agree?" Ryder grinned wider when Trey only furrowed his brows. "It's not like I'd do it for free. I know I scrambled your neurons pretty well, but I think you've got enough synapses to work this one through. I've been after your little girlfriend there for weeks. Her coming after me was just a happy accident that made it all a little easier. So, take it one step at a time, but what do you *think* she offered me?"

Trey let out a dark sound, one that suggested he'd figured it out. He didn't turn his back on Ryder, but he turned his head slightly, as though he wanted to ensure I could see exactly how pissed he was. "Please tell me he's kidding."

"Who's to say, really?"

"For fuck's sake, Grey. I knew you were stupid, but what the hell?"

"Wow, harsh. You could just say thank you."

"I'm not about to thank you for sacrificing yourself on some stupid fucking pipedream! There's no way that he'll actually help me—assuming he even could. So this is all for nothing—you end up hurt and for fucking what? For nothing."

"And you think instead I should have just sat back and done nothing?" I asked, then shoved his back in frustration. "Sorry, but that's not the sort of person I am. I wasn't about to just accept that you were going to die because of me, because I put you in a place to get hurt. So kindly fuck off, if you don't like my choices."

Ryder watched the back and forth as though it were some amusing television show in the background, something not worthy of his full attention but also not boring enough to stop watching.

"Oh, how about *you* fuck off," Trey responded, curling his lip up and into a snarl that bared his teeth. At the same time, the mist that signaled a change had started to envelop him, seeping out through his pores.

"And this conversation isn't over." With that, he locked his focus on Ryder, and I found myself damn glad it wasn't locked on me.

Except, the moment he did, Ryder lifted his head, the action so subtle it could have almost been missed. What *wouldn't* get missed, though, was the sudden blast of power that dug into my mind with all the finesse of an ice pick. It seemed the same wave must have hit Trey, because he dropped to his knees and clutched his head. I didn't know if it was worse for him because Ryder had targeted him or if he took it harder due to the damage already done. Maybe it was like hurting a wound not yet healed—it hurt a lot worse than a new injury.

Whatever the reason, I couldn't keep myself awake, couldn't resist that blast of power. It was the first time he'd attacked me so directly, and I had no hope of resisting before everything went black. The last thing I heard was the angry roar of a bear.

* * * *

I woke later, my head feeling like someone had poured a cupful of gravel into my skull. When I moved at all, it shifted around, battering my mind and leaving small cuts in its wake. All in all, I had to say I didn't much recommend consciousness at this point.

However, as the events that had brought me here came back to me, I knew that just going back to sleep wasn't an option, so I forced my eyes open.

The room was light, something that struck me as odd. Would have figured Ryder would know the first step to being a proper villain was dramatic lighting. He should have lowered those bitches until even the ugliest guy at a bar started to look good.

Of course, Ryder was every bit as handsome as his brother, so it wasn't like he needed it for that particular reason.

Asshole. Just one more reason to hate him — and he'd already given me plenty of those.

"You up?" At first, the sight of Ryder's face let me relax. It was stupid — I *knew* this was Ryder, after all — but my brain went back to Harrison. How was it I was close enough with him now that even the sight of him would ease me, would make me feel safe? Ryder tilted his head slightly as he crouched beside me, making me realize I was flat on the floor in the center of a rather massive shop. The large windows at the front were all covered with brown paper, as though the place were getting ready to open.

The scent told me the truth, though. It was almost shockingly sweet, a sure sign that he'd used this place to make Cloud. Part of me was surprised he'd let me come here, but then again, he was probably about done here, ready to move on to the next little hole he'd crawl into. I pushed myself up to sitting as I considered the truth behind that. Ryder expected to destroy Harrison with this. He knew he'd blame himself for my death, and he wanted to take everything from his brother. Between pouring Cloud into the community and destroying me, he'd have finished his plan then slunk off into the sunset.

Which reminded me of the other important thing, so I looked around the room. "Where's Trey?"

Ryder smiled as though he found my stupidity oddly charming. "He's over there." He gestured toward the corner of the shop, where I spotted Trey's form in a heap. "He's stronger than I would have expected. Weres usually are, but I'm used to dealing with wolves. He's the first bear I've ever met, and I'd like for it to be the last."

"Did you fix him?"

Ryder let out a loud sigh as though the conversation bored him. "I did what I could. I told you from the start that it wasn't a for sure fix, but I patched up what I could."

"What does that mean?"

"It means I did what I said I would and gave it a shot. He'll probably not have to get put down anymore, but fuck knows for sure. He's never going to be totally normal."

I curled my hands into fists, frustration eating away at me with how little he seemed to care. *He'd* done this. He'd caused this pain. Sure, I had a hand in it, but he should feel worse than I did about it, yet he spoke as though it was the last thing he gave a damn about.

And fuck if that didn't make me want to end his pathetic life. I wasn't all that bloodthirsty normally. I was far more the type who'd get petty revenge when pissed off. I'd screw with people for *years* when they made me mad, but even with the worst of the worst, I'd never really wanted to kill them.

Maybe Ryder deserved an award for that shit.

"How do I know you're telling the truth?" I asked.

"Does it matter? You've already given up your leverage, so it doesn't really matter if I'm telling you the truth or not. You can't do anything either way."

"You underestimate *just* how much of a problem I can be."

"I don't think I am. I've seen just how much you've screwed with my plans. Besides there's no reason for me not to do as you asked. It's not like I plan on killing you right away, so my life will be far easier if you behave yourself. If I screwed you over and lied from the jump, it'd just create more issues for me."

I stared at him, trying to determine the truth. I didn't trust that I could spot every lie from him, but he seemed to be telling me the truth. I had no idea if that meant Trey would recover, if he'd fixed enough to make a difference, but it was better than nothing.

"Okay," I answered. "I'll believe you."

"Good girl. Now, we need to get going."

"Where?"

"Well, we can't stay here. I've got no idea if you gave anyone else the information or if Harrison could track you somehow. I know you wouldn't have told anyone right away, but you could have left a note. It's better to leave the bear here and we go. I've finished my time in this area anyway—I've managed to take everything away from Harrison, to make sure he knows exactly how I've felt all these years. My work here is done." He rose, then grabbed a stack of clothing off one of the tables. When he tossed it, it landed in a pile before me. "Change into this. I want everything off so there's no chance of you wearing some tracker. You'll leave your jewelry, your phone, your shoes, everything."

"You're just like all men, telling me to get naked as soon as we meet," I muttered, then stared at him with one eyebrow lifted.

He rolled his eyes but turned his back on me. Him giving in surprised me, but I'd guess that was a timeline thing. If he had to fight with me, everything would take *far* longer.

"Don't think I'm going soft," Ryder said, his back still to me. "If you cause me problems, I have no problem tearing the bear's mind apart again. I just want to get this done as fast as possible."

I stripped, hating again how bright the room was. I'd rather have it dimmed so I didn't feel like I was stripping under a fucking spotlight. I ignored that, though, I went as quickly as I could. It wasn't for Ryder's comfort, but rather I wanted to be dressed again as soon as possible. I disliked the idea of being buck-ass-naked in a room with an unstable Werebear and a drugged-up Mind. Nope, that was about the time I'd prefer a full suit of armor.

However, the black sweats and sweatshirt that Ryder had given me would have to do. At least they were butt-fuck ugly. If he'd put me in some frilly bullshit, I'd have been even more annoyed. No one could see this get up and get an erection, though.

And if they could? They were into shit way too weird for me.

"Done," I said as I pulled on the second shoe. He'd left sandals for me, ones that used a single strap over the top of the foot. It meant that despite them being a tad too big, they'd work well enough. I scrambled to my feet once I'd finished.

"Keys?" he asked.

"Left them in the car."

"Phone?"

I held my hands out, unwilling to answer that one. "I don't have anything, as you can see."

His gaze moved over me, sending less than pleasant shivers through me. "How can I be sure you haven't hidden anything?"

"Yeah, thanks, but I am so not into the idea of some weird cavity search kink right now. I'll pass." Even as I said that, I lifted the hem of my sweater to show off my stomach and the waist of the sweats, trying to sell the fact.

He came closer, and the sensation of his hands patting over my clothes turned my stomach. Still, I didn't move, didn't jerk away as he checked my pockets for anything I might use against him. When satisfied, he made a slight grunt.

Was he sorry he couldn't keep this up longer? *Bastard*.

"All right, then, let's get going."

I turned toward Trey, the idea of leaving him there passed out not sitting all that well.

Ryder waved him off. "He'll wake up in a few hours all on his own. At that point, he'll see how it went, but it's not my problem anymore. Come on." Ryder wrapped his hand around my arm, his grip tight enough for my crow to object. He pulled me toward the back of the shop.

I caught one more glimpse of Trey, surprised to find his eyes open, though it didn't seem like they locked on anything. Fear bubbled inside me, but I kept quiet. It was probably just his mind recovering — at least, that's what I told myself as Ryder led me out the back.

"You're going to just leave all that stuff there?" I asked.

"Why not? Cleaning it up would be a pain. The items needed to make Cloud aren't that hard to get, save for what I need from Harrison, which I already have packed up. It's easier to just start over in a new city with all new shit. Besides, it isn't like everyone doesn't know it was me — no reason to get rid of any evidence." He opened the door to a large crew cab truck. I grabbed the 'oh shit' handle, annoyed by the lack of running boards. *Short people exist, damn it!* I

Jayce Carter

hauled myself into the truck just before he slammed the door shut.

The engine roared to life after he hit the start button, then put it into reverse. The back seat was full of boxes—evidence that he was planning on running.

I laughed, unable to help it.

Ryder peered to the side, frowning. "Not sure there's much to laugh about right now. What, have you lost your fucking mind already?"

"I was just thinking about how many times I thought about running off over the past years. When I got myself into trouble, when I was framed for murder, when things were so fucking hard, I'd always think—I could just run away. I could disappear and none of this would be my problem anymore. I think it's hilarious that when I finally do, it's with *you*." I wiped my eyes, which had started to water. "Gotta say, I never saw that one coming. Life does like to be random."

Ryder steered the large vehicle with ease, a sign that he was used to it.

It shuddered when we hit a pothole, but Ryder didn't seem to notice. The lights of the shop disappeared into the distance, the darkness growing and along with it—my anxiety. It was like now, with just the two of us, I really had to face the uncertainty of my future, the reality of my position. I'd gotten trapped here with a guy who not only wanted to hurt me, but who was looking forward to it.

And here I was, sitting in his truck, headed away from any chance of help. I was leaving behind everything in my life. I was leaving behind the life I'd created, my home, my family, the people I'd surrounded myself with. I didn't look for them to save me, but fuck if it didn't hurt that I wouldn't see them again.

I thought about how pissed Harrison would be when he learned about this, and worse, how he'd blame himself. I thought about the way Galen would rage, cursing me not coming to him. I could only picture the retribution Kelvin would rain down on Ryder—and I was pretty sure that asshole would track down Ryder all on his own. Was it some sort of petty revenge that I felt sure Ryder would pay for what he'd done?

Too bad it would be too late to actually do me any good, with me being six feet under by that point.

Hopefully. Sure, dying wasn't included in my best-case scenario usually, but considering the other choice? Thinking back to how it had felt when Ryder had dug through my brain before? I really thought dead might have been a better option.

"Do you really hate Harrison this much?" I asked.

Ryder's hands tightened on the steering wheel. "Wouldn't you? What if you knew someone who stole everything from you? I was born to powerful parents as well—I should have become Clan head. Instead, he took it all from me. I have to live every day seeing him, hearing all about him, knowing that I should have gotten that all. Do you know what that feels like?"

I thought back to the person who had changed my entire life. I recalled the way I'd hated him some of the time for it. "I was there, once."

"Oh, yeah?"

I nodded, then stared out the window as I spoke. "Yep. I wasn't born like this, you know? I had a life, plans. They weren't *good* exactly, but they were mine. Then someone showed up, and they changed that all.

They didn't ask my opinion, didn't give me an option, just turned me into *this*."

Ryder frowned, as though trying to get a handle on our conversation. "So you should get how that changes a person. Don't you want to make them pay? You might not get your old life back, but you've got to want to do something so they feel the same pain?"

I hated that I couldn't fully deny his words. How many times had I cursed *him,* had I lashed out because of everything I'd lost, all the things I'd suffered. "There was a time when I thought that, too," I admitted softly. "When it first happened, when I first changed, I was so angry. All I could see was everything I'd lost. I've always been difficult, but along with that anger? I just couldn't help it."

"So how can you blame me for what I'm doing?"

"Because I grew up. I look around me now and, well, it's not so bad. Is my life the one I thought I'd have? Fuck, no. I thought I'd have more money, more orgasms and far fewer annoying men in my life. That's not what happened, though. By clinging onto what I thought I was supposed to have, it only dragged me down, it only made me angry. Now, though, when I see what my life is like, it isn't that bad. I have friends, I have family, I have things that I would have never had if that hadn't happened."

"Sounds a lot like putting lipstick on a pig."

"Maybe it is, but if you have to kiss that pig, you can't tell me lipstick won't help. Look, we all end up in the position we end up in. You can stomp your feet and act like a victim or you can just fucking get on with it. Instead of you still getting a good life, you ruin the rest of your days yourself. I'm a huge fan of self-sabotage, but is that *really* what you want?"

Ryder pressed his lips together, his gaze hard. Clearly, the boy didn't much like getting a taste of reality. Then again, I'd found a lot of Minds tended to not like arguments since they were so used to being able to influence those around them. "You don't understand," he said finally, his tone was lower than before. "You can't understand. You were turned into something more, not something less. Harrison was taken for training to become the next Clan leader. Me? I got shipped off to a human boarding school because they saw no use for me. I didn't even get to be raised with my family because of Harrison. I wasn't welcomed in the Spirit world, but I wasn't human, either. I became a person unwanted everywhere. You got a second world—I lost mine. We are not the same."

I shook my head. "You're just comfortable in your anger. You feel safe there, hating everyone, blaming Harrison for everything. Life is a lot simpler when you're never at fault for anything, isn't it? When you're able to point your finger and make it all someone else's problem? That's the coward's way, and I won't pretend like I haven't done it a hundred fucking times myself, but at least I can admit it. I don't hurt others just because it makes my life easier."

"You really are stupid, aren't you? Calling me a coward when I'm in charge of you?"

I laughed, the sound bouncing off the interior of the truck cab. "You're going to do what you want to do with me. I know I don't have long left—why the fuck would I spend it kissing your ass? *Please*, bitch. If I'm going to kiss a man's ass, it'll be one who's a lot fucking better than you."

I barely got the words out before pain echoed through my skull, a blast of power that was sickeningly familiar. It hit me so fast, I nearly missed Ryder's words. "You don't seem to understand your position, but you will. I'll take your mind apart bit by bit until you realize who the better man *really* is."

"It'll always be Harrison," I forced past my lips despite the pain. "He isn't better because of his power, but because he doesn't *abuse* that power!" I turned my face from his, to look out of the windshield, the darkness of the back road lit only by the glow of Ryder's headlights. I still had no idea where we were headed, but I had a sinking suspicion we wouldn't make it that far.

Good riddance.

There, in the center of the headlights, something appeared. I couldn't make sense of the dark shape at first, but Ryder must have noticed it as well. He slammed the brakes, sending me forward, catching myself on the dashboard. The pain in my head, at least, disappeared. It seemed Ryder had bigger problems to deal with.

The truck came to a hard stop, metal groaning around us. I looked forward, where golden eyes met mine.

Trey?

How the fuck had he gotten here? His huge paws were against the hood of the truck, the metal dented to show that between him and a truck, he easily won. He had his teeth bared, and I really couldn't tell if he was any saner than he'd been before.

"Fuck," Ryder muttered, and a glance toward him showed red streaking down his face. He must have hit his head on the steering wheel. As he peered out of the windshield, spotting Trey, he narrowed his eyes, a sure sign that he planned to undo any work he'd done to fix him.

Not on my watch, asshole.

I pressed my back against the door and brought my legs up, then kicked as hard as I could, aiming for Ryder's head. I made myself a nuisance for him, which was enough to distract him from focusing on Trey.

I'd sacrificed enough — I wasn't going to let that go to waste by allowing Trey to get brain-fucked now.

Ryder turned his attention on me, grabbing my ankle just as I went to kick him again. Before he could do anything else, the door behind me opened, and I toppled backward. I expected to hit the ground, but to my amazement, that didn't happen. Instead, someone caught me.

I craned my neck to find Harrison there, relief all over his perfectly crafted face as he stared at me. However, as though all he needed was to find out I was okay, he tore his gaze away from me and focused instead on Ryder.

And fuck if that wasn't one nasty look. I didn't see it much from Harrison, but that expression held so much anger. It seemed he'd hit a point where he wasn't as able to control himself anymore.

Ryder stared back, the two of them looking so damn similar that it threw me. How could two people be so much the same, even share DNA, and yet end up entirely different?

Ryder's door opened, and Trey reached in — still fully shifted — and yanked him out.

Harrison helped me backward, until I got my feet under me.

"Trey —" I started to say, pulling away to ensure Ryder didn't attack him again.

"He can't do anything, not while I'm here," Harrison assured me. "My powers are far stronger than his, so with me here, even his Cloud isn't enough to overcome."

His words reassured me, and before I knew what happened, my knees gave out. Harrison's hands were still on me, which kept me upright yet again. I let him hold me, thrown by the fact that I'd just been ready to die but now…it didn't seem that would happen. I'd just been tumbling over a cliff, certain of my own end, but now I had Harrison's arms around me.

"How are you here?" I asked. "You can't track me."

"Galen called me and told me the location of the car. I went there and sensed Trey nearby. I found him at the shop and woke him."

"But we aren't anywhere close to there anymore, and you can't find me or Ryder."

Harrison shifted me so I turned, facing him. He stroked his fingers over my cheek, the touch so gentle it made my chest ache. "Bears have a fantastic sense of smell. He was able to track Ryder by scent." He peered down at me, noting the changed clothing, stared hard at my face—which I must have hit on the dashboard when the truck came to such an abrupt stop. "You were hurt again because of me."

"Not because of you. I made the choice to come here, to save Trey. I couldn't let him get killed when I could stop it."

"Trust me, you are not the only one who will have to deal with that," Harrison said. "You'll have to answer that to a few people. I suspect Galen will get here soon, and Kelvin as well. I doubt they will find your penchant for self-sacrifice to be as charming as you think it is."

I sighed, thinking about facing off against *those two* after everything else. No doubt they'd be pissed, but what other options did I have?

I turned to find Trey coming closer, easily holding the much smaller Ryder by the back of his neck. They got to just in front of us, and I was really damn happy to have the huge Trey there. Ryder had appeared angry before, but it was nothing compared to his look right now. He stared at the way Harrison touched me, an anger in his expression that was terrifying.

I'd learned that emotion that deep could twist people, could make them do things that would be unimaginable at any other time. In other words? It could push a person to things even I didn't want to think about.

"This is *over*," Harrison said, speaking to Ryder. "I have tried to help you, tried to protect you for my entire life. I ignored when you came after me, when you targeted me, but you have now gone too far. I will *not* ignore your actions when they endanger those I care for."

"Please," Ryder snapped back. "You're fucking loving this. You love when you get to be the hero, when you get to be the big man over me."

"You think that because you see the world as you and everyone else against you. You have no idea how to exist in a community, how to interact with others without dominating them. You are fearful of others, and due to that, you go straight to hatred. You want to harm others before they harm you, and you don't care if they were going to at all."

Ryder laughed, the sound lacking any genuine sense of sanity. "So what now? You'll kill me? Let's not play stupid games like that—you don't have it in you to do that. You feel too guilty about everything you stole from me. Are you going to take my life, too?" He tossed the question out like a challenge, and no matter how much I knew Ryder deserved exactly that, I also suspected Harrison wouldn't.

"No," Harrison said, his voice softer. "But I will have you locked up so you can't hurt anyone again. You can live your life in isolation, so you don't have the chance to carry on as you have been."

I sighed, wanting to tell him he was an idiot, but knowing better than to do so. This was Harrison's choice, and I understood how he wouldn't want to be the one to kill his own brother. If I pushed him into it, if I made him do that, he'd only come to resent me for it later. At the end of the day, this had to be his choice.

His wrong fucking choice…

Except, before I could say anything else, a startling fear overcame me, and right on its heels — a pain in my head. I looked toward Ryder, familiar enough with his tricks to identify it immediately. Whatever he'd done must have surprised everyone, because Trey had dropped to his knees and even Harrison stumbled. Ryder took his new freedom to come forward, his hand out. I couldn't move, couldn't do anything to stop what happened as Ryder shoved his palm against Harrison's face.

At first, I thought maybe he was trying to smother him, until he pulled back and I spotted the familiar clear powder on his palm. Worse, more of it rested on Harrison's face.

Harrison blinked, stumbling and catching himself on the side of the truck.

"Harrison?" I asked, unsure what to say.

He looked up at me, but his eyes held a strange vacancy, as though he weren't truly awake.

Ryder started to laugh, moving backward. Trey appeared unconscious in the dirt.

"What did you do?" I asked.

Ryder gestured toward his brother. "What does it look like? You know, in all the time he made Cloud for me, all our attempts, he never took it. Not once. He knew it would increase his power, that it would take away that pesky sense of responsibility he had, but he still never took it. I wonder what the effects will be."

"Maybe it'll be that he tears your mind apart, you fucking idiot," I shouted.

"I doubt that. Look where his eyes are locked. You're way too interesting for him to take notice of anything else. I'd wanted to fuck you up myself, but maybe this is better. Harrison will sober up sometime tomorrow and he'll have to live with what he does to you."

"He would never—" I started to say, but a sudden pain shot through my temples.

It wasn't the same as when Ryder. In fact, it made Ryder feel like some ham-fisted virgin trying to figure out where a girl's clit was. Harrison, on the other hand, sliced through any defenses I had with such speed and dexterity that it terrified me. It went to show that no matter how much he tried to hide his power, how much he tried to never scare another person, never do things they wouldn't want, he was more than capable of it.

I managed to look back at Harrison for a moment before I felt him fully take over my mind.

Fuck. This didn't look good.

* * * *

The world had disappeared around me so I existed in some void with only Harrison across from me. He stared at me, his expression different from the one I'd grown used to. He seemed distant, not himself.

"You can resist this," I said when the silence became too much. The pain had lessened, but I was still fully aware that he was there, inside my mind, and that he could tear me apart from the inside easily.

"But why would I?" Harrison tilted his head but came no closer. "Do you know how hard I work to control myself? All my life, my powers have been enough to affect others even when I try not to, even when I exhaust myself attempting to hold it back. Day in and day out, I have to keep myself from doing what comes natural to me."

"That's because you don't want to hurt people," I said, trying to break through to him, past the Cloud, past the madness that created.

He shook his head. "You don't understand. You can't. You have no idea the pressure on me to resist or the drive inside me to taste the minds of those around me. It is like constantly walking through a buffet and not being allowed to sample anything. You steal—I saw your home, the countless shiny baubles you'd taken to please that other side of you, the crow inside you that demands that. However, me? I'm expected to always resist, to never give in, to be perfect."

I forced myself to walk closer to him, hoping that by seeing me more clearly, I might shake him back awake. It wasn't like I suspected this fake distance between us made a bit of difference when it came to his ability to harm me. "It's not about being perfect. You just know the man you want to be. Ryder tried to tell me that he was better than you, but I told him that was bullshit.

You wake up every day and want to do more for those around you. You want to protect others, want to keep them from getting hurt. You are a better man than he could ever be."

Harrison let out a low groan, as though he loathed that I had to say such a thing. "Will you hate me, then? I don't think I can resist, so will you hate me later for what I'm about to do?"

"Can't you resist it?" My voice trembled.

His answer was his expression, one mixed with both excitement and anguish, as though the Cloud fought with his conscious and he was sure the Cloud would win. No, he couldn't resist. The best I could hope for was Trey to wake up, for Galen or Kelvin to arrive, which meant the most important thing was to survive this.

It meant when he came forward the last few steps that separated us and placed his hands on my cheeks, when the pressure in my mind increased, I forced myself not to fight it. Sure, I tended to much prefer my privacy. My crow pecked at the inside of my skull, hating the idea of anyone taking anything from me — especially my thoughts, my memories. Still, I didn't fight, didn't resist it at all. I understood that resisting would only make the damage worse.

And as weird as it sounded, my biggest fear was Harrison when he woke from this drug later, when he saw what he'd done. If I fought this, I'd be dead, but him? He'd have to live with it. That felt like letting Ryder win, and I was too petty a bitch for that.

So I tried to ignore the pain when he slipped deeper into my mind, the touch of him against my thoughts so much more personal than when we'd had sex. It was a whole different level of intimacy that I honestly never fucking wanted. Still, I kept myself relaxed.

The first thought that popped open, the memory that swarmed through me wasn't one like Ryder had pried from me. He'd wanted the painful ones, the ones I'd hated. Harrison, instead, woke a memory of a family dinner. I couldn't even recall exactly when it had happened, only that it was before I'd changed.

I saw myself, a few years younger, and my family all around the table at my mom's house. My siblings were still underaged, looking so young and innocent, but me?

I almost laughed at the troublemaker I appeared. Instead of my now normal blue hair, I'd had the locks dyed a bright red. I think I'd been kicked out of an apartment after a dustup with a neighbor, and my mom had let me spend a few nights there to gather myself.

"I've never had a family dinner." Harrison's voice made me turn to find him behind me, his gaze locked on the table. "It looks nice."

At least he sounded a bit less…crazy.

"We did them a lot. Once my brother and sister moved out, they became a little less often, but we still do them at least once a month. Maybe you'll come with me next time."

"I doubt your brother would like that."

"He never likes the men I bring to dinner." I frowned. "Why this memory?"

"It was easy to access. I know you're trying to give me space, to not resist, and I'm trying, too. If you were anyone other than you, I would have turned your mind to nothing but sludge already. Only you could get me to hold back, even with the Cloud."

"That's oddly terrifying and romantic, which I'm pretty sure is the only type of romantic I'm willing to accept."

Harrison let out a noise full of pain before clutching his head. I didn't need to ask why, because someone else suddenly stood in the room as well.

Ryder.

"I can't believe I underestimated you," he said, looking my way with an expression that didn't bother to hide any of his disgust. "I thought that Cloud would be enough to deal with Harrison and you, but imagine my surprise when I figure out that somehow, you got through to him."

"I don't want to hurt her," Harrison said, his voice full of pain. "I don't want to cause any harm to her."

"Of course you do—you just resist it. I know you, because we're so much alike. You want to hurt her, to dig into her thoughts and own them all for yourself. You want to taste every memory of hers, to roll around in her brain. It doesn't matter how well you think you know a person, there's no way to get closer, to own them more than to dig into their mind, into every piece of them that they try to hide from the world. You hide from it all you want, you pretend that you're somehow different, but I know the truth. You see, no matter how little time we spent together, you and I are *exactly* the same. You just won the lottery, and I lost it. But if anyone understands the darkness inside you, it's me. You don't need to hide it, not from me."

Harrison shook his head, his hands still clutching tightly. Even though he denied it, I could see the truth in his face. He did want to hurt me, at least in this moment. It might have been the Cloud along with the years of self-restraint snapping, but he wanted to crawl through my head, damage be damned.

"You see," Ryder said, this time to me, "Harrison might act high and mighty, but at the end of the day, he's a scared little boy. We didn't spend much time together as kids, but we did a few times. Once, I got to come stay where he was being trained for a weekend. I guess they thought it would be good for him to have me there. It was pretty fucking cruel to make me witness everything I didn't get access to, but what did they care about me? The thing is, I got to see the *real* Harrison then. He was nothing but a little boy trying to live up to the expectations of others, knowing he'd never manage it. I knew then that I should have been the one to get the powers, that I could have ruled better. I'm stronger than he is. He's the same now, too, just a kid trying to pretend to be an adult."

I went over and shoved Ryder, my helplessness turning to anger. "I told you before and I meant it. You will *never* be half the man he is!"

Ryder smirked. "I hope you think that when he rips you to pieces. I wish I could have done it, but I'll enjoy watching it just as much."

The room disappeared, and instead, I found myself in another memory. The car where I had my first real conversation with Harrison? After he'd saved me when I'd been in my crow form? As quickly as it happened, it changed again. Sparks of my life flashed by so fast that I couldn't keep track. A dull throbbing in my head was impossible to ignore.

"You see," Ryder said, whispering into my ear, "He will always pick me. He could kill me now if he wanted to, but he won't. He feels too guilty, like if he can just fix me, then everything is okay. It doesn't matter how much he cares about you, he will *never* kill me—not even to save you."

I cried out as the pressure in my mind grew, as I struggled to stay conscious in some form. Everything swirled around me, the pain growing.

Until it slowed for just a moment, as if between blinks it had stuttered. Across the space, in the darkness, I spotted a figure.

Kelvin? It made no sense, since we were in my memories, my thoughts, and only a Mind could enter there. I was sure of it, though. I wouldn't ever *not* recognize Kelvin, especially with those bright eyes. He offered me a mocking smile as though to kick me in the ass.

What the fuck was I doing? I wasn't the type to give up, to give in, to accept bullshit.

This was *my* mind, for fuck's sake. It was a twisted, broken place, but it was mine. As the world twisted around me, as everything became harder and harder to keep up with, I focused, taking us back to that first memory of the family dinner. It took form around us, younger me sitting there in the chair almost like she could see me.

"What the fuck?" Ryder asked, his eyes wider, as though he'd figured out something had changed.

I ignored his question though and reached toward the table, wrapping my fingers around my goal. "You made one big fucking mistake," I said. "You know that Harrison is too noble to kill you, but you forgot one thing."

I approached Ryder, ignoring Harrison, ignoring the room, ignoring everything other than the man currently in my sights.

"And what's that?"

I tightened my grasp around my weapon. "That I'm not a good person like he is." I drove the steak knife from the table up and into Ryder, aiming it to slip beneath his ribs. After sinking it in, I twisted it, needing to do as much damage as possible.

Ryder reached out and grasped my wrist, his expression full of shock. It seemed he really hadn't realized what I was capable of to protect those I cared about. I didn't love the idea of ending a life, but I'd do it in a heartbeat if needed.

"You…" he said, the one word broken.

"You're right—Harrison would never hurt you, but I'm not him. If it takes me ending you to protect him, I'll carry that weight."

He let out a laugh, one full of pain. "This wasn't how I thought this would go, but it's not that bad. I still fucked Harrison over."

"No, you didn't. I protected him."

"And you think that he's going to thank you for it? You think he'll forgive himself for what he did to you? That he'll thank you for killing the brother he's been trying to save?" He laughed, the sound breathless and confident.

I turned my head to find Harrison staring at us. Had this woken him? Broken the hold the Cloud had on him? I took a step toward him, but he backed away. The rejection hit me hard, Ryder's words still ringing in my head.

I opened my mouth to say something, anything, but I didn't get the chance. Instead, Harrison collapsed, and when he did, the false world around me dissolved.

"She's coming around," came a voice I instinctually turned toward. It was familiar and safe and fuck if I didn't need that right about now.

I forced my eyes open to find Kelvin there, my head in his lap, with Galen beside me.

"Harrison," I said, scrambling up only to have Kelvin hold me tighter so I couldn't go anywhere.

"He's breathing. What the fuck happened, Grey?"

And fuck, I really didn't want to tell this story...

* * * *

Hours later, I was back home. It was strange how my house didn't feel like mine anymore. The world hard changed too much.

No, that wasn't right. I'd changed too much.

"You okay?"

I nodded and forced myself to smile even if I didn't feel like it as I turned around to face Kelvin. "Yep. Of course."

He sighed, a half-smile on his lips. He saw right through the attempt, didn't he? Instead of calling me on it, he wrapped his arms around me and pulled me against his chest. I breathed in the scent, one I used to hate. Was it because of our bond? Had that changed it? I didn't know, but it didn't matter right then, either. All I knew for sure was I needed to feel like things were steady.

The way Harrison had looked at me still haunted me, that look of betrayal, Ryder's words. I'd done it to save him, but I might have lost him at the same time.

"It'll be okay," Kelvin said.

"How do you know that?" I asked. "How can you be so sure?"

He pulled back enough to look down at me. "Because I know you. You are an annoying little pest who never gives up—but that's one of your strong suits. I know none of this went the way you wanted it to, but you'll get through it. You'll figure out a way to make it okay, because if anyone could, it would be you." He leaned in and pressed a kiss to my forehead, the touch achingly sweet. It made me realize just how tired I really was.

And instead of fighting it, I wrapped my arms around him and held on tight.

I'd have plenty of other things to deal with later. My life was still a fucking mess, after all. I was still a seat on the Council, I had a job to worry about, a werewolf who insisted I become his mate, a vampire who had made me his thrall and one pissed-off Mind who might just hate me now.

I'd won, right? I mean, we'd dealt with the Cloud dealer, we'd found my stalker and we'd come out on top. Trey was healing—so far as I knew. He had to live with Galen for safety, and he certainly wasn't entirely sane, but who amongst us was? Harrison and I had gotten closer, learned to rely on each other, had some mind-blowing sex, but now?

It felt like Harrison was light years away. He'd woken up—Ignis had called me to let me know—but he'd yet to reach out to me. And I, being a coward, hadn't tried either.

I was supposed to be happy, wasn't I? We'd succeeded even when it didn't seem possible.

However, as I wrapped my arms around Kelvin, as I let him support me because I just couldn't bear the weight of even my own body, I knew the truth.

Everyone was a little bit out of their flocking minds at the end of the day.

Epilogue

I looked around the empty council room, my stomach somewhere in my throat. Even if I knew that wasn't physically possibly, it sure as fuck felt that way.

"We could have pushed this back another week." Ruben came to stand beside me, the bastard somehow looking entirely at ease here. Then again, this was home field advantage for him, wasn't it?

"I have no idea what you're talking about." I crossed my arms, more than willing to pretend that nothing was bothering me.

Of course, Ruben knew. The bastard seemed to know everything, so the events that happened that night, everything with Harrison and Ryder, Ruben somehow knew it all. He wasn't the type to come right out and talk to me about it, to ask me how I was feeling—neither of us were that type—so instead we pussy-footed around the truth.

Which was that even after almost a week, I'd yet to hear from Harrison. I'd been ghosted enough times in my life to see it coming.

So when I heard that the monthly council meeting had been called — and I was expected to attend — I said yes. Could I have had Ruben move it? Probably, but why?

I had a feeling that anything that bothered me now would bother me in another week as well. None of that would resolve, so why put it off?

"Is everyone coming?" I asked to change the topic.

Ruben sighed but nodded. "As far as I am aware, yes. This will be your first official meeting, but I don't expect anything will be too bothersome for you. You will most likely be able to simply sit there and remain silent."

"If you think I can do that, you clearly don't know me that well." I smirked as I sat in the chair in front of the blue crystal, the place set out for me.

Ruben opened his mouth to say something back, but the opening of the door shut him up before he could.

Galen walked in, his expression softening when he spotted me. I smiled back at him while he went to his seat. Next came Kelvin, who had the nerve to come over and steal a kiss before taking his seat, the show off.

But fuck if it didn't feel nice... We were just about at the point where I'd need him to bite me again, and I hadn't started to think about how to handle that. I had a feeling Harrison wasn't interested in helping out there again.

Next came Porter, making me realize it had been a while since I'd seen him. Then again, he behaved like a skittish deer, someone that lived his own life and cared little for being a part of others'. Even still, he nodded my way despite ignoring everyone else.

Which left just one person…

My stomach tightened when the door opened one last time, and I sat up, unsure what to say but certain I needed to say *something*. Except it wasn't Harrison who walked in. Instead, it was Beth, dressed up and looking every bit the part of Council Head.

A line appeared between Ruben's brows, telling me he hadn't known about this, either. "I was under the impression Harrison would be here."

Beth looked his way and gave one hell of a political smile. "Something came up and he was unable to attend. He sent me in his stead."

Ruben pressed his lips together, then gestured toward the Mind seat.

I guess Harrison can't even stand the idea of seeing me. I stared down at my lap, the pain greater than I would have expected. Somehow, I'd held out hope that he'd forgiven me, that if we could just see each other, just speak, we could get past this. That night had been hard on us both, but I wanted to move past it.

It seemed he didn't.

"Thank you all for coming," Ruben said, taking his spot, standing at the head of the table, his voice strong. I had to admit, he looked rather stunning the way he took control of a room full of powerful Spirits like that. He didn't so much as flinch when dealing with such strong personalities. He started to go over the list of issues they were dealing with, the new problems, the resolved issues.

I zoned out partway through because, fuck it, I really didn't care. The entire point of the council was to keep the peace between the clans, and given my position as a clan of one, none of it really had anything to do with me. They could fight out every little problem between them all on their own while I imagined what underwear each person was wearing. It was a good way to pass the time, at least.

Beth was probably in something cute and practical. Porter was likely in boxers, because I couldn't imagine him caring much about such things. Kelvin was probably not wearing anything, the kinky bastard. He looked my way, lifting his eyebrow and smirking as though he could tell I was thinking something filthy.

I rolled my eyes and kept going with my little game. Galen would be in boxer briefs, no question about that. Ruben? I dropped my gaze toward his waist, trying to picture what was beneath those shockingly tempting black slacks. I decided to imagine briefs, partly because it was fun to picture something snug and that didn't leave much to the imagination.

"Grey?" Ruben said, startling me.

"A thong!" I yelled back, then frowned as I realized how little that would mean to anyone else. Worse, no one seemed even startled about the weird statement, as though they all expected that nonsense from me.

"Anyway"—Ruben pushed forward—"what do you think?"

"Clearly, she thinks thong," Kelvin said. "You're as useful as ever, Grey."

Ruben shot Kelvin a sharp look, then went back to me. "We were talking about the influx of Weres—especially strays. Does your clan have any opinions on the matter?"

"Oh. Not really? I mean, do you want me to adopt a few or something?"

Galen choked, then patted his chest as though trying to fix his erratic breathing.

"So the Chaos clan stands mutes," Ruben said, which was probably a much more appropriate way of saying what I had. "Then we will leave the issue to the Weres for now—however, if you cannot bring this under control, if stray Weres continue to cause problems for the other clans and the humans, the Were Clan will be held responsible for it."

Galen nodded, but a tension in his face suggested this issue was far from over.

After that, the meeting wrapped up quickly.

At the end of the meeting, once Ruben had closed it, I rushed over to Beth. "Harrison didn't come?"

She said nothing back, her poker face impressive. After a moment, she shook her head. "No, as I said, something came up."

"Don't bullshit a bullshitter," I muttered softly. "He just didn't want to see me, right?"

She swallowed hard, the answer clear in that one tiny action. Still, she was a professional, and answered with the same careful expression as before. "As I said, he simply had other matters to attend to. If you'll excuse me." She nodded respectfully before walking out, leaving me there, staring at her back.

"Two vampires," Kelvin said.

"I doubt you were close with them," Galen snapped back.

I turned to find the two men speaking in the corner of their room, but their deep voices carried. Even more than their voices, the threat there.

"No fights in the council room," I said as I slid between them. "I *just* got a chair. Let's not ruin it, hmm?"

Galen offered me a bored look, then darted his gaze to Kelvin's. "The council room also isn't the place for such displays as earlier."

"What? Am I not allowed to offer my thrall a bit of affection? Perhaps you should find yourself a mate so you can enjoy such benefits?" Kelvin spoke with such false sweetness in his voice, he could have sent a diabetic into a coma.

"You're lucky she still needs you," Galen snapped.

"What are thralls good for if not shields?" He stayed behind me as though he'd ever actually let me protect him. "Well, I suppose they are good for a few other things."

At that, I threw my arms up. "Fine, you can both fuck off." I stepped out from between them and headed toward Ruben.

"Grey," they both said, their tones so similar I had to fight a laugh.

"Nope. I'm out. Maybe if you both fuck one another you'll get over this whole rivalry thing, because neither of you are fucking me until you work it out." I slid my arm through the crook of Ruben's, pulling him to get him going.

"What if they really do have sex? In my council room…"

I shrugged. "Well, I'm not cleaning up the mess."

And just like that, I felt like no matter how crazy my life got, how lost I felt, how unsure I was about my path, things would be okay.

If my biggest worry was cleaning up after a little sword-crossing fun?

I'll be just fine.

Want to see more from this author?
Here's a taster for you to enjoy!

Flocking It Up:
Flock Around and Find Out
Jayce Carter

Excerpt

Sex toys got the job done, but at times like this, I had to admit an actual cock—and the man attached to it—could still prove himself useful.

I didn't like giving blood, but somehow the sensation of fangs in my skin never failed to get me off. Did I have some weird kink?

If so, I really didn't give a fuck, at least not right now. It felt too damn good to care. And from the grinding of a hard cock against my back when he rolled his hips, I had to guess that Kelvin felt exactly the same.

He had his lips latched on my throat, the suction rushing shivers through my body, the swallowing sound far sexier than it had any right to be.

I arched backward, losing myself in so many competing sensations. It was always like this, though—always overwhelming and too much and not enough at once. No matter how many times we found ourselves like this, our bodies intertwined, our breaths a tangled, panting mess, it never failed to surprise me just how deeply I felt every last touch of his.

Kelvin withdrew his fangs and licked across my neck, his saliva cool against my skin, a way of showing that he'd sealed the wound. It soothed the pain from the bite, but it didn't douse the flames inside me. If anything, it made me want him more.

My brain was a mess, nothing but need and desire and heat. I dug my nails into his back, through his shirt, desperate to yank the fabric from him. I wanted him bare to me, without a stitch hiding him.

"Please," I begged, ragged and broken. Any other time, my wanton pleas would have humiliated me, but right now, I only knew what I wanted. Nothing else mattered.

He grasped my chin and kissed me, his tongue still coated in blood, but I didn't give a fuck. I sought the warmth of his mouth, teased his agile tongue, anything to have just a little more.

"This is enough." The words came out rough through his panting breaths. They made me lightheaded, made me want to hear him say far filthier things in that same tone of voice.

Except, I knew better. Even as far gone as I felt, I knew better. This was his line, the one he always drew.

I'm not the sort of girl who has to rely on a reach-around. It was great when I got one, don't get me wrong, but if I didn't? I could handle my own shit just fine.

So I reached down, between our bodies, and slipped my hand beneath my skirt. The flowy fabric hadn't been the reason I'd picked this outfit, but it sure proved a benefit. I snaked my fingers into the crotch of my panties to find my already soaked cunt.

It reminded me that it had been far too long since I'd had someone stretch me just right, since I'd experienced that slight burn when a hard cock filled me. I had plenty of toys, but they just didn't do the job the same way.

It hadn't been for weeks, not since...

A momentary vision of Harrison hit me, and I shoved it away.

I'd be damned if that mess fucked with my orgasm. It had hung around in my head for far too long, ruining my mood time and time again—I wasn't about to let it ruin this, too.

"You're killing me," Kelvin whispered, his words harsh, but he didn't stop me. "How do you expect me to hold back when you do things like this?"

"So don't hold back." I nipped his full bottom lip, biting it in retaliation for him denying me what I wanted.

"I already told you. If you want me, you have to tell me *before* I bite you. I won't do it, not when my bite has already fucked with your head."

Which he had told me, and somehow, he'd stuck to it no matter the temptation. No matter what I did, how badly I wanted him, he *never* crossed that line. He never touched me beyond the needed bite, the contact to make sure I didn't go through withdrawal from the venom in his bite.

It really was annoying how he could hold himself back and I had all but zero control.

Pathetic.

Thankfully, that remained at the back of my mind, hidden behind the waves of want that filled me. I teased my clit, the hardened nub begging for attention.

What wouldn't I give to feel Kelvin's lips on it?

I pulled back enough to stare at his mouth, the fantasy so real and reality so close but unattainable.

"I can't," he whispered back, upset and thin. "You have no idea how much I want to push you back, spread your thighs, and lick you until you scream, Grey, but I can't."

"Why not?"

"I've already told you why — because I've already seen you stare at me like you hate me. I can't have that again. I'll wait until you're sure you want it, that you want me. Until then? I'll just suffer." He dropped his gaze, but the folds of my skirt hid the way my fingers teased my slit. "Fuck, am I suffering... This is why I don't usually do noble, because it's unpleasant. A hedonist like myself prefers enjoying life to the fullest."

"So why are you resisting?"

He lifted his gaze to mine, staring into my eyes in a way that shook loose my thoughts, that felt far more personal than the intimate way we sat, than anything else we'd done. "Because you're about the only thing in the world worth doing this right for."

And just like that, the asshole got me off with that declaration like I was some love-struck virgin.

This really is sad.

* * * *

Why was dressing in front of someone so much more embarrassing than undressing? I could strip down and not think twice about it, but somehow, standing here, in the center of the hotel room, straightening all my clothes, felt like being on full display.

Kelvin made it no easier, sitting in the chair in front of the desk, staring right at me.

"We don't have to meet at places like this." He gestured at the hotel room.

"What? You think I'm going to invite you over to my house like some guest?"

He didn't react, and that almost made me feel worse. Had he pretended to be hurt, it would have been a sign the words hadn't hit. Him not snarking back suggested they'd stung.

"You could come to my place."

"Thanks, but I'll pass. My last time at your place wasn't that pleasant." I recalled staying there, with him, after I'd gotten framed for a murder I for sure didn't commit. It hadn't been a good time.

He pressed his lips together, then sighed. "I could rent a place, if you'd prefer."

The idea had me shaking my head. My headache and body pains had disappeared due to Kelvin's bite, but the muscles in the back of my neck tightened, suggesting one was still coming.

"You want to play house?"

"It doesn't have to be playing house."

"It would be, though. We aren't anything like that."

"Why can't we be? I know you're angry still. I know you aren't happy about how things have gone, but can't we get past that? I've come to help you every time you've called for months, but you still can't even consider something more between us?" He stared straight at me, not breaking eye contact, not giving me a moment of space to think.

And it was *far* more terrifying than if he had snarled and shown his fangs. Kelvin mad—that I could take. I could handle him yelling and cursing at me, wouldn't so much as flinch at that.

This, though? A moment of him being so fucking vulnerable?

Fuck this.

He let out a broken laugh, one dark and desperate. "I guess I put myself in this position. This is the finding out after fucking around, isn't it?" He got to his feet, then went to the closet and took his jacket out, sliding it on and buttoning the front.

"That's it?"

"I've waited this long. I have little choice but to continue until you understand. Are you ready to go?"

"I don't need an escort."

"I've never been much of a gentleman, but I'm not about to let you walk out of a hotel room alone that we used together."

And fuck, how was I supposed to argue with that?

I didn't have an answer, which was exactly why, fifteen minutes later, I found myself in the lobby of the hotel, Kelvin to my side.

The reason was obvious. No one came to a hotel in pairs at this hour for anything other than sex. With him all dressed in his suit, it probably appeared he was cheating on his wife, meeting some girl in the middle of the workday.

In reality, the middle of the day meant fewer chances that we were seen by any other vampires, and this place had a good underground garage to use. That had been his only real requirement, though he'd wanted to pick far nicer amenities than I did.

I would have been fine with something that charged by the house, since it wasn't like I was planning to spend all that much time here and the ambiance didn't matter. Kelvin had fancier taste than I did, though, so he wanted something nicer.

This place had been our compromise—something that probably didn't have bedbugs but also didn't cost a small fortune. In the end, I'd picked it, probably because Kelvin was still trying to win me over.

Good luck.

Turned out that no matter how nice someone seemed, how kind their actions, I just couldn't forget being forcefully bound to them — even if they'd done it for my own good.

My crow screeched in my head at the very reminder of the indignity. It valued freedom above all else, and Kelvin had snatched that from me, making me his thrall — or at least some twisted version of it.

It meant that even when I thought for a moment that I might be able to forgive him, that I might rethink how angry I was, that he could slip beneath my walls again, my crow reminded me, *no fucking way*.

The lobby had that old world money feel, with metal detail on the ceiling and over-the-top trim on everything. I held the key card between two fingers, then headed for the check-out desk.

Somehow, checking out was always the worst part. It felt like they could see what we'd just been doing, checking out only a few hours after checking in.

Not that I cared all that much. What did it matter if they suspected we'd been having steamy, forbidden sex just before?

Jealous much?

I turned in the key, suffered through the suggestive stares — *they probably figure I'm a working girl* — then headed away from the prying eyes of the staff.

"Should we meet here next week again?"

I shook my head. "No. I'll just call you when it's time."

"Why? We end up meeting at the same time every week anyway. It makes more sense to expect it at this point."

Except, I couldn't. Sure, I understood his reasoning, and yeah, it made more sense. If we knew we needed to see each other at this time, why not plan it ahead? It'd end up easier on us both.

I couldn't, though. "This way is better."

He sighed, the same sound as before, full of the same frustrations. "You can't even stand the idea of a planned time with me, can you? Is it me, or is it the schedule of it?" He ran his fingers through his hair, pushing the locks from his face.

It made me question, for just a moment, if he'd grow sick of this. So far, he'd focused on getting what he wanted, on winning me over, but what would happen if he changed his mind? If he decided this was too much?

I tried to picture a future where Kelvin *wasn't* there. Where I couldn't just call him up if I wanted. The truth was, if I couldn't see him, I'd be the one to suffer — not him.

It was like recognizing a terrifying future I hadn't realized was possible before.

He set his hand on my cheek, his skin flushed and warm — probably from my blood. "Don't worry about that," he said, his voice sweeter than I usually heard from him, as though trying to make up for worrying me. "I'll be here no matter how long it takes."

I went to answer — though what I'd say, I had no idea — when a shout echoed through the lobby. Not a *'you cheated on me, you asshole'* yell of a woman who'd found her husband her with some woman, but one of real fear.

I twisted to find someone barreling from the elevator just as the doors opened — a woman whose eyes were bloodshot and full of madness. Blood coated her hands and stained her shirt. She must have gotten hurt unless she was just a *really* messy eater.

Or both…

The woman was small, only an inch or two taller than me, but she rushed with the confidence of a football player going in for a tackle.

She'd have slammed right into me if not for Kelvin yanking me aside and out of the way with less than a second to spare. It left me falling against his chest.

Funny, he could have leveled the person if he wanted to, but instead chose to save me.

Probably since we were in public, and he didn't care for leaving evidence that might bite him in the ass later. It was best to keep a low profile at such times, after all. No one wanted humans getting a whiff of the real world.

The woman ran forward, toward the door, but before she reached it, a familiar figure stepped inside.

Galen.

It was hard not to notice him. Not because of his looks—he actually looked a bit like a computer nerd, someone who might get glanced over at any time. Instead, a glance at his face showed the immense power at his disposal, the incredible will of his wolf, that he became so impossible to ignore.

"Wonderful," Kelvin muttered, the word so soft that I doubted he'd intended for me to hear.

The woman skidded to a stop just before Galen, who stood as though entirely unworried. He didn't prepare for a fight, didn't appear any different from a man walking up to a stranger.

I took a step that way, wanting to warn him, but Kelvin held me tight. "Stay out of it."

Sure enough, Galen's voice rang across the lobby despite how quietly he spoke. "Stop this."

The amount of force in that voice sank into me, a part of it demanding even I obey. I rarely heard him use his position as alpha, rarely saw this side of him. It reminded me that he did in fact rule over all the Weres in this area of the country, that he could force any of them to his whim.

And the immediate reaction from the woman told me something else — she was a Were.

She dropped to her knees, tears filling her eyes, the anger draining away and fear replacing it. She sobbed out broken words and I could only catch *sorry* among them.

Galen crouched before her, balancing on the balls of his feet without effort. "You're tired, aren't you?"

She nodded.

"You knew you shouldn't run. There is no help out there, not for people like you." His words struck me as vicious, yet he said them without venom. Instead, there almost seemed a strange kindness in them, an acceptance, a truth.

"I don't want to die," she said.

"Do you want to harm others? Do you want to hurt those you care about? No? Then you know that the only place for you is in the pack."

His brows inched toward each other before he lifted his gaze, finding me so fast it felt as though he'd known I was there. A new tension entered his body, different from before. He'd shown no fear or worry before, yet now? Now he seemed on edge. He moved his gaze over me — was he checking for injuries? — and when he seemed satisfied, he returned his focus to the woman.

This time, when he spoke, however, a sharp edge rested in his words. "You could have done serious damage. This proves your lack of control, that you cannot be allowed to roam free."

"Not the cage," the woman pled.

He rose, then gestured toward her. For the first time, I noticed others behind him — three men in police uniforms — who came forward. Funny that he made it impossible to pay attention to anyone else. They grabbed the woman, who had started to fight, and hauled her out despite her screams. Another officer went to speak to a hotel employee, no doubt to smooth that over.

I'd known, of course, that spirits kept people in different positions of power to help keep our secret, but seeing it always unnerved me.

Galen didn't leave. He headed our way, his shoulders pulled back, his steps sure. Then again, he'd just faced off against a Were — he wasn't that worried about me, and he knew Kelvin wouldn't do anything here.

"Your strays are becoming a problem," Kelvin said, making it clear we were skipping pleasantries. "You should keep them on a leash."

"I'm taking care of my own. Last I heard, no Grave has gotten hurt by a stray."

"Yet that one nearly mowed over this Crow, and I doubt either of us would have liked that."

Galen's nostrils flared, the only show of temper.

Leave it to Kelvin to get beneath Galen's skin.

"What's wrong with her?" I asked to derail whatever they had going on between them.

Galen turned his gaze from Kelvin and focused instead on me, his expression softening. "She's a stray. She can't control her beast, so she can't be allowed to roam free. She didn't listen to that and tried to run."

"She seemed afraid."

"No one likes to face reality when that reality isn't what they want and isn't likely to change." He shrugged, though a certain discomfort said he didn't like it.

Or perhaps he just didn't like me to see it.

"What'll happen to her?"

He didn't answer, and that sure told me the answer.

I recalled Trey, the werebear who'd had his mind ruined by a Sprit, the way that they'd expected to have to kill him. No doubt this was the same sort of situation.

A Were who couldn't control its beast was beyond dangerous. In that state, the beast was agitated, vicious, reactive. I knew logically Weres like that couldn't be allowed to just go along as they wanted — they were far too dangerous.

Knowing something was logical and accepting it was a whole different matter, though.

"You won't actually hurt her," I said with a soft laugh, as though I knew he was kidding even if he wasn't.

His gaze hardened, looking every bit the alpha he was. "If Kelvin hadn't been here, she could have hurt you. She could have slammed into you, could have taken you apart right here in the lobby."

"She wouldn't have —"

"Did you see the blood on her? She hurt three other people in this hotel alone, not to mention whoever else she ran into before that. She definitely could have hurt you, and that isn't something I'll allow. Don't worry about it, though, it isn't your problem." His gaze moved between Kelvin and me, a question there.

Kelvin didn't answer it and I sure didn't plan on it. Galen knew something was going on between us, but the last thing I wanted was to have to explain it.

Not only was that awkward as fuck, but it took me back to Kelvin denying me — as he always did — and how pathetically I'd begged.

Nope, that was not the sort of thing anyone else needed to know. It was humiliating enough that Kelvin, Harrison and myself knew.

"When do you plan to have this situation dealt with?" Kelvin pressed.

"I'm working on it."

"Should we convene the council? If you can't deal with it on your own, I'd be happy to offer my people to clean up your mess."

I'd never known that an offer of help could sound that threatening, but leave it to Kelvin to manage that little gem.

And of course, Galen took it exactly as intended. "No, thank you. I believe we can take care of it." He looked at me once more, his expression guarded this time. "Call me later, Grey. I'll have to deal with this, but afterward, I'd like to see you."

I nodded, unsure of what else to say. Seeing Galen wasn't uncommon, and it had been a few days. Still, agreeing with Kelvin behind me felt odd.

Especially when I drew such distinct lines with Kelvin.

Galen offered one more glare Kelvin's way before turning on his heel and walking out, not glancing back. I had to admit, he managed to look pretty bad ass...

As soon as he left, Kelvin let out a soft snort. "Well, as fun as that was, I'm afraid I need to get back. I have work to take care of."

Which of course reminded me that he did manage to drop everything for these little get togethers, and I should probably be more thankful than I felt. He could have said no, after all.

So instead of causing more problems, I offered a smile. "Yeah, sure. I've got shit to do, too. Well, thanks." I took a step back, ready to bypass the whole awkward goodbye thing. A walk of shame was bad enough, but the goodbye just before was downright painful.

Before I could shuffle away, though, Kelvin caught my wrist and pulled me in close. I expected a kiss, something passionate, the way he always did. His voice reached my ear, instead. "Be careful around Galen. The Weres aren't in a good place, and their territory isn't safe."

With that, he released me and stepped away, then turned toward the elevator, his warning ringing in my ears.

The warning against the Weres didn't feel personal, not like he just hated Galen—which he did—but instead like he knew things going on that I didn't.

My phone rang, stealing my attention. I pulled it from my pocket and looked at the screen.

Porter.

I answered the call, wondering what weird and horrible luck had me talking to these three men one after another.

"Hello?"

"Can you meet me right now?"

So much for niceties.

I almost said no, just to play hard to get—and because it felt weird to see him while I still likely had Kelvin's scent all over me—but Porter had never reached out like this. He'd helped me when I'd needed it, but he hadn't ever been the one to make the first move. He was more aloof, less concerned with me or the rest of the real world. The curiosity was enough to get me to agree. "Sure. Where?"

A quickie at a hotel, a feral Were, and now a druid asking for my help?

Well, wasn't today shaping up to be one weird fucking day?

About the Author

Jayce Carter lives in Southern California with her husband and two spawns. She originally wanted to take over the world but realized that would require wearing pants. This led her to choosing writing, a completely pants-free occupation. She has a fear of heights yet rock climbs for fun and enjoys making up excuses for not going out and socializing.

Jayce loves to hear from readers. You can find her contact information, website details and author profile page at https://www.totallybound.com

Home of Erotic Romance

Sign up for our newsletter and find out about all our romance book releases, eBook sales and promotions, sneak peeks and FREE romance books!